Katharine Swartz wrote her first story at the age of five, *The Christmas Rose*, which had a print run of one. Since then she has written many stories and serials for magazines. After living for six years in England, she now resides in Connecticut, USA, with her husband and three young children.

DOWN JASPER LANE

1904. Twelve-year-old Ellen Copley leaves the rail yards of Glasgow behind and travels to America with her father. They hope to start again in a small Vermont village with Ellen's aunt and uncle. But, abandoned by her father, Ellen has to suffer life with her inhospitable relatives. Then she travels to Canada to live with her father's sister and family, and for the first time she finds acceptance. Torn between love and duty, her life becomes a fractured existence in both Vermont and Canada as she struggles to carve a place for herself in a changing and increasingly turbulent world.

KATHARINE SWARTZ

DOWN JASPER LANE

Complete and Unabridged

ULVERSCROFT
Leicester

First published in Great Britain in 2009 by
Robert Hale Limited.
London

First Large Print Edition
published 2010
by arrangement with
Robert Hale Limited.
London

British Library CIP Data

Swartz, Katharine.
  Down Jasper Lane.
  1. Scots- -Canada- -Fiction. 2. Scots- -Vermont- -
Fiction. 3. Canada- -Social life and customs- -20th
century- -Fiction. 4. Vermont- -Social life and
customs- -20th century- -Fiction.
  5. Domestic fiction 6. Large type books.
  I. Title
  813.6–dc22

ISBN 978–1–44480–065–4

Published by
F. A. Thorpe (Publishing)
Anstey, Leicestershire

Set by Words & Graphics Ltd.
Anstey, Leicestershire
Printed and bound in Great Britain by
T. J. International Ltd., Padstow, Cornwall

This book is printed on acid-free paper

1

'There she is, Ellen. There she is.' Douglas Copley put an arm around his daughter's shoulders as they stood at the rail of the *Mary Rose*. In the harbour before them, under a glittering summer sun, the Statue of Liberty stood, one elegant arm raised, ready to greet yet another shipload of hopeful immigrants to the shores of America, and the streets of gold fabled to lie beyond.

Passengers jostled at the railings, eager for this first view of their new country. After a week on the crowded steamer, most were ready to step on to land, and into the dreams they'd spun for themselves.

Ellen Copley couldn't wait.

'What do you think to it, Ellen?' Douglas asked as he looked down at his daughter. Her hair had blown loose from its ribbon and framed her face in chestnut tendrils. Laughing, she held it away from her eyes and squinted into the sun.

'It's wonderful, Da. Wonderful.'

He nodded in satisfaction. 'It's about time we had something wonderful, lass.'

Ellen merely nodded. She didn't want to

1

think about the past, about her mother's grave only three months old, left in Springburn. She didn't want to remember the months tending her in the stale air of the sickroom, the way hope slid into despair, and how Mam turned her face to the wall, an invalid these many years and far too ready to die.

Ellen was ready finally to live. The future lay before them, as shining as the sea that stretched to a crowded shore, and it held a promise she couldn't wait to fulfil.

The Copleys had been planning to emigrate to the United States when Ellen was but three years old. Douglas had planned to begin life anew there with his older brother Hamish and their younger sister Rose.

There was opportunity in New England, businesses to start, fortunes to be made, or so you would believe if you listened to Douglas as he and Hamish dreamed in the flat's tiny kitchen, their booted feet stretched out to the coal stove.

Ellen never understood just exactly what the Copley brothers planned to do; she heard snatches of conversation, talk of opening a shop, a business, making decent money, breathing clean air. She didn't care what the nature of her father's dreams were; she just liked the way he smiled and snatched her into his arms, throwing her so high in the air that

2

her mam scolded that she'd hit her head on the ceiling.

The dreams by the stove had stayed vague, for Douglas's wife Ann fell ill just weeks before their ship was set to sail. Douglas had urged Hamish and his wife Ruth, along with Rose, to emigrate without him. Ann would recover soon, and they would all be together. It had seemed so simple.

Ellen remembered going with her father — Mam was home in bed — to the docks to see the other Copleys off. Hamish, Ruth, and Rose were no more than blurred faces in her memory, figures standing at the railing of the ship as her father waved with determined cheer and Ellen felt the sting of tears and disappointment. She wanted to be on that ship, and she clung to her father's hearty words as they finally turned away, the ship no more than a speck on the horizon.

'It'll be us soon, lass. Another month or two. When the weather's warm and your mam can catch her breath.'

Ellen nodded, wanting to believe, yet even at that young age doubts struck at her heart. She lay awake in the night, listening to her mother wheeze breathlessly before she finally erupted into hacking coughs that tore as much at Ellen's soul as they did Ann Copley's chest.

The weather warmed, the pallid sunshine streaking through the windows of the flat, bathing Springburn's engine yards in gold, and her mother never did catch her breath.

The spring slipped into a damp, muggy summer, and then autumn again, and all the while her mother seemed to shrink and fade. Her times away from bed, cooking and cleaning and taking care of her family and flat were farther and farther in between, and the careworn look on her face told Ellen that her mother could no longer pretend that they would be heading westward when the weather turned . . . again.

Douglas still pretended, though. Ellen knew he needed to; he clung to hope. In a place like Springburn, it was sometimes all you had. In the evenings he brought the ships' timetables to their flat, poring over them by the light of the stove. Sometimes Ellen would sit on his knee and watch as he traced the ship's passage on a map with a work-grimed finger.

'Across all that ocean, see Greenland there . . . a cold place, that! All the way to New York City . . . a city of islands, Ellen, covered in buildings, some touching the sky! Imagine that.'

The journey, however, did not stop in New York. Hamish and Ruth had settled in

Vermont, opening a general store in the small town of Seaton. The letters were infrequent, but treasured. Ellen loved to hear her father tell of it.

'Plenty of trees, and fields as far as the eye can see. And the rivers! The fish fair jump into your hand.' He spoke with such certainty that Ellen half-believed he'd been there and seen it for himself. She loved to hear about the farmhouse he'd build, with her own bedroom with a window looking out on an oak tree. They'd have kittens, of course, and a cow or two, and perhaps some sheep.

'And a dog, Ellen,' her father would say seriously. 'A man has to have a dog.'

'May I name the kittens?' Ellen asked eagerly. 'And may they be grey ones?'

Her father nodded thoughtfully, drawing on his pipe. 'I reckon so.'

Sometimes Ellen's father took her to the Glasgow docks, to watch the ships set sail.

'We'll be waving from the deck one of these days,' he'd say cheerfully, his arm around Ellen's shoulders, the dream firmly in place.

Yet the doubt that had gnawed at Ellen's heart began its treacherous work on Douglas's. Ellen couldn't remember when they stopped going to the docks. She wasn't sure when her father stopped bringing the timetables back to the flat. She did remember

5

the day her father asked her to leave school to stay home and nurse her mother.

He drew her on his knee, as if she were a child, even though she had turned eleven months ago. 'I'd do it myself, lass, if I could. But I need to be at the rail works.'

Ellen nodded in understanding, for without her father's job as an engine repairman they would be out on the street. Yet she could not suppress the sharp stab of disappointment at the thought of leaving school, those neat rows of desks and the respite from the small, stuffy flat, and this showed on her face.

'It won't be long,' her father said, and his voice trembled slightly. 'God be with us all, it won't be long.'

Ellen slipped off her father's knee. At that moment, she felt as grown-up as Mrs MacDougall upstairs. She didn't belong on her father's knee any more.

Ellen took on the responsibilities of their small household with grim determination. She haggled in the market, and hung out the washing in the courtyard in the back, and made soups with what vegetables were left in the basket, pursing her lips and rolling up her sleeves just like any other housewife in Springburn, whose man made his living in the engine yards, where a quarter of the world's trains were made, or so it was said.

6

She watched with a cool detachment when other children lined up by the railway-owned steamboat for a school trip to Broughty Ferry. And if she thought of another ship they'd planned to go on, she told no one.

Every once in awhile a letter from America would come, and Douglas would read it aloud in a flat, even voice. Ann would smile faintly, as if listening to a fairy story, to hear of the trees and fresh air, the simple living and the easy prosperity.

Ellen remained silent, but there was a deep burning within her, a burning to leave the cloying air and damp walls of the sickroom, and the narrow, grimy streets of Springburn beyond.

Sometimes she would meet her father's eyes, and he would look away quickly, folding the letter up without speaking of it, as if to speak of it would be to let go of their dreams.

Then Ellen's mother died. It had been a long time coming, and when Ann Copley finally breathed her last, Ellen could only feel a weary sorrow, coupled with the guilty stirrings of relief. Her memories of Mam were of a feeble woman, a tired smile or weak hand patting her own, and little more. Towards the end there hadn't even been that.

Yet the flat seemed strangely empty without her mother's presence, and although Douglas

7

once suggested Ellen return to school, it didn't seem practical. Who would scrub and cook and wash? Who would go to market, darn her father's socks?

Besides, Ellen admitted quietly to herself, she wouldn't fit in with the other children, children who hadn't yet left the schoolroom for the reality of work. She felt years older, yet she wasn't quite thirteen.

Two months after her mother died, Douglas Copley brought home the timetable of the *Mary Rose*. He handed it to Ellen silently, and she gazed at it for a moment before looking up at him.

'She leaves in three weeks,' he said quietly. 'I haven't saved quite enough for two tickets yet — '

Ellen went into the pantry and took out an old flour tin. She handed it to Douglas and he looked inside, his mouth dropping open in surprise. 'How — '

Ellen smiled. 'I've been saving too.'

His eyes glinted with emotion as he looked up. 'You're a good lass,' he said, his voice hoarse. 'A good lass.' He rested one roughened hand on her hair, briefly, and Ellen wished she could put her arms around him. A few years ago, she would have, and he would have given her one of his old bear hugs, yet with the cares and worries that had weighed heavily on both of their shoulders, that easy affection had slipped away.

She didn't know how to get it back.

With their pooled savings, they were able to buy two third-class tickets on the *Mary Rose*, departing Glasgow on 3 July 1904 and arriving at Ellis Island Immigrant Station, New York, on the tenth.

And now they were here, their new lives — their *real* lives — about to begin. Ellen lifted her face to the air, letting the salty sea breeze cool her cheeks.

The blank, staring face of the Statue of Liberty gazed across the harbour as the ship passed, and Ellen found something chilling about that impersonal face with its patrician features, a face that had coolly watched thousands — hundreds of thousands — of hopeful immigrants pass this way.

Shrugging aside such thoughts, Ellen closed her eyes and pictured her room in Vermont as she imagined and hoped it to be, a patchwork quilt on the bed, a window looking out to fields of flowers. She could almost feel the crisp pages of new books, hear the shared laughter of new friends. She hadn't had many friends in Springburn after she'd left school. In truth, she hadn't had any. There had been no time, and she'd felt so different from the children who could still go to school, dirty their knees and pull each other's plaits. While they were playing games in the schoolyard, she was bartering over a vegetable barrow, or counting her pennies to make the coal last.

Yet surely in Vermont, when she was in school, that would change. There would be no bartering, no counting pennies. Ellen didn't want to be a child again; that was impossible. But she wanted to feel young.

The steamboat was cutting quickly through the harbour to its destination, the immigrant station at Ellis Island. Ellen had heard whispers of this place on the ship, heard the tales of flinty-eyed customs officers who barked questions, turning back anyone whose accent was funny, whose English too broken.

And then there were the doctors, who poked and prodded and even lifted your eyelids with button hooks, all to make sure you were fit enough to enter this land of dreams.

'And if you aren't?' Ellen asked once, and a woman with a nursing baby had regarded her with pity.

'Pray you are,' she said grimly. 'Pray you are.'

Ellen's father dismissed anyone's concerns over 'the Hall of Tears' with a jaunty laugh. 'That's not for us, Ellen. We're both fit and strong, and we've family waiting for us. That's not for us.'

And Ellen knew it wasn't as well, felt it as surely as if they'd already passed through. Optimism, bright and shiny, buoyed her spirits along like a sail, and she clung to it.

The ship was soon moored, bobbing amidst many others, and they were being herded off its decks like a flock of muddled sheep.

'Women to the right, men to the left,' a man barked, and when Ellen made to follow her father, he pushed her none too gently in the back, to the other side. 'Women to the right,' he snapped, and Ellen stared at him with wide eyes.

'It's all right, lass,' Da called. 'I'll see you on the other side, after you're through.' He called to a young woman they'd befriended on the ship. 'Annie McCready, see to my girl, won't you?'

'Aye, I will,' Annie promised, and hustled Ellen along with her four other children.

Ellen barely had time to register the huge hall, filled with a dense, heaving mass of humanity. Huge, grimy windows streaked the dusty floor with sunlight.

Ellen looked for her father, but could not seem him anywhere. Around her, a dozen languages were being spoken, shrill voices raised in anger and fear. People clutched bundles and children, guarding against the worst. Deportation.

Ann McCready threw her a quick, harried smile. 'It will be all right. You're little, but you're strong enough, aren't you?'

Ellen didn't know how strong she was. She felt a sudden, plunging fear at the thought of being sent back, then resolutely dismissed it. Hadn't Da said that wasn't for them? Her future was here, and a customs officer couldn't change that.

Still, her heart beat fiercely as she clutched the tatty carpet bag that held her most dear possessions, her old rag doll, a silver-plated brush and her mother's Bible.

'Come along, lass,' Ann said, jiggling her baby on her hip. 'Stay with us, now. Though I imagine it will be awhile.'

They waited three hours, standing in that hot, crowded hall, before it was finally their turn in front of the customs officers. By that time, it was midmorning and the immigration hall was stifling. Ellen felt sweat trickle down her back, and knew her face was flushed with heat. Her legs ached from standing so long, and she swiped at a damp tendril of hair.

'You!' A surly man in a blue serge suit pointed at her. 'Come up, then.'

Ellen glanced at Ann, but the older woman

just gave her a little push in the back. 'Go on, then. Families go separate. Your Da's on the other side.'

Ellen walked up the officer. He eyed her in an unfriendly way.

'You alone?' he demanded and she shook her head, her throat suddenly too dry to speak.

'Do you speak English?'

She nodded. 'I'm Scottish,' she said, but her burr must have been too much for him to understand, for he rolled his eyes.

'Someone waiting for you?'

'My father.'

He understood this much, for he made a mark on her card. He jerked a thumb and a doctor scuttled up to her. Ellen flinched in surprise as he flourished a button hook to pull her eyelids up and check for trachoma. He slapped at her cheeks. 'Flushed, isn't she? Feverish, I'd say. Was there illness on the ship?'

'Not so as I heard,' the customs officer said in a bored voice, and the doctor pursed his lips.

'Still, she's on the scrawny side. I don't like that brightness in her eye at all.'

The customs officer shrugged. The doctor took a piece of chalk out of his pocket, and Ellen grabbed his arm.

'Please, sir, it's just the heat. I'm perfectly well — '

He shrugged her off as he marked a large 'x' on the shoulder of her coat. 'Go to the desk there, girl. They'll see to you.' There was the merest flicker of pity in his eyes before he moved on.

Ellen tasted fear, cold and metallic. She swallowed, watching as streams of people flowed by her, people who did not have chalk 'x's on their shoulders, people who were heading towards the large, double doors that led to the outside, to freedom.

She didn't know what the 'x' meant, but it could be nothing good. At the best, a delay while she suffered through another physical exam. At the worst, passage back to Scotland.

Ellen took a deep breath and looked around. The McCreadys were gone, prodded onwards by the officers, no doubt assuming Ellen was already on the other side, reunited with Da.

No one was watching her. And no one, she thought, was going to keep her from joining Da on the other side of this wretched hall.

Quickly, her fingers trembling, she took off her coat and put it on inside out. The 'x' was no longer visible. Her heart thudding so fast she felt dizzy, she moved to the double doors.

A customs officer squinted at her suspiciously, but Ellen lifted her chin and gazed evenly back, her heart thudding so loudly she felt it in her ears, and he looked away.

She walked with her shoulders stiff, quivering with tension, expecting the meaty hand of a customs officer to grab her, turn her around, and demand for her to return. What was the punishment for what she'd done, she wondered sickly. Deportation? Prison?

Still, she kept one foot in front of the other, oblivious to the sweaty, heaving crowd around her, everyone desperate to be released from this place, to the promise of freedom and hope.

The doors loomed closer, and closer still, and no one stopped her. Then she was through, jostled on either side, and she stood outside, breathing the salty sea air once again and blinking in the bright sunlight, weak with relief. All around her the water shimmered, as brilliant as diamonds.

Someone grabbed her arm, and she nearly screamed.

'It's me, lass!' Da laughed and hugged her. 'I told you it'd be all right, didn't I?'

Ellen looked at her father's light, happy face, and swallowed her fear. She would never tell her father about the 'x'. She knew she couldn't.

'You did, Da,' she said with a little smile, and he chuckled.

'That tug there, it's a transfer boat. It'll take us to Manhattan. Look at the buildings, from here even! They're taller than smoke stacks. By this time tomorrow we'll be in Vermont, Ellen, in the country air, with family again.'

Ellen nodded. Vermont. She repeated it silently to herself, like a promise. Vermont, with her own room and the house they would build. She was going to name the kittens Silk and Satin. She could already see their dear, little velvety faces.

The next few hours passed in a blur, as they moved from tender to dock to streetcar, tramping wearily around this alien city until they were directed to the train station. Ellen was amazed at the noise, even louder than Springburn. And the buildings were so high! It hurt her neck just to look up for a tiny glimpse of sky.

In the train station a newsboy shouted the day's headlines. 'Twenty die in factory fire! Women and children perish in the flames!' He spoke with obvious relish and Ellen turned away with a shudder.

Da put his arm around her shoulders. 'Never mind, lass. It's to Vermont we're going, not here. It's different there.'

16

'It had better be,' Ellen replied smartly, and Da grinned. Ellen knew he was always pleased when she showed some spirit. She grinned back.

By the time they'd purchased their tickets to Seaton, Vermont, boarded the train, and eaten sandwiches purchased from a pushcart, Ellen was exhausted. She leaned her head against her father's arm, his coat still smelling faintly of tobacco and the engine grease from the railway works. Within minutes, lulled by the rhythmic chugging of the train, she'd fallen asleep.

It was nearly dark when she awoke, stiff and disoriented. For a moment the movement of the train made her think she was on the ship again, lying on her bunk. Then she sat up and looked outside, dusk falling softly on open fields, farmhouses and fences speeding by in a blur.

'We've been travelling all afternoon,' her father said with a chuckle. 'It's nearly evening now.'

Ellen blinked the sleep out of her eyes. 'How much longer?' she asked.

'We change at Troy. I think we should be there in an hour. We'll spend the night there, get the first train in the morning. Should be with Hamish and Ruth by dinnertime tomorrow.' He settled back in his seat. 'It's grand, this, isn't it? Travelling in trains, instead of working under them!'

'Grand,' Ellen repeated. She'd never stayed in a hotel before, but just the word conjured images of chandeliers and velvet seat cushions, fancy meals eaten with silver forks.

The reality was rather more ordinary, but Ellen was no less pleased with the simple, spare room in a boarding house. She ate her sausages and potatoes with relish, and fell deeply asleep in her little bed, too tired even to dream.

It felt only moments before Da was waking her again for the morning train.

It was a hot, sluggish sort of day, and Ellen wished she had a prettier summer dress as they waited on the platform for the train to Seaton. She wanted to give a good impression to her Uncle Hamish and Aunt Ruth. She knew they'd had no children of their own, for Da had said so. Somewhere in her deepest, most private imaginings she saw herself fulfilling some need in them that she couldn't even name.

She looked down at her plain dress of yellow wincey. It was serviceable, but she'd like a dress in sprig cotton, something with flowers. She'd seen a girl her own age in the city with a dress covered in little blue forget-me-nots and a straw boater with a matching ribbon. She'd like something like that. She thought about asking Da, but he'd promise her the moon in the mood he was in, and what did he know about dresses?

Ellen chuckled to herself, and her father raised an eyebrow. 'What's that funny, then?'

'I'm just happy,' she admitted. She didn't care what she was wearing, not really. She leaned into his arm as she had so many times before, felt the comforting weight of his shoulder, that easy affection starting to return after so many years. They'd survived the ocean crossing, passed through the Hall of Tears, and surely now only good was ahead. Only happiness.

2

The sun was hot as Hamish Copley waited in his buckboard for the noon train from Troy. Sweat gleamed on his balding head and he slapped his hat against his thigh. A few bees buzzed lazily around the wild raspberry bushes that sprang up in a thorny tangle against the station wall.

'Any sign of her yet?' Hamish called to Orvis Fairley, the station master. Orvis looked down at the watch gleaming heavily against his large stomach.

'She's not due for another eleven minutes. The Central New York Railway always comes on time.' Hamish nodded, and Orvis glanced at him in open curiosity. 'Who are you waiting for, then? You're not one to leave the store at midday.'

Hamish fidgeted in his seat. 'My brother Douglas is coming in,' he admitted, 'with his daughter. They've come all the way from Scotland, on the ship, you know.'

'I didn't think they'd come all the way on a train,' Orvis replied with a smug chuckle, and Hamish suppressed a sigh. It seemed he was always saying the wrong thing.

He leaned back in his seat, enjoying the sun on his face. Ever since he and Ruth had opened the Seaton General Store eight years ago, he'd spent most of his time indoors, behind the counter. It worked better that way; the people of Seaton liked to see Hamish, jovial and easygoing, slip the children barley sugar and chat with the old-timers. But they preferred to do business with Ruth.

Orvis stuck out his head to look down the railway line. 'Nothing yet,' he announced cheerfully. 'Three more minutes.' He leaned back, looking again at Hamish. No one else was at the station, and sometimes nobody got off the train at Seaton.

'Your brother, you said? What made him finally come, then?'

'His wife died.' Hamish didn't remember Ann Copley too well. She'd been a fragile, wispy little thing, although he knew Douglas had loved her to distraction. He wondered how his little brother had changed in the last ten years. Before they'd emigrated, Douglas had been the one with the energy, the dreams.

'The secret,' Douglas would say, tapping a row of advertisements in the newspaper, 'is to find your market. Something that hasn't been made before. Something that's needed.'

21

Hamish always nodded, although he didn't quite see himself as an inventor. And whenever he asked Douglas just what they'd be inventing, his younger brother would shrug and laugh.

'Who knows, as long as it sells?'

It made sense, of course, and there were hundreds — thousands — of men in America who had invented something no one else had even known was necessary. What about Coca-Cola, that funny, fizzy drink, and even the iceboxes to keep it in?

Hamish chuckled to himself. It had all been nonsense, of course. He wasn't an inventor, and running a general store suited him admirably. He'd done well enough so now he could put Coca-Cola in his own icebox, if he so desired, no matter who'd done the inventing.

Would Douglas still have the old dreams, he wondered, the ambitions to invent something and be a man of the world? The thought gave Hamish a vague sense of alarm.

'It'll be good to see him again,' he told Orvis with more heartiness than he actually felt. 'Him and the girl.' He wondered about Ellen, the child he barely remembered from Springburn. He liked children, always had a kind word for the schoolchildren who came into the store for sweets. Of course, he'd be seeing more of Ellen since she would be living with them . . . even now, Hamish wasn't quite sure how it was all meant to work out.

When Ruth had read the letter from Douglas, she'd merely pressed her lips together and said, 'That will be some help.' They hadn't talked about it since.

'The train's here,' Orvis announced with pride. 'I see her coming down the line.' A few minutes later the black engine came into view, with two dusty, tired-looking passenger cars behind. Hamish swallowed and jumped down from the buckboard, cramming his hat back on his head.

As the train slowed to a stop, he saw a face in the window, little more than wide eyes and a tangle of hair. Then the train stopped, Orvis threw the passenger door open, and Douglas Copley stepped out, the girl behind him.

'Hamish?' Uncertainty flickered in his eyes for the barest of moments before he went forward to embrace his brother. Hamish's arms closed around Douglas automatically. 'It's been awhile, eh? You look well.'

'Lost most of my hair,' Hamish said self-consciously, for he'd removed his hat when Douglas and his daughter stepped from the train. 'And you — ' Hamish did not finish for he did not know what to say. The truth was, the sight of his younger brother had shocked him. He may have lost his hair, but Douglas had lost his vitality.

Ten years ago, Douglas had been young, dark haired, handsome and charming. Now his hair was grey, his face tired and lined, his shoulders stooped.

'It's been a long time,' Douglas acknowledged, 'but we're finally here.' He moved aside, bringing his daughter forward with an arm around her shoulders. 'This is my girl, Ellen. She's been a blessing to me and her mam.'

'I'm sure she has.' Hamish smiled at the girl, who looked, he thought, pale and underfed, with far too much hair. It surrounded her face in a dark tangle, and she regarded him out of wide, hazel eyes that were unsettlingly serious.

'Pleased to meet you, Uncle Hamish.'

Uncle — ! The realization surprised Hamish into giving her an awkward, little hug. 'Well, of course I'm pleased to meet you, little miss. Though I suppose I knew you, when you weren't higher than my knee.' He laughed, a rather forced sound, and said, 'Let's get your bags.'

Hamish received another shock when he saw what they were travelling with, just one worn carpet bag and a small, battered steamer trunk. Sometimes it was hard to remember that he and Ruth had come to America with little more. Prosperity had a way of dulling the memories, sweetening them.

'You must be tired,' Hamish said. 'I'll take you right home. Ruth's minding the store. We live next door, you know, built our own house five years ago, when the store started doing well.' He found himself swelling proudly, and then looked away, ashamed of his own smugness.

'We can hardly wait to see it,' Douglas said cheerfully, and Ellen smiled. Hamish felt soothed as he put their cases in the wagon and helped Ellen climb aboard. Perhaps it would be all right.

They were silent on the short journey from the station into Seaton. Out of the corner of his eye Hamish watched Ellen gaze at everything with wide eyes. He thought of Springburn, with its grime and noise, and vaguely remembered his own surprise and delight at the simple greenness of Vermont. The grass was soft, vivid, and hopping with crickets; the clouds in the sky looked like bits of cotton wool. Hamish smiled.

'You'll like Seaton,' he said, and Ellen regarded him seriously.

'Yes,' she said. 'Yes, I will.'

Hamish tipped his hat to most everyone in

Seaton, murmuring his greetings. Douglas and Ellen stared and nodded, and Hamish tried to imagine the village through their eyes.

Ten years ago Seaton had been a few shabby farmhouses and not much else. Then one of the big manufacturers had built a mill, and another company had discovered a quarry. People came for the work, and began building. First houses, then a doctor's surgery, a blacksmith, a church and even a school. The rail line was extended, and the Copleys built their general store.

Now Seaton bustled with folk. On the corner across from the store was the unlikely combination of a barber and ice cream parlour. The blacksmith had even started selling bicycles.

'Here we are,' Hamish announced. The Copleys' house wasn't too grand, because Ruth said it wasn't Christian to be showy. Still, Hamish thought it was impressive, with its wide front porch and two rows of double windows. 'You head on in,' he continued. 'I'll just put the wagon away. Poor old Polly needs her oats.'

When Hamish rejoined his brother and niece in the sitting room, they were both standing, Douglas with his hat twisted in his hands.

'You've done well for yourself, Hamish,

and that's a fact.' There was no rancour or jealousy in Douglas's voice, merely awe. Hamish blushed and fidgeted.

'Ruth made lemonade earlier. She thought you'd be thirsty, from the train.'

'Lemonade!' Ellen whispered, and Hamish felt another prickling of discomfort.

'I'll go get it.' He hurried to the kitchen, and Ellen followed him. She watched from the doorway as he took a pitcher from the icebox.

'Is that an icebox?' she asked. 'A real one?'

'Yes. We have ice delivered every day.' He paused uncertainly. 'Almost everyone in Seaton has an icebox, you know.'

Ellen didn't say anything for a moment. Hamish was unnerved by her clear, knowing stare. 'I see,' she said quietly, after a moment, and went and fetched three glasses from the cupboard.

Hamish watched as she moved about the kitchen, first looking for the cupboard with glasses, then putting them on the table. This girl surprised him, he realized, because she wasn't like the girls he knew, the girls with plaits and pinafores who came into the store for hair ribbons and sweets.

'I'm sorry about your mother,' Hamish said, realizing he should have mentioned Ann before.

'Thank you,' Ellen said simply, and together they walked back to the sitting room.

The lemonade was cool and sweet and Hamish drained his glass in one gulp. He sat, twisting the cool, empty glass between his sweaty palms while both Douglas and Ellen sipped at it carefully.

'I'll show you the store, afterwards,' he said. 'And your rooms, of course. Ruth got them all ready.' There was a brief, charged moment of silence, or so it seemed to Hamish, so he kept talking. 'She'll be back any moment, I expect. Couldn't wait to see you, really she couldn't.' Realizing he was talking too much, Hamish smiled shame-facedly and stood up. 'I'll take your bags upstairs.'

Before he could move any further, the front door opened, and sunlight slanted through on the scrubbed pine floor. Hamish looked up to see Ruth, and smiled.

'Ah, here she is. Ruth, come see my brother and his daughter. We're so glad to have them, aren't we?'

Ruth eyed him coolly for one moment before moving into the room to meet her relatives.

★   ★   ★

28

Ellen's mouth seemed dry, even though she'd just taken a sip of the cold, sweet lemonade. She wasn't sure why she was nervous to meet her Aunt Ruth. Perhaps it was because of the way Uncle Hamish spoke of her, in that timid way. Almost as if she were somebody to be afraid of.

Ruth moved into the room, her skirts sweeping the floor. She was tall, with greying blonde hair swept up into one of the new, loose styles. She wore a simple but well-made blue dress, with leg-o-mutton sleeves and shiny black buttons. Ellen thought it was the most elegant dress she'd ever seen. Over the dress, Ruth wore a clean, starched apron trimmed with lace. Ellen had never seen such sparkling white cotton.

'Well, here you are.' Ruth moved to Douglas and shook his hand. Douglas returned the handshake with a deferential awkwardness Ellen didn't recognize. Da had always been his own man, confident in himself, yet since they'd stepped foot in this place he seemed like someone else entirely, apologetic and overwhelmed. Ellen realized she felt the same way . . . as if she didn't belong, and didn't know if she ever would.

'It's good to see you, Ruth. Been a long time, then.'

'So it has.' She moved to stand in front of

Ellen. Ellen looked up at her. Her aunt's face was handsome rather than pretty, but when she smiled suddenly Ellen felt a little spurt of relief. Ruth reached down to press her cool cheek against Ellen's.

'Dear Ellen. Douglas has written about what you've been through. Such a help to your mother and father. A credit to them, and us, to be sure.' There was a pause as she touched Ellen's hair with one fingertip. 'No doubt your hair is so dirty and tangled from the journey. The trains are frightful.'

Ellen's cheeks turned red and she struggled to murmur an appropriate response. 'Yes, ma'am. I apologize for my hair, ma'am.' She wouldn't humiliate Da or herself.

'Listen to that!' Aunt Ruth laughed, the sound a bit sharp. 'You'll have to get rid of that burr, my girl. No one in Seaton will understand you. Now, why don't you go upstairs and clean yourself? I'm sure you wish to make yourself presentable to us.'

Recognizing that she was dismissed, Ellen walked woodenly to the stairs. She turned once. 'Which way to my room, ma'am?'

'The little box room, at the back,' Ruth replied. 'I'm sure you'll find it suitable to your needs.'

Ellen nodded her acceptance and gave one fleeting look to her father, who was staring at his feet. She walked slowly upstairs.

Her room was small, but to Ellen, who had slept in a cot in the kitchen, it seemed like heaven. There was a pine bed frame with a feather mattress and a white and blue patchwork quilt. A small bureau with a washbasin and pitcher stood across from the bed, and a little mirror hung above it. Above the bed was an embroidered Bible verse, Proverbs 11:29.

'He who brings trouble on his family will inherit only wind, and the fool will be servant to the wise,' Ellen read aloud. She'd heard the verse in kirk before, but somehow it now seemed like a bad omen. She thought of Ruth's dismissal of her, and the coldness she was afraid she'd seen in her eyes.

Ellen turned to the window. Her own window, the blue checked curtains ruffling in the breeze. It looked out on to a scrubby yard with a wilting kitchen garden and a hen house, and no trees.

Perhaps she would plant one.

Ellen took her brush from the carpet bag, which Hamish had left by the bed. She drew it fiercely through her hair, which tended towards unruliness, till it lay flat against her head, her eyes stinging from the pain. She set her mouth in a determined line.

Now was not the time to feel sorry for

herself, simply because her aunt and uncle had not welcomed her with loving arms flung open wide. They had to get used to her, just as she and Da did to them. It was silly to dream of fairy tales, of emotional reunions that belonged in the Treasury of Much Loved Stories she'd read once, in school.

Ellen put the brush on her bureau, then decided to unpack the rest of her belongings. It didn't take long. Her two dresses went on the clothing pole by the door, and her second set of undergarments and stockings in the drawer. She put her mother's Bible in the bureau as well, and her rag doll, Celia, on the bed.

Mam had sewn her in her better days, and Ellen had made several dresses for Celia with scraps of cloth. Now she looked far too worn, the red stitching of her mouth half undone, one glass bead eye gone, but Ellen loved her.

For a moment her eyes stung again, this time from memory, as she remembered Mam lying propped up in bed, her pale face glowing, as she handed Celia to Ellen.

'It's not much, but I know you'll take care of her.'

Ellen fingered her doll now, wishing she'd taken better care of the one thing Mam had given her. She'd almost forgotten how Mam had spent many days sewing so laboriously, but always with a quick, tired smile. Sometimes it was hard to remember the good days her mother had had. They had stopped so long ago.

There was the sound of footsteps in the hall, and then Aunt Ruth opened the door. Ellen looked up guiltily, Celia still in her hands.

'Now you look a bit more presentable.' Aunt Ruth's eyes narrowed. 'What is that dirty thing you're holding?'

Ellen clutched the doll. 'It's my rag doll, Celia. Mam — '

Ruth plucked Celia from her hands. 'It's dirty, and most likely contaminated from the ship. I suppose all manner of dirty little immigrants held it?'

'No, only me — '

'We'd best throw it out, just in case.' Ruth's face softened slightly, and her lips curved in a smile Ellen didn't like. 'You can pick a new doll from the store. We've got some lovely ones, porcelain faces and painted lips. They put this one to shame.'

Ellen drew herself up. Rage was coursing through her, and she fought to keep her voice steady. 'Thank you very much, Aunt Ruth, but I'd like to keep my doll all the same. My mam made it for me and I don't have much left from her.'

There was a moment of silence that seemed to Ellen worse than any rebuke. She could hear the breeze blowing the curtains against the wall, a small, pleasant sound so at odds with the way Ruth smiled coolly at her.

'Very well, Ellen. But the doll will have to be boiled in the washing, in any case. I won't suffer dirty things in my house.' Ruth turned, her skirts swishing across the floor. 'You should come downstairs. I'm showing your father the store.'

Ellen counted to ten before following her aunt. Her heart was still beating fiercely, and she strove to keep her face as pleasantly expressionless as possible.

The Seaton General Store was a two-storey building, a large sign in painted red letters out front, with a wide porch underneath that displayed barrels and bins of fresh fruits and vegetables.

Inside was no less impressive. A long, polished counter ran along the back, behind which were shelves stacked straight to the ceiling.

There was everything imaginable in that store, Ellen thought. She walked by sacks of beans and rice, tins of every food imaginable, from Arbuckle's Ariosa Coffee to Gold Medal Flour, with the slogan 'Don't get counterfeits, get gold medal' written in curly gold script on the front.

Behind the counter were what looked like a hundred glass-stoppered jars, each filled with a different kind of sweet. Ellen read an advertisement next to stacks of chewing gum: 'Wrigleys: Get the Parasol, Not the Girl!'

'We did an offer,' Hamish explained kindly, for he had come to stand beside Ellen. 'We gave away a free parasol for every one hundred packs of gum bought.'

'One hundred packs of gum?' Ellen repeated incredulously. 'But who would ever — ?'

Uncle Hamish chuckled. 'They saved, of course. The boys, especially. Wanted something for their mothers.'

Ellen nodded slowly, although she could not imagine anyone buying so much gum, even in their whole lifetime.

'Why don't I get you something?' Hamish suggested in a conspiratorial whisper. 'What do you like? Humbugs? Lemon drops? Liquorice twists? Or what about jellybeans?' He went behind the counter and took a little wax paper bag from a large stack. 'What it'll be?'

Ellen watched as Uncle Hamish beamed at her, and the rows of jars with their brightly coloured sweets seemed to blur in a dizzying rainbow. She swallowed nervously.

'Er . . . jellybeans.'

Uncle Hamish took a large metal scoop and poured a multicoloured stream of jellybeans into the little bag. 'There you go. Welcome to Seaton, Ellen. Welcome to America, for that matter!'

Ellen clutched the bag and smiled back at him.

'Try one,' Uncle Hamish said, and with a little giggle, Ellen popped one into her mouth.

She'd had sweets before, of course, but not very often and the sudden burst of sugary flavour made her eyes widen. Uncle Hamish chuckled, pleased.

'Look around, Ellen. We've got just about everything.'

Still holding her bag, and nibbling a jellybean every few minutes, Ellen continued to wander around the store. She passed by buckets of nails and screws, rows of rakes and hoes, coiled ropes and balls of string and twine. Another row was filled with medicines: Dr Morse's Indian Root Pills, Chamberlain's Cough Remedy, and Brown's Iron Bitters (for All Manner of Wasting Diseases).

Further on, she came to Austen's Forest Flower Cologne, which smelled lovely even without pulling out the stopper, and Ladies'

Lavender Soap wrapped in purple paper and tied with a satin ribbon.

Then there were the toys: balls and hoops, draughts and chess sets, and a row of proud, porcelain dolls that truly did put poor Celia to shame.

Ellen stopped in front of the bolts of fabric and reels of hair ribbon, satin, silk, polka-dotted, and striped. She gazed longingly at a bolt of flower-sprigged cotton.

'Lovely, isn't it?' Aunt Ruth asked, coming to stand beside her.

'Yes,' Ellen couldn't resist stroking the fabric, and gasped in surprise when Aunt Ruth sharply slapped her hand.

'You mustn't touch, Ellen,' she said calmly. 'See, look what you've done.'

Ellen saw a small smear on the cotton, and realized it was from eating the jelly beans. She hid her sticky fingers in her skirt.

Her hand stung, and so did her cheeks, with shame. 'I'm sorry, Aunt Ruth.'

'Now you know.'

A bell jangled on the front door and Aunt Ruth turned crisply away.

'Elmira Cardle, so good to see you. And I see you've brought Hope, as turned out as always. Come meet my niece, Ellen. No doubt you can be a pleasing influence on her.'

Ellen stepped forward, willing herself not

to blush at her aunt's implied rebuke. A girl about her own age with fat yellow braids, wearing a pink cotton dress stood there, smiling uncertainly. Her mother, a stout woman in forest green with a smart green and white striped apron, bristled proudly.

'Say how do you do, Hope.'

'How do you do,' the girl murmured dutifully.

'I'm pleased to meet you,' Ellen replied, trying to keep her voice as clear as possible. Still, Mrs Cardle exchanged a quick look with Aunt Ruth.

'You arrived recently, dear?' she asked, and Ellen nodded.

'She came with me.' Da strode forward, and Ellen felt a wave of relief at seeing his cocky smile, his sure handshake. 'I'm Hamish Copley's brother, Douglas is my name. We arrived this very day.'

'I see.' There was a coolness to Mrs Cardle's voice even as she said, 'I'm sure any friend of the Copleys is a friend to us.'

Douglas nodded, and the Cardles moved on to conduct their business in the store. Ellen saw her father grin and wink at her, and she smiled back. Some things wouldn't change, she thought, not between her and Da.

Later that evening, after Ellen had helped

Aunt Ruth with the washing up, she joined Da on the back porch. He sat on the bottom step, his legs stretched out, his face thoughtful.

'Have you ever heard it so quiet, Ellen?'

'The crickets are loud,' Ellen replied, sitting next to him. Their chirping was like an incessant whine in her ears.

'Ah, but I don't mind the crickets. It's the city noise I'm glad to be rid of. That unholy din. A sound of misery, it was.'

Ellen nodded, and Da gave her a quick smile. 'You're glad to be here? Your room is just as we said it would be. Imagine that.'

Ellen could only nod again, resting her chin on her knees. Her feelings were so mixed up, a tangle of terrible sorrow and wild joy, she wasn't even sure which was which. Her room *was* lovely, but it was a room in a house her father had built which she'd dreamed of.

She wondered what had happened to those dreams.

'I'm glad, Da,' she said, and then, compelled by honesty, added quietly, 'I think.'

To her relief, Da only chuckled. 'I know it's strange,' he said in a low voice, 'and Ruth always was a wee bit prickly. But you'll stay on the right side of her, Ellen. You'll be all right.'

A vague sense of unease crept over Ellen at

her father's words. 'What about you, Da?'

'What about me?'

'You've always said I'm to go to school, but what about you? Will you work in the store?' Somehow she couldn't imagine her father behind those gleaming counters.

'Ah, Ellen, don't worry about me.' Her father gazed out at the hills, now inky purple in the twilight, an embroidery of stars above them. 'I'll find my way. We both will.' But he didn't look at her as he said it.

'What way?' she pressed, and her father only shook his head.

'We'll see . . . we'll see. I may have plans, but it's nothing to worry about now.'

The screen door squeaked open and slapped closed, and Ellen turned to see Ruth.

'It's time little girls were in bed,' she said sharply, then softened it by adding, 'you look fit to drop, Ellen. Tomorrow's a busy day. I thought you could visit Hope Cardle, and we must see about your things.'

'My things?'

'You'll need some new dresses and the like for school,' Aunt Ruth said briskly. 'Nothing fancy, mind.'

Ellen could not suppress her grin of delight. 'New dresses?' And a possible friend? At that moment she felt perfectly happy to be in Seaton. 'Thank you, Aunt Ruth!' She almost reached forward to embrace her aunt, but stopped at the last moment and ducked her head in thanks instead.

'Upstairs, miss.' Aunt Ruth's lips twitched in something like a smile, and Ellen hurried upstairs.

She would get used to it here, she told herself as she slipped into her thin nightdress. She would come to love it. She *would*.

Ellen lay in bed, watching the moonlight shift patterns across the pale wood floor, and tried to cling to her sense of satisfaction.

Yet as sleep descended, she couldn't shrug off the faint unease caused by the way her father had looked to the hills and told her not to worry.

Why would she worry, Ellen wondered. What did her father have planned?

3

'Sit still, child,' Ruth said, her voice caught between annoyance and amusement.

Ellen immediately stopped wriggling, though her shoulders positively itched to twist and turn, to catch a glimpse of the girl in the mirror who looked so grown-up in navy muslin.

Aunt Ruth had been as good as her word, taking the morning to see Ellen with three new dresses. First they'd gone over to the store, and Uncle Hamish had taken down the bolts of cloth while Ruth sized them with a knowledgeable eye.

Ellen had held her breath, not saying anything, not daring to ask for the pink-sprigged cotton with the little clusters of yellow flowers. When Aunt Ruth clucked her tongue and chose the navy muslin, her heart had plummeted just a little bit, but she smiled all the same.

New dresses were still new dresses, after all.

'They'll do, I suppose,' Ruth said now, taking pins from her mouth and sticking them firmly into a little pink pincushion. 'They fit at any rate, and they should last through the winter. You're a small thing, aren't you?'

Ellen shrugged, remembering how the immigration officer had almost sent her back because of her smallness.

In a quick, strong movement, Ruth took Ellen's chin in her hand. 'You may answer when I speak to you, Ellen. Otherwise you're being rude.'

'I . . . I didn't know you asked me a question,' Ellen stammered, and Ruth's eyes narrowed.

'I said you were small. You may answer, 'Yes, Aunt Ruth'.'

Uncertain and a little afraid, Ellen nodded her head like a puppet. 'Yes, Aunt Ruth.'

'Very good.' Ruth let go her chin and gave a small smile. 'The dresses should be ready in a few days. There's an ice cream social at the church on Saturday. You can wear the navy to that.'

Since they were all navy, Ellen didn't see the need to respond . . . until she saw Aunt Ruth's expectant gaze. 'Yes, Aunt Ruth,' she said dutifully, and her aunt smiled tightly.

'Do we actually eat ice cream at the social?' Ellen asked, realizing at once that the question sounded stupid, especially when Aunt Ruth raised her eyebrows incredulously.

'Of course we do. What do you suppose it's

called an ice cream social for?'

Ellen nodded thoughtfully. 'It's just I've never eaten ice cream before. Is it very cold?'

Ruth pursed her lips and jabbed a pin in the dress pattern. 'You'll find out soon enough.'

Ellen watched her aunt covertly, the strong lines of her jaw and throat, the way her hands moved gracefully across the fabric. She must have been very pretty when she was young, and even now she possessed a sort of queenly beauty.

She wanted to say something, something about how the feelings inside her were so strange — joy and excitement and a terrible confusion and even grief all mixed up into one tight ball of emotion that always seemed to get stuck in her throat — but the determined set of Ruth's mouth, the cool distance Ellen felt she saw in her eyes, kept her from saying anything at all.

While Ruth busied herself with the dress patterns, Ellen wandered out into the little yard. She liked to sit on the porch steps and breathe the clean air, away from prying eyes.

She watched the chickens scratch in their little yard. That morning she'd asked Aunt Ruth if she could gather the eggs.

Ruth had pursed her lips, eyeing Ellen thoughtfully, before giving one decisive nod.

'I suppose you could, couldn't you.'

'Do they have names?' Ellen asked and her aunt looked at her as if she'd sprouted another head. Ellen was getting quite used to that look.

'No, of course not, child. They'll be supper eventually, after all.'

Ellen decided she would still name them. She just wouldn't tell anybody.

Now she kicked at the steps and wondered what she should call them. The speckled one who always flapped her wings could be Breezy. Ellen sighed in sudden, pent-up frustration.

Perhaps it was a silly thing to do. She'd rather draw the hens, and in her mind's eye she could see the bold pencil lines, imagine how she would shade the sun slanting across the dusty yard.

Ellen knew she could ask Uncle Hamish for paper, but something kept her back. She wasn't ready, somehow. Drawing was still so precious, so secret, that she didn't even want to share the knowledge of it. There was Mam to think of, after all.

Mam would want me to keep drawing. Ellen could almost hear Mam's voice, telling her she had a gift, and that gifts weren't to be wasted.

Yet she'd been wasting her gift for years, it

seemed, doodling on scraps of papers with bits of coal or lead. She hadn't even told Da about her drawings, and she felt silly now to even think of it.

Ellen sighed and kicked her feet some more. The activity kept her from growing melancholy, and she wouldn't give in to tears.

The truth was, she wasn't quite sure she fit in here . . . or if she *ever* would. She hadn't even dared to sit on the front porch yet, for fear of being watched like she was an oddity in a zoo or museum. She hadn't liked the way Mrs Cardle had looked at her in the store yesterday, as if she were something almost dirty.

Ellen knew she wasn't like the people here, who ate ice cream and rode in motor cars, and did things she hadn't dreamed of back in Springburn. Her accent was too strong and raw, her manners strange and perhaps even coarse compared to what they were used to, but she knew underneath — she hoped anyway — she was still the same. Eating ice cream didn't make you that different, did it?

This was her home now, Ellen reminded herself, for better or worse. She would have to get used to it, and, she determined resolutely, it would get used to her.

★   ★   ★

46

Ellen twirled in her new dress, even though there wasn't enough fabric to make it float out. Still, she pressed her hands down the soft, new material and took in a deep breath of pure pleasure.

'Like it, do you?' Ruth asked, a faint thread of laughter in her voice. Ellen smiled up at her.

'Oh, yes, thank you, Aunt Ruth. I'm sure it's the nicest dress I could ever have.'

Aunt Ruth pursed her lips in a gesture Ellen was becoming used to. 'Well, perhaps we'll make something flowered for you in the spring. No doubt you'll have grown again by then.'

Ellen found her father in the kitchen, sticking his tongue out in concentration as he tried to flatten his hair with a bit of water from the pump.

'I look a sight, don't I?' he said ruefully, then whistled softly. 'Ellen Copley, if you aren't the loveliest thing I've seen this side of the Atlantic!'

Ellen laughed in delight and twirled again. Her hair, brushed hard by Ruth's relentless hand, lay against her shoulders in shiny chestnut waves. Aunt Ruth had found a matching navy hair ribbon, even if it was plain cotton.

'You look fine too, Da,' she said, and he made a face.

'I'm not used to this dressing up. I think I prefer my work coat, grease stained as it was.' There was a wistful look in his eyes that made Ellen prickle in alarm.

'But you'll get used to it, won't you?' she said in what she hoped wasn't too pleading a voice. 'You do look smart, Da, in a tie and those new trousers.' Douglas had also been given goods from the store.

He glanced down at her, a gentle smile softening his features. 'Oh, aye, I'll get used to it. Have to, won't I?'

Ellen nodded, but a faint uneasiness continued its prickling along her spine. Since their arrival in Seaton, her father had not worked in or even familiarized himself with the store. He hadn't met anyone that she could see. In fact, he hadn't done much of anything at all.

Sometimes, at night, Ellen would gaze out at the star-pricked sky and think of how large the world was, how the sky covered them all, from sleepy Seaton to the noisy rail works of Springburn. And she wondered where her father belonged, because she was beginning to suspect he couldn't be happy in either place.

Ruth and Hamish entered the kitchen, Ruth looking imposing in a summer dress of lavender silk, Hamish pulling at his celluloid collar.

'Well, then.' Ruth looped her reticule over one silk-clad arm. 'Shall we?'

The whole town seemed to be out on Seaton's one main street, as far as Ellen could see. Girls and boys in their Sunday best, with scrubbed faces and straw boaters. Women bearing baskets of food or cake platters, chatting amiably while their husbands loitered and laughed, hands stuffed into trouser pockets.

It was hot, hotter than Ellen had ever known, and the sun shone down on her bare head. Aunt Ruth had given her a straw hat with a navy ribbon tied round its brim, but Ellen was afraid to wear it. She couldn't see properly with the thing on, and she didn't want to trip and ruin her whole outfit, so she held it in her hands. Besides, there was her perfectly tied hair ribbon to think about.

Everyone was making their way to the village green across from the Congregational Church, a large white building with a spire that seemed to pierce a sky so blue it looked to crack right open.

Long trestles had been set up on the grass, with big buckets set in ice — whole chests full of ice — and inside the most delicious looking ice cream.

'This is my niece, Ellen Copley,' Aunt Ruth introduced her to a series of forbidding looking matrons, their faces sober as they inspected her dress, her shoes, the hat she held awkwardly in her hands. Da seemed to have disappeared with Uncle Hamish, leaving Ellen to trot obediently after Ruth, speaking when spoken to and not before, which she couldn't imagine doing anyway.

Finally, after Ellen had been introduced to so many names she couldn't remember and her head ached from the heat, Ruth dismissed her. 'You may go get some ice cream, Ellen, and introduce yourself to the children. I'm going to sit here and take some refreshment.'

Ellen walked away from her aunt with a certain amount of trepidation, for now that she was free she didn't know where to go. She wanted to try the ice cream, but what if she made a fool of herself? She wished she knew where Da was, for she'd enjoy sharing the experience with him, but he hadn't made an appearance, even though Uncle Hamish was now fetching Ruth some lemonade.

Squaring her shoulders, Ellen marched to the chests holding ice cream. She'd faced much worse than this. She'd haggled with every peddler and street seller in Springburn, and nearly always came out the victor. Why was she so afraid of this world?

Because it's so strange, a timid little voice inside herself answered. Ellen ignored it.

A jolly looking man in a striped apron was serving the ice cream. Ruth had pointed him out to her as Mr Edwards, the man who ran the barber shop and ice cream parlour.

'And what may I get you, missy? Vanilla, chocolate, or strawberry?'

'Strawberry, please.'

He smiled as he handed her a dish with two glistening pink scoops. 'You must be the new girl living with the Copleys,' he said. 'A relation, are you?'

'A niece,' Ellen said, her hands clasped tight around her bowl. 'My da's here too. He's Uncle Hamish's brother.'

'I'll be pleased to meet him as well, I'm sure.' Mr Edwards handed her a spoon, and Ellen made her way across the lawn.

A group of girls with beribboned plaits and spotless dresses were sitting, giggling and chatting, under the shade of a clump of oak trees, but Ellen knew she could no sooner join them than she could sprout wings and fly.

Slowly, so as not to disturb the mound of ice cream before her, she walked to an empty stretch of grass near enough to the girls so they could be friendly to her if they liked, but far enough so she could still be on her own.

The first taste of ice cream was strange, cold and slippery and surprisingly sweet.

51

Ellen closed her eyes to savour the taste.

'I know you.'

Her eyes flew open in surprise and a little embarrassment. Hope Cardle stood in front of her, dressed in drab green, her fair hair in two fat plaits, her face red from the sun. There were freckles on her nose, standing in relief to her ruddy skin.

Ellen bobbed her head. 'Ellen Copley. You came into the store the other day.'

'May I sit with you?' Hope asked, and Ellen scrambled to make a space.

'Of course.'

Hope sat down, hands folded primly in her lap, her expression filled with glum longing.

'Do you want some ice cream?' Ellen asked uncertainly, and Hope shook her head with obvious regret.

'Mama won't let me have any. She says I'll spill it on my dress, and this is my best one. It's true, I suppose. I'm terribly clumsy.'

Ellen nodded, for she couldn't think of a polite answer. Hope eyed her ice cream with envy and she took a reluctant spoonful. Eating ice cream while someone watched you hungrily wasn't all that fun.

'Do you want some of mine?' Ellen asked after she'd managed several mouthfuls under Hope's beady eye. 'I could give it to you off the spoon so your dress didn't get mussed.'

Hope darted a look around her, but no one was paying attention to the two girls off by themselves. 'I suppose I could, couldn't I?' she said nervously, and Ellen found herself laughing.

'Go on. If Aunt Ruth is letting me have some in my new dress, I don't see why your mam has to be such a stickler about yours.' Besides, Ellen thought, Hope's dress was one of the ugliest she'd ever seen, even if the material was shiny and stiff. The olive colour didn't suit her at all.

'All right.' Hope opened her mouth like a little bird, and Ellen stuck a spoonful of ice cream in. Hope's eyes widened in delight. 'Oh, isn't it delicious!'

They both giggled then. 'Have another,' Ellen said but Hope bit her lip in uncertainty.

'I shouldn't — '

'Don't be a bampot,' Ellen said with a laugh, 'it won't get on your dress!'

Hope tilted her head to one side, her blue eyes wide with guileless curiosity. 'You do talk funny, don't you?'

Ellen returned her spoon to her bowl. 'What do you mean?'

'Mama said that yesterday, but I hadn't heard you well enough to know. But now I see — ' Hope stopped midsentence, her mouth dropping open. 'Oh, I'm sorry! I didn't mean to be rude, honestly. Mama's always saying I can't keep two thoughts in my head — '

'Never mind.' Ellen could feel her face flushing but she strove for a smile. 'I probably do sound funny to everyone here. None of you seems to realize that you all sound rather funny to me.'

Ellen knew her words sounded bitter, and to her consternation Hope's cornflower eyes began to fill with tears. 'Oh, never mind,' she said hurriedly, 'have some more ice cream.' And she thrust the spoon at Hope before she could begin to truly cry.

Hope swallowed, sniffing. 'I'm sorry. I meant to come and be friends with you.' She gave the group of nearby giggling girls one yearning glance. 'I don't have many friends. The girls at school think I'm stupid.'

'You're not,' Ellen said loyally, for Hope was the closest thing she had to a friend, and Hope smiled tremulously.

'I don't think I am, but I am awfully clumsy. Oh, look, there's Mama. I suppose we're going now. I'll see you at church?'

Hope clambered to her feet as Ellen nodded. As she started forward, she tripped over the hem of her dress and sprawled forward in an untidy heap on the grass, knocking Ellen's elbow as she did so.

The bowl of ice cream flew from Ellen's hand and a scoop of strawberry ice cream landed on the front of her dress, sliding down in all of its sticky pink glory to land in a melted puddle on her lap.

Ellen stared at it in horror. Hope struggled to her feet.

'Hope Cardle!' Mrs Cardle marched over to the girls, her dress billowing out behind her like a sail. Her expression was an alarming mixture of fury and embarrassment.

Hope hung her head, her face scarlet. 'I'm sorry, Mama — '

Mrs Cardle's gaze swung to Ellen, still sitting in the grass, paralyzed by the disaster. 'I see you've managed to befriend the only girl in Seaton as clumsy as you,' she said.

Hope opened her mouth to reply to this unjust accusation, but her mother took her by the elbow and began marching away. Hope threw Ellen a look of desperate apology over one olive-green shoulder.

Ellen's cheeks burned. The little spectacle had not gone unnoticed, and she saw the group of girls, like a gaggle of geese, glancing at her as they laughed behind their prim little hands.

Ellen dabbed at the sticky mess as best as she could with her handkerchief, dreading what Ruth would say when she saw her.

She walked slowly over to the table in the shade where she could see her aunt chatting with several other grown-ups.

'Ellen Copley!' Ruth spoke in a hiss, and Ellen hung her head. 'Can you not even manage a simple dish of ice cream?' Ruth seemed to be about to launch into a diatribe, but perhaps something in Ellen's expression, or the public arena for the confrontation, made her purse her lips and give a brisk nod.

'You'll have to walk home and clean yourself up. I hope that dress isn't ruined, young miss.'

Uncle Hamish rose from the table, smiling easily. 'I'll take her home.' He bent to whisper in Ellen's ear. 'Talking with Hope Cardle, eh? That explains it.'

Tidied and changed, Ellen sat with Uncle Hamish on one of the rockers on the front porch, her feet barely skimming the floor. He handed her a tall glass of lemonade, which she sipped gratefully.

'I think I like lemonade better. Less sticky.'

'So it is,' Hamish agreed.

Ellen twisted the cool glass between her palms. 'Uncle Hamish, do you know where Da is?'

'Why, at the ice cream social, I imagine! Enjoying himself like everyone else in this town.'

'But I didn't see him there,' Ellen said slowly. A certainty was growing in her that Da hadn't stayed at the social. 'I don't think he's happy here.'

Uncle Hamish cleared his throat, an uncomfortable sound, and patted Ellen's knee. 'It takes some getting used to, you can be sure. But your father will become accustomed, Ellen, just as you will. Wait till you start school! We'll have you talking like a Yankee in no time.'

Ellen gazed at the street, empty with everyone still at the social. Outside the barber shop there was a red and white striped glass pole, the colours spiralling round and making her dizzy. 'I suppose I'll have to, won't I,' she murmured, and at Uncle Hamish's questioning glance, explained. 'Talk like a Yankee, I mean.'

'You won't be able to help it.'

'But what about Da?' Ellen pressed. 'Will he work in the store with you?'

Hamish shrugged, one finger inching towards his collar to give it an unconscious tug. 'Your father will have to do whatever he has to do,' he said at last. 'A man has to find his way in this world, Ellen, as best he can for himself. And that's all I can tell you.'

That, Ellen thought disconsolately, was no answer at all.

Ellen had been at Seaton for several weeks when she woke up to a crisp September dawn. School was starting next week and she could hardly wait. She could already imagine the crackle of paper, the squeak of chalk on the blackboard, the desks, the books . . .

The house was silent as she sat in bed, sunlight streaking over her quilt in long, yellow fingers. For a moment, she allowed herself to be, if not happy, then content.

Perhaps things would be all right, after all.

In the dawn stillness, she heard a faint creak, followed by the slapping sound of the screen door. Someone was up.

Ellen tiptoed to the window and watched as her father, his old rail-worker's cap pulled low over his face, walked across the hen yard and out into the dew-damp grass, the meadows and woodland stretching behind, out of town, to an unknown horizon.

Ellen bit her lip, quelled a pang of indecision, and then slipped into her dress, one of the new navy muslin ones. Aunt Ruth had burned her old wincey dresses.

She tiptoed downstairs, her heart skipping a beat when she heard Uncle Hamish let out a rumbling snore, and Aunt Ruth gave a dry little cough. Then she heard the steady breathing of sleep, and tiptoed on.

Outside she hurried to catch up with her father, who had disappeared from view. Ellen had not walked very far from the house yet, both from her own sense of caution and Aunt Ruth's stern reminders not to sully her new dresses.

Now, however, with sunlight bathing everything in bright, yellow light, the air as clean and fresh as a drink of water, she wondered why she had not ventured on an exploration sooner.

The Copleys' house was on the edge of Seaton's main street, and Ellen was surprised to see how quickly the ordered civility of the town dropped off into wilderness. The rolling, sweet grass meadow she hurried through was tame enough, but it was skirted by a dark-looking wood Ellen was hesitant to enter.

She scanned the fields rolling into the distance and saw only a few black and white spotted cows who gazed back at her balefully. Ellen wasn't precisely frightened of cows, but she wasn't well acquainted enough with them to want to get too close.

Da must have gone into the woods, she decided and, squaring her shoulders, she headed towards the trees.

Sunlight dappled the shady ground, and

she could hear a ceaseless twitter of birds still awakening the dawn.

'Da?' Ellen called out, and her voice seemed little more than a whisper among the trees.

She kept walking, slowly, looking left and right, until she heard the sound of a stream, and she pushed her way through some raspberry brambles to find herself on the crest of a slope leading down to a merry little creek. Her father was standing by the shore, skimming stones across the water.

'Da?' Ellen picked her way down the hill, and her father turned to look at her in surprise.

'I must have woken you when I left.'

'I heard the door, but I was awake anyway.'

She joined him at the bank and gazed into the clear water, catching sight of a few minnows darting in the shallows.

'Remember what you said? Fish to jump into your hand?'

'I said that, didn't I?' her father agreed after a moment, his gaze on the water, and Ellen felt the prickle of unease that had plagued her nearly since their arrival.

'We ought to fish,' she said brightly. 'Uncle Hamish has some poles, I should think.'

'He has a lot of things,' Da said, and there was an edge of bitterness to his voice.

'It could be a laugh,' she ventured. 'We'd bring home dinner! Rainbow trout, perhaps — '

'Ah, Ellen.' Da shook his head, and when he turned to her, his eyes were so full of sad regret that Ellen wanted to turn away, to forget that she'd ever followed him here. 'I don't know how to fish.'

'You could learn.'

Da sighed and shoved his hands in his pockets. 'I suppose I could.' He shook his head. 'I just don't know if I want to, Ellen, and that's the truth.'

Ellen stared at the rushing stream. The water was clear, tumbling over a few mossy rocks in a crystalline waterfall. 'What are you trying to tell me?' she asked at last, for she knew well enough Da wasn't really talking about fishing.

'I'm moving on, Ellen,' he said quietly, after a moment. Both of their gazes were fixed on the water. 'There's need for men out in New Mexico, building a rail line right down to the border.'

'But you're an engine repairman,' Ellen said faintly. She felt as if the safe, little world they'd just begun to construct for themselves was cracking apart. 'You don't lay tracks.'

'No, but I could see the way of it pretty quick, I reckon. And the country, Ellen

— take a look for yourself!' He took a crumpled leaflet out of his pocket, and Ellen stared blankly at the desert vista emblazoned on it.

She pushed it away with her hand. 'You said you didn't want to learn new things. It seems to me that's a lie.'

'Don't be calling me a liar, Ellen,' Da said, his voice taking on a warning note.

'No? What should I call you, then? How can I call you Da when you're leaving me as surely as Mam did? Except she didn't have a choice! You do!'

'I couldn't be happy here, Ellen. I thought I could.' Da turned to her, his face full of sudden desperation. 'I thought I'd help in the store, or perhaps even get our own bit of land. I thought there'd be a way.'

'There is — '

'No, Ellen, not for me. Don't you see? I didn't sweat my soul in Springburn to live the same stifled life in a town with a different name.'

'But it's so different here!' Ellen cried. 'There's fresh air, and trees, and school — '

'For you — '

'You breathe the same air as me!'

Da chuckled, but it was a sad sound. 'It doesn't feel the same.'

Ellen was silent for a moment. She felt the

sting of tears and forced herself to blink them away. She could hardly believe Da was telling her this, that he was planning to leave her with two strangers. For in a moment of stark honesty, she realized that's just what Hamish and Ruth were. 'When do you go?' she finally asked.

Da didn't meet her eyes. 'There's a train pulling out tomorrow, heading west.'

'Tomorrow?' Ellen felt shock streak through her. 'Were you ever going to tell me?' The tears were close again, blurring her vision. 'Or were you going to sneak off?'

'I planned to tell you!' Da looked both angry and abashed. 'I was just thinking about how to tell you. I'm sorry it came out like this. I'm not a man of words.'

The sun was rising in the sky, causing Ellen's dress to stick to her shoulder blades. She shook her head as if to deny all Da had said. She didn't dare speak, her throat was too tight.

'You'll wish me off?' Da asked. 'I'll write. I'll come back. I promise.'

Ellen nodded, her jaw clenched. Da put a hand on her shoulder, and she shook it off.

'Ellen — '

She shook her head, backing away, tears spilling from her eyes. Then she ran.

4

'You want some paper?' Hamish looked at Ellen's small, determined face and gave her an encouraging smile. He was glad the girl was showing some interest at last. She'd found out about Douglas leaving this morning, and even Ruth had possessed enough heart not to rail at her for her sodden dress.

'She'll make herself sick, crying like that,' she said with pursed lips as they both listened to Ellen's stormy tears coming from behind her closed door.

'Let her be,' said Hamish. 'It's hard for her, poor mite.'

When Ellen finally emerged her face was pale but composed. She found Hamish behind the counter in the store, devoid of customers in the late afternoon heat, and asked for paper and some charcoal.

'Charcoal, eh?' he said as he put a pad of paper on the marble topped counter. 'What are you planning with that?'

'I want to draw,' Ellen said simply, and Hamish leaned forward, impressed.

'Are you an artist then?'

He meant to tease, but Ellen gave him such a grown-up look of polite disdain that he felt quite uneasy.

'Yes,' she said, and took the paper and charcoals. 'Thank you very much for these, Uncle Hamish.'

Later, Hamish confessed to Ruth, 'She seemed quite set on it, poor thing. I wonder what she'll draw?'

'Girlish nonsense, I shouldn't wonder,' Ruth replied shortly. She sat in front of their bedroom mirror, plaiting her long silvery blonde hair. 'I didn't think Douglas was such a ne'er-do-well.'

'Ruth!' Hamish shifted uncomfortably. Douglas slept in the room next to theirs, and might be able to hear Ruth's strident voice. 'He's all right. He just needs to find his place.'

'Which isn't here, apparently,' Ruth returned. 'I thought he was going to help at the store! Make a life for himself and the girl, rather than go haring off on his own foolish dreams and leave us with the consequences.'

Hamish could not think of an adequate reply. He was barely able to admit to himself that he actually felt relieved Douglas was going. His brother's restless presence, the difference in their circumstances and experiences, had all conspired to make Hamish feel quite nervous around his brother.

Douglas had even mentioned it once, when he told Ruth and Hamish he was leaving. 'We had dreams once, didn't we, Ham? It's strange the way things turned out, after all.'

Hamish had nodded, flustered. 'Yes . . . I suppose it is a bit odd,' he said.

'Ellen will be a help to us,' he said now to Ruth.

Ruth finished her plait and tossed it over one shoulder.

'That remains to be seen.' She glanced out the window, the sky inky black, the pale glow of one of the town's new street lights casting an orange circle on the pavement. 'She might be of some use,' she relented after a moment.

Hamish got into bed. Sometimes Ruth seemed a hard woman, he knew, but he'd seen a moment of softness here and there with Ellen, and he hoped that might continue and grow yet. Perhaps without Douglas here, Ellen would look on them more kindly.

'Ruth,' he said hesitantly, 'do you ever wish we'd been blessed with children?'

Ruth raked him with a quick, contemptuous glance. 'That, Hamish Copley, is a foolish question.'

She blew out the lamp and got into bed, and Hamish knew that was the end of the conversation.

Ellen woke up early again, this time to work on her drawing. She'd done with tears, the hours on her bed clutching a newly washed Celia having spent her, and now she felt as empty and hollow as a shell. She knelt on the floor, the paper spread out before her.

She was drawing from memory, a sketch of her and Da on the deck of the ship. They were both laughing, looking out to sea, their elbows leaning on the rail.

Since she hadn't seen it from the outside, she could only imagine what it looked like, remember how it had felt. The waves, the sparkling sun, the hope.

It would be her parting present to Da.

Ellen had decided earlier not to accompany him to the train. She wouldn't pretend she approved of his plan, wouldn't act as if he was going on a grand adventure with everyone's blessing.

Yet after she'd wasted her tears on broken dreams, she realized her relationship to Da was too precious to hurt in that way. He knew how she felt about his going. The least she could do was put a brave face on it.

Ellen concentrated on her drawing, the world around her seeming to dissolve as she focused on line and shape. It had always been like this, so when she was nearly finished and looked up from her drawing, she had to blink to bring the world back into focus.

She was still in her nightgown, and the morning light showed it couldn't yet be seven o'clock. Still, she didn't know when Da was leaving, so she hurried to wash and dress, rolled her drawing up carefully.

Downstairs it was surprisingly quiet. She heard low, murmuring voices from the kitchen. Ruth was counting eggs and Hamish was still in just his shirt and trousers, drinking coffee. They both looked grim.

'It's shameful,' Hamish said. 'What was he thinking?'

'About himself, no doubt,' Ruth replied. 'As he has been since he arrived in this country.'

Ellen's heart lurched at the sharp words and she stepped into the kitchen. Sunlight fell in a dappled pattern on the wooden floor.

'Why are you talking about Da that way?' she demanded.

Hamish looked up, surprised and abashed, but Aunt Ruth simply pursed her lips, her eyes narrowed.

'You won't talk that way to your elders, miss,' she said shortly, and Hamish muttered, 'Ah, give her a break, Ruth. This once.'

Ellen ignored them both. Something awful

was building inside her. 'Where's Da?'

There was a silence, tense and terrible, and then Ruth gave a slight shake of her head. 'I'm sorry, Ellen. He took the morning train to Chicago without telling anyone. He's gone.'

Ellen felt a rushing in her ears, as if a river were flowing right through her. She reached out to grab the back of one of the kitchen chairs, the smooth, solid wood comforting under her hands. It steadied her.

'What do you mean he's gone?' she asked in a voice that didn't quite keep from shaking. She knew what Ruth had meant; it was plain enough. Da had taken the morning train. He'd sneaked out of the house like a naughty child or a boy playing hooky. He had not bothered to tell Ellen. He'd not bothered to say goodbye.

Still, she needed to hear it again.

Ruth just shook her head. 'I'm sorry, child.' The harsh lines of her face had softened into pity. Ellen's grip tightened on the chair.

'No.'

'Ellen — ' It came out as half-warning, half-plea, but Ellen wasn't even listening.

'He left a note. A letter.' She turned to Uncle Hamish who was starting to look uncomfortable. 'Didn't he?'

'I don't know, sweetheart,' he said quietly.

'That's the truth. Maybe he slipped some-thing under your bedroom door.'

Ellen brightened. 'He must have done that! I was so busy, I wouldn't have even noticed.'

'Busy?' Ruth's eyebrows rose in suspicion. 'I thought you were sleeping.'

Ellen did not reply for she'd already scurried from the room on bare feet, catching her dress around her knees as she took the stairs two at a time.

'Ellen Copley!' Ruth cried in exasperation. 'Walk like a lady!'

Ellen pushed open her bedroom door and dropped to her knees. There was nothing. The floor was bare.

She looked under the bureau, the bed, the washstand, even her pillow just in case he'd come in while she was still sleeping, or even last night.

Nothing.

She sat back on her heels and blinked back tears. She would not cry. Not now. She'd cried too much already, and a new hardness in her heart made her think her father was not worth so much sorrow.

Why had Da left without saying goodbye?

Gazing out the window at a slice of blue sky, the sunshine dappling the floor, Ellen wondered if he were planning on ever coming back.

She got up slowly and walked downstairs. Uncle Hamish and Aunt Ruth were still in the kitchen. Aunt Ruth busied herself with breakfast, and Uncle Hamish put down the coffee cup halfway raised to his lips, regarding Ellen uneasily.

'Did he leave anything?' Hamish asked. 'A note for you?'

'Hamish.' Ruth hissed under her breath. 'Can't you see her face? Of course he didn't.' She put two eggs, a rasher of bacon and a thick slice of bread fried in bacon grease on Ellen's plate. 'There. Sit down and get that inside you.'

Ellen sat at the table and gazed down at her unwanted breakfast. Under Ruth's beady eye, she forced down a few mouthfuls.

'How about helping me in the store this morning, Ellen?' Uncle Hamish asked brightly after a long, tense moment had passed. He winked. 'I'm sure we could find something to cheer you up.'

Ellen smiled wanly. Sweets and hair ribbons from the store seemed to be her uncle's way of making things better, but she knew now that some wounds did not heal so easily. Still, it would take her mind off things and the only other option was staying home with Ruth and being put to work in the kitchen or garden.

71

'All right. Thank you, Uncle Hamish.'

They walked over after breakfast, when Seaton's Main Street was just stirring to life. The Vermont State Bank, an impressive brick building on the corner, was getting ready for business and one of the clerks was polishing the marble steps.

Across the street, Mr Edwards smiled and winked at Ellen. She watched his barber's pole spin around in a blur of red and blue, and two men went inside for their morning shave.

Hamish unlocked the door and led Ellen inside, flicking on the electric lights that had been installed last year.

Ellen had been in the store many times by now, but she still loved the hugeness of it, barrels and boxes and bins stretching to the ceiling.

She stood by the counter while Hamish dusted off his ledger book and scales, two of the most important tools of his trade.

'We've quite a morning,' he told her cheerfully. 'Elmer Pyles is coming in with three chickens and a passel of green beans. Then sometime before noon I'm expecting a shipment of hammers and things from The Kilby Tool Company in Rutland. You can help me unload the boxes.'

Ellen nodded, running her fingers along

the smooth marble-topped counter. She'd come to realize that running a successful general store required a great deal more than simply standing behind the counter and taking orders.

Many of the farmers traded their goods for merchandise, and only last week Ellen had watched Uncle Hamish wrestle a pig into his barn while the happy farmer drove away with a wagonload of tinned peaches and several bolts of chambray.

Several times a week the store took deliveries from Rutland, and Hamish went to the depot to oversee the unloading of goods from the train.

Hamish was in his element, however, when he could put on his big, white apron and measure flour and sugar, slipping sweets to the children while the old-timers sat on the pickle barrels and played draughts with bottle caps.

Then, with his thinning hair and ruddy cheeks, he reminded Ellen of a beardless Father Christmas. Thinking of it now, she longed to draw her uncle in the store, could even picture the way her charcoal would cut across the paper. She sighed aloud, and Hamish looked at her with a half-smile.

'Cheer up, sweetheart. He'll write.'

She nodded mechanically as her heart

plummeted once again. For a moment, she'd almost forgotten about Da.

'Why didn't he, though?' she asked in a small voice. 'He wasn't going to leave till noon. Why did he sneak out like that?'

'I don't rightly know.' Uncle Hamish scratched his head. 'I can tell you this, though. Scenes always made your da uncomfortable. It was ever like that when we were boys.'

Ellen looked up at her uncle with a start. She'd somehow forgotten that Hamish was Da's brother and had known him since he was in the cradle. They were just so different.

'What do you mean, scenes?' she asked.

'Well . . . crying and carrying on and such.'

'I wasn't going to cry!' Ellen protested indignantly, and Hamish was hasty to appease her.

'Not even tears, I mean, just the scene itself. Saying goodbye. As I recall, when we left for America, he said goodbye as if it were any other day, and went off to work, whistling.'

'I suppose I know what you mean.' Now that she thought about it, Da had never liked any messy emotion. Even when Mam had been at her worst, she'd always smiled bravely and Da would look faintly relieved.

'Where's he gone, exactly?' Ellen asked after a moment. She recalled the brochure with the desert scene on its front, but she hadn't read it properly.

'Out to New Mexico. New land is opening up there, for cattle farmers and the like. There's plenty of land, but it looks a hard place to me. Dry and hot as . . . well, you know. Hot.' He smiled, abashed, and Ellen frowned.

'It must be quite far, then.'

'Couple thousand miles. Your da will take the train till it stops, I expect, and then he'll start laying the rails. Eventually they want a rail line all the way from Santa Fe to the border of Mexico.'

'He doesn't lay rails,' Ellen said quietly. 'He repairs engines.'

'I'm sure he'll put his hand to that as well,' Hamish said a bit too heartily, and Ellen fixed him with an earnest stare.

'Will he come back, Uncle Hamish? Do you think he will? Tell me the truth.'

Uncle Hamish rubbed his chin uneasily. 'Ah, Ellen, what a question! Of course he'll come back. It's hard for a man to come to this country, you know. He's got to find his place. It was Ruth who thought of fixing up a store, and I was lucky enough to like it. But your da needs to find his place, and it wasn't here.'

'Then where is it?' Ellen asked. 'I don't suppose they have schools and places for children along the rail lines.'

Uncle Hamish looked horrified for a moment before he managed a weak chuckle. 'No, indeed. But there's a school here, a new one, built of brick only a few years ago, and you'll do just fine there.'

Ellen knew she'd asked too much of her uncle, and with a little smile she set about dusting the long rows of shelves. She was looking forward to school, although there were a few nerves jangling around inside of her when she thought of all the other children she didn't know, children who seemed so different from her.

She'd seen Hope at church and occasionally in the store, but their friendship hadn't gone beyond that. Her mother seemed to keep a stern eye on her, and for some reason was not keen to develop the friendship with Ellen.

'Chin up, Ellen,' Hamish called to her as she half-heartedly dusted a shelf full of Mrs Alston's Rheumatic Bitters. 'I see Elmer Pyles's wagon outside and I'll need you to take those chickens to our coop!'

* * *

The first day of school was one of those clear, crisp September days where it felt as if nothing could possibly go wrong. Ellen slid out of bed, her feet falling into a puddle of sunshine.

Aunt Ruth had laid out one of her new, navy dresses, and had even put extra starch in the collar.

Ellen dressed, brushing her hair till it lay flat and then tied it back neatly with a new white silk hair ribbon Uncle Hamish had given her last night, along with two new pencils and a composition book.

'In my day, we had slates,' he told her ruefully, 'but it's all paper now.'

Ellen rifled through the stiff pages and smiled happily. 'Thank you, Uncle Hamish.'

Downstairs Aunt Ruth had prepared pancakes with syrup bartered from one of the farmers, a golden pat of butter swimming in the middle.

'We don't have pancakes every morning, mind,' she said severely, but an awkward smile cracked her stern features, and Ellen grinned back.

She felt, if not happy, then content.

The Seaton Central School was a four-room brick-fronted building on Maple Street, a short walk from the General Store. A few years ago, it had been a one-room school-house like the dozen others scattered around Seaton, serving the local farm children.

As Seaton grew, however, the one-room schoolhouses closed, and the children were driven in, or more likely walked, to the Central School. Recently, Vermont had passed a law requiring children between the ages of eight and fourteen to attend school, but Uncle Hamish had told Ellen that everyone looked the other way during harvest time.

When Ellen arrived at school, children had already started forming lines to be let in to the imposing building. The school yard was no more than a dirt yard with grassy patches and a flag pole, but it somehow managed to convey the impression of importance all the same.

Ellen looked at the different lines, and saw that they were separated by age. Quickly she scuttled into the line for oldest children, behind a prim looking girl with two beribboned plaits.

'Ouch!' Ellen grabbed her head, turning around in surprise. A gap-toothed boy grinned at her, her hair ribbon in his hand.

'Got you. You're the Scotch, aren't you? Seen you at the store.'

'Yes, I am.' She held her hand out. 'Please give me back my ribbon.'

'How're you gonna make me?' the boy taunted, holding it above his head.

'Look, Artie Dole wears ribbons!' Two boys farther back in line cackled, and Ellen's tormentor scowled.

'I wasn't wearin' 'em, anyway,' he muttered, tossing the crumpled ribbon back to Ellen, who took it with stiff dignity.

The whistle blew, and the lines of children began filing in the now open double doors. It was too late to tie her hair back, so with a dark look at Artie Dole, Ellen slipped the ribbon into her pinafore pocket.

The classroom for twelve to fourteen-year-olds was a bright, sunny room with ten desks, each meant for two pupils, and a chalkboard at the front.

As everyone found a seat, girls linking arms with their friends, Ellen realized there were thirteen pupils in her class, and she was the thirteenth. Swallowing hard, she slid into a desk alone at the back.

'Good morning, class, and welcome to a new school year! I am your teacher this year, Miss Evans.' The teacher smiled at everyone in turn, and Ellen liked the look of her.

Miss Evans was young and pretty, her dark hair caught up in one of the newer, looser styles. She turned to the chalkboard, and Ellen saw a boy in the back slip another boy an alarmingly large bullfrog.

Miss Evans turned around. 'I'll have that frog, please, Jeremy Bentham.' She held her hand out, smiling, but there was a steely glint in her eye that Ellen rather liked. Shamefaced, the boy walked up front to hand Miss Evans his contraband frog. She took it firmly with two hands, deposited it out the window, and then turned back to her class.

'Now, then. Shall we start with a hymn?'

The morning passed quickly enough, with Miss Evans administering tests to the children to see how proficient they were in all the subjects.

Ellen managed her penmanship well enough, but she struggled with her arithmetic. Since she'd left school several years before, she hadn't had a chance to catch up with her learning, though she'd read nearly any book she could get her hands on. That didn't learn her the multiplication tables, she soon realized.

When everyone was dismissed for lunch, Miss Evans called her to the front.

Ellen stood by her desk as the other children filed out of the room, more than a few shooting her covert, curious looks.

'Hello, Ellen.' Miss Evans smiled kindly, but it had too much compassion in it for Ellen to feel comfortable.

'Hello.'

'You've just arrived here, haven't you? I know we haven't met formally, but I know your aunt and uncle, of course.'

'Yes, ma'am.'

'Did you go to school in Scotland, Ellen?'

Ellen squirmed. She could feel a hot blush stealing over her cheeks. 'I did, but I had to stop when I was ten. My mam was ill.'

'I see.' Miss Evans looked down at something on her desk, which Ellen realized was her arithmetic paper. It had a great deal of crossed out answers on it, and she squirmed some more.

'I think you're a very bright young lady, Ellen,' Miss Evans continued after a moment. 'And I'm sure you'd do very well in this class. When you read aloud for me, it was really quite perfect, despite your accent.'

'Thank you, ma'am.' Ellen waited, for Miss Evans was looking at her with a faint frown line between her brows.

'I'm afraid, however, your arithmetic and grammar are simply not up to task,' she continued. 'I can't have you continue in this class at your current rate of progress.'

Ellen's stomach dipped. But it was only the first day! 'You mean I have to go home?'

'No, of course not. You may go in the class for the ten to twelve-year-olds. And when your arithmetic and grammar improve, you may join us again.' Miss Evans smiled tentatively. 'It happens quite often, dear, especially with the farm children. They take time off for the harvest, and it's difficult to catch up. You understand, I'm sure.'

She did, but it did not make it any easier — or less humiliating — when Ellen transferred her pencils and composition book to the other classroom.

Mr Phillips was her new teacher, and he regarded her sternly, without a flicker of warmth in his small, shrewd eyes.

'Weren't up to scratch, were you? We'll soon get you in shape, miss.'

Taking her lunch pail out to the yard, Ellen decided she liked Miss Evans much better.

The rest of the day passed in an unhappy blur. As much as she hungered for knowledge, administered by Mr Phillips's stern hand, Ellen found it much less palatable.

Even worse perhaps was the blatant unfriendliness of the other children. No one was mean, of course, and no one bullied her. Ellen thought she might have preferred that. Instead, in their little clumps in the school yard, they regarded her with cautious curiosity, or worse, indifference.

To them, she was a nobody. Ellen wondered how anyone made friends in this town.

'Why, we don't,' Hope said in surprise when Ellen had gathered up the courage to approach her. She glanced worriedly over her shoulder at the cluster of girls she'd been talking to, whose heads were bent together as they whispered. 'We've all known each other forever. No one really moves to Seaton, you know. Or if they do, they just — '

'Just what?'

'Stick it out, I suppose. Of course, there are the quarry workers' children, and the factory's, but they have their own schools.' Hope gave a little shudder. 'They come and go like gypsies, you know, so we wouldn't be getting to know them. They certainly wouldn't come here. Mama doesn't even like to go to the store when they're in there.'

'She doesn't sound like a very nice person,' Ellen said sharply. 'My father worked in a rail factory.'

'Did he?' Hope's eyes were wide. 'Oh, I didn't know!'

Somehow Hope's apologetic ignorance didn't make Ellen feel any better. Would the other children be just as snobbish?

Ellen walked home alone that afternoon, dragging her feet through the dust. She knew Aunt Ruth would scold her for dirtying her shoes, but somehow she couldn't dredge up the effort to lift her feet.

School — that great, shining promise — now seemed just another thing to dread. Even Hope, her one possible friend, had apologized and run straight back to a bunch of girls who sashayed past Ellen, their noses in the air.

Why couldn't she fit in? Ellen knew she was different, was even willing to change herself a bit if necessary.

But that didn't matter. The problem was, everyone else knew she was different, and they wouldn't even *let* her change.

5

A few weeks after school started Ellen woke up in the night to a ferocious storm. Rain lashed the window and thunder cracked overhead. She stood by the window and watched the trees lining Main Street bend and sway in the wind.

She wondered where Da was. Had he reached New Mexico yet? Was it raining there? Did it even rain in the desert?

Ellen doubted it. She'd looked on a map at school, and New Mexico was far, far away. As far away as Scotland was, only separated by an ocean of land.

It wasn't until the rain pattered to a stop that Ellen heard the low murmuring of voices downstairs. It had to be the middle of the night, but Ruth and Hamish were obviously awake.

Hesitating only a moment, Ellen opened her door and tiptoed downstairs.

'I don't know what she expects us to do,' Ruth said in a low, querulous tone. They were sitting in the kitchen, and Ruth's long, silvery blonde hair was bound in a plait that lay over one shoulder.

'I expect she just wants some help,' Hamish replied mildly. 'Five little ones all down with the scarlet fever. It sounds bad to me.'

'They're over the worst of it, apparently,' Ruth replied, 'or so it says in the letter. I don't suppose her good-for-nothing husband helps at all!'

'There's nothing wrong with Dyle,' Hamish said, 'except that he's Irish.'

Ruth harumphed, her sharp eyes glancing over Hamish's shoulder to rest on Ellen's toes, visible under the crack in the kitchen door.

'Ellen Copley!' she called sharply. 'Come in here at once! How dare you eavesdrop on us?'

Ellen came forward reluctantly. 'I'm sorry, Aunt Ruth. The storm woke me up and I heard voices downstairs.'

'And you didn't think to make your presence known?' Ruth replied with one eyebrow arched. Ellen hung her head.

'I . . . I didn't think.'

'That's not a surprise,' Ruth snapped, and Hamish held up one hand in appeal.

'Ruth — '

'Well, she's hardly the brightest child!' Ruth replied, her glance raking over Ellen. 'Still in the younger class, and Mr Phillips has no plans to move you up at all, or so he told me when he came into the store. Seems to think you need a lot of help.'

Anger burned, a hot lump in her chest, but Ellen forced her voice to stay calm. 'I suppose I do.'

'Of course, I don't know what good it will do,' Ruth continued relentlessly. 'You're thirteen soon, aren't you?'

'Next month.'

'And I expect you'll stop school after this year. There's no point going on, is there, the way you've been getting on? Artie Dole is two months younger than you and Mr Philips says he'll be ready to move up before Christmas.'

Ellen tried to keep her face blank as she shrugged, but inside she felt as if her fragile hopes were being torn to shreds. No school after this year? She realized she'd assumed since she wasn't needed on a farm, she could continue school for as long as she liked, perhaps even go to the high school in Rutland. Formless dreams as of yet, but now dashed in their infancy.

Ruth's eyes narrowed as she gazed at Ellen thoughtfully. 'Of course, there could be another way — '

'What way?' Hamish asked, a thread of anxiety in his usually genial voice.

'Rose needs someone to take care of her little ones, and I certainly can't be spared.' Ruth nodded decisively. 'We'll send Ellen instead. She isn't fit for schooling anyway, and I'm sure she'll be a help to Rose.' She fixed Ellen with a gimlet stare. 'Won't you?'

'Send me?' Ellen repeated faintly. 'Where?'

'To my sister's, in Ontario,' Hamish explained. He threw a troubled look at his wife. 'Rose McCafferty. She lives on an island in Lake Ontario, and has five children all down with the scarlet fever, but I don't think — ' he trailed off under Ruth's fixed stare.

'You don't think what, Hamish Copley? It makes perfect sense. Ellen can be of some use to someone, and I'll be able to stay here.'

'But she's just a child.'

'You've nursing experience, don't you?' Ruth demanded of Ellen. 'You nursed your mother for over a year, as I recall.'

Ellen nodded. She felt as if her carefully constructed world, difficult as it was, was collapsing around her. Move again? To nurse someone else's children? The McCaffertys were kin, of course, but they were still strangers.

And worse yet, she would not be able to go to school.

This wouldn't have happened if Da hadn't left, Ellen thought. She gazed at her aunt's determined face, a face she'd come to know, hiding, she'd hoped, a fledgling affection.

If Aunt Ruth harboured any warm feelings for her, she was certainly adept at hiding them now. She nodded once in Ellen's direction.

'Now that you've finished eavesdropping, you can go upstairs and get some sleep. Tomorrow you'll tell your teacher you won't be back to school after this week, and I'll arrange your train fare.'

★ ★ ★

Ellen was amazed at how quickly things could change. In just a matter of days, Aunt Ruth had bought her train passage to Millhaven, Ontario, from which she would take a ferry to Amherst Island, where the McCaffertys lived. She'd sent a telegram ahead to warn them of Ellen's arrival, muttering darkly all the while about the unreliability of telegraph services on the island, so Ellen wondered if anyone would even know she was coming.

Three days after Aunt Ruth made her decision, Ellen found herself at the train depot, a valise at her feet, while Aunt Ruth and Uncle Hamish said their goodbyes.

'You'll change at Rouse's Point and Ogdensberg, to Millhaven,' Aunt Ruth said briskly, although she'd gone over Ellen's itinerary several times already. An all-day train to Rouse's Point, on the Canadian border, where Aunt Ruth had arranged for the landlady of a boarding house to look after her for the night. The next day, she would take the train to the shore of Lake Ontario, where she would board a ferry to Amherst Island. 'The conductor will help you,' Ruth continued bracingly. 'Just ask if you're unsure.'

Ellen felt dizzy. Two rail changes and a ferry, not to mention an overnight stay, by herself? She wanted Da desperately, and yet at the same time she couldn't help but feel a sharp stab of resentment that he wasn't here to help her.

He'd made his choices. And hers were being made for her.

'I wish one of us could go with you, Ellen,' Uncle Hamish said in a low voice. 'It's a long way, I know.'

'Nonsense, it's all taken care of,' Ruth snapped. 'She'll be in good hands. I've promised Rose she can have you till Christmas. After that I expect she'll want you sent back here.'

Ellen felt like a parcel, and an unwanted one at that. She couldn't help but wonder what had turned Ruth so cold towards her.

'I'm sorry, Aunt Ruth,' she said hesitantly, 'if I've offended you in some way.'

'Offended me? Of course not.' Ruth looked vaguely uncomfortable for a moment, but then the train whistle blew and Uncle Hamish picked up her valise. 'I just want to put you to some use,' Ruth said, and marched towards the train.

Ellen didn't remember much of the journey. She felt as if she had a fragile enough hold on her composure, and to remark all the strangeness of it would make her relinquish it completely.

She did notice the leaves, the trees creating a blurred rainbow of reds and yellows as the train sped by. They looked, Ellen thought, as if their tops were on fire. The sky was a deep, aching blue, so bright and solid a colour it hurt to look at it.

The conductor was friendly enough, and at noon Ellen ate the sandwiches Aunt Ruth had made for her, wrapped in wax paper, washed down with a bottle of sarsaparilla.

It was six o'clock when she arrived at Rouse's Point, and was met by a stout, brisk-looking woman in bottle-green bombazine.

'Don't talk much, do you?' she commented when Ellen had given several monosyllabic replies to her questions.

'I'm sorry, I'm very tired,' Ellen murmured, and the woman, Mrs Cranby, nodded sympathetically.

'It's a long day, at that. Well, you won't find anyone to say boo to. I cater to the soldiers at Fort Montgomery, and they won't bother with a child like you. Mind, we've some traders staying with us just now, but they speak French. They're Quebecois, not American like you or me.'

'I'm not American,' Ellen said startled, and Mrs Cranby nodded knowingly.

'Scottish, aren't you? Well, you're American now.'

After a huge dinner of venison stew, Ellen was escorted to her room, a small box room off the kitchen set up with a cot bed.

The next morning Mrs Cranby took her back to the depot, and she boarded the train to Ogdensberg.

It was late afternoon when she finally arrived on the shores of Lake Ontario, a wide expanse of blue-green water with a few islands no more than grey-green specks on the horizon.

Ellen boarded the ferry to Amherst Island, a small craft with a cheerful, red-cheeked captain.

'You're my only passenger today,' he told Ellen, 'so I guess we can leave.'

Ellen looked at him in surprise. 'It's only half past three. I thought the ferry wasn't due to leave until four o'clock?'

'It ain't,' the captain agreed cheerfully, 'but I'm in charge, so I am. I suppose I can decide when it leaves. Besides,' he spat neatly into the foaming water, 'no one left the island this morning, I'd have known. So no one's comin' back.' He pointed to his head, covered in white wispy hair that made him look like he'd dipped his head in cotton wool. 'I keep it all in here.'

Ellen nodded, murmuring faintly, torn between liking the man and thinking he was quite barmy.

Still, she enjoyed the crisp, lake breeze as it blew against her face, and the water of Lake Ontario was a deep, foamy blue-green, clear and beautiful. In the distance she saw a faint, green smudge that the captain told her was Amherst Island.

'It's not a big place, mind,' he said. 'No more than twelve miles long and four miles at the widest point. But it's a happy place, I'll tell you that. The islanders are fierce proud of their little slice of land.'

'Do you know the McCaffertys?' Ellen asked hesitantly, and was rewarded with the captain spitting into the lake again.

'Do I know the McCaffertys! A fine family. Everyone knows everyone else on this island, child, and that's a fact.' He rubbed his chin thoughtfully. 'Got more children than sense,

Dyle has,' he continued. 'He used to run the inn in Stella, a fine place, good taproom, but the island just can't support that kind of business now the shipping's down. It's all going by rail, these days. He sold it up to the town, and they turned it into the new school. Of course, all the old ladies were fair scandalized, the children learning their letters in an old taproom! As for Dyle, he bought a farm out on the shore, nice piece of land, but . . . well, Dyle's not much of a farmer, and that's a fact.'

'I see.' Although truthfully, Ellen wasn't sure she saw at all. She'd heard Ruth call Dyle a good-for-nothing, and now she wondered uneasily if it were true. Just what would the McCaffertys be like? And would they like her?

Ellen felt an ache inside her, of both longing and loss. She was tired of living with strangers, of feeling like a stranger herself. She wanted the comforts of home, of being known and loved, and yet she knew they were denied her, at least for now. For a long while.

'You'll like the island,' the captain assured her. 'Everyone does.' He grinned, and Ellen saw that both of his front teeth were missing. 'You say hello to Dyle for me, missy, say hello from Captain Jonah.' His grin widened. 'There ain't no whales in Lake Ontario, so

94

don't you be worryin'. I think my mum had a laugh when she named me, to tell the truth.'

The ferry office in Stella was a humble, wooden building, empty of people when Captain Jonah tied his little boat up at the dock.

'Harrumph,' he muttered. 'And if I don't know where Bill Lawson has gone!'

'Where has he gone?' Ellen asked.

Captain Jonah gave her a dark look. 'Just because Dyle McCafferty sold up his inn don't mean there aren't any other taprooms on this island.'

With that pronouncement, he went striding off down Stella's only main street, a pleasant dirt road lined with white, painted wooden buildings.

'Captain Jonah,' Ellen called, her voice edged with desperation. 'What shall I do?'

'Wait,' came the reply, over his shoulder as he continued striding down the street. 'Someone's bound to come for you.'

Ellen wasn't so sure about that. What if the McCaffertys had never received Aunt Ruth's telegram? Considering what she knew so far about the island, it seemed entirely possible.

The sun was setting low in the sky, turning the waters of Lake Ontario to burnished gold, and there was a nip in the air.

The leaves, copper and crimson and deep

yellow, rustled dryly in the breeze.

The little ferry office was shut up, so Ellen sat on the weathered bench outside. She peered down the street, but Captain Jonah had disappeared and she couldn't see a soul.

'If no one comes, what shall I do?' she murmured to herself, the first stirrings of panic fluttering in her breast.

Surely Captain Jonah would return . . . or someone else would happen by. She could always walk up the street and knock on someone's door.

Ellen leaned her head against the back of the bench and closed her eyes. Right then she wished to be anywhere else, even the old flat in Springburn, or under Mr Phillips's beady eye at school, than alone in the oncoming darkness in such a strange place.

Her eyes still closed, she heard the clip-clop of a horse's hoofs and its low nickering.

She opened her eyes to see a rather dilapidated wagon slow to a stop in front of the ferry office. A sullen-looking boy of fourteen or so with scruffy black hair gave her an impatient look.

'Well, I'd suppose you'd better get in, then, Ellen Copley,' he said.

Ellen gaped at the boy in surprise. 'Get in?' she repeated, her voice little more than a squeak. 'But who are you?'

The boy tugged at his cap irritably, his expression little better than a scowl. 'Name's Jed, and I've been sent to fetch you. So get in.'

Ellen swallowed. It wasn't as if she had much choice. Darkness was falling like a soft cloak, and the air was decidedly chilly. 'All right.'

She stood up, her valise banging against her legs. 'Shall I . . . shall I just put this . . . ?' She gestured helplessly to the back of the wagon, which looked dirty and half-filled with old straw.

Jed muttered something under his breath and swung out of the wagon. 'Here.' He took the valise from her and threw it into the back of the wagon where it landed with a muffled thud.

He turned to stare at her, and Ellen saw his eyes were a startling, light grey.

'Aren't you going to get in?' he demanded.

'Er . . . yes.' Clumsily Ellen grabbed the side of the wagon and swung herself up. Behind her she heard Jed snort in derision, and her face flamed. This was not how she envisioned her arrival on the island.

Jed swung himself up beside her in the wagon and took the reins. He didn't speak, just clucked softly to the horses which started a slow, steady trot out of Stella.

The buildings fell away to rolling meadow, now cloaked in twilight, with tumbledown stone fences lined with maple trees on either side of the dirt road.

'Are you my cousin?' Ellen asked after a moment, her voice only a bit quavery.

Jed turned to look at her incredulously. 'Me? No.'

'Oh. Well, I've never met them, you see.'

He snorted. 'So it would seem.'

Ellen bristled. She couldn't help it. She was tired and anxious, and her whole body felt as if it were strung tighter than a bow. 'You haven't exactly introduced yourself,' she pointed out sharply, and was glad to see a faint blush stain Jed's cheeks.

'I told you, my name's Jed,' he said. 'Jed Lyman. My pa's farm is next to the McCaffertys.'

He stared straight ahead, his mouth a grim line. Ellen gazed around at the meadows now covered in darkness, the lake just a sound of water lapping against a distant shore. She shivered.

'You cold?' Jed demanded in a surly tone, and Ellen quickly shook her head.

'No. No, that is — ' she shivered again. Her dress and thin shawl were little protection against the now decidedly nippy air.

With a scowl, Jed shrugged off his woollen coat, draping it over Ellen's shoulders with a decided lack of grace.

'Thank you,' Ellen murmured, silently concluding that Jed Lyman was one of the most unpleasant, ill-mannered boors she'd had the misfortune to meet.

They rode the rest of the way in silence, the horses trotting slowly but surely over the rutted road, knowing the familiar path even in the oncoming darkness.

By a large archway of oaks, Jed pulled the wagon to a stop. 'Here we are.'

Ellen merely looked at him, for the lights of the farmhouse were mere twinkling pinpricks in the distance, up a long drive, the oaks flanking each side. He surely wasn't going to make her walk up all that way with her valise?

Muttering under his breath, Jed turned the wagon up the lane. The oak trees arched over the dirt track, making it seem as if they were going through a tunnel.

'Jasper Lane,' Jed told her after a moment. 'The McCaffertys' place.'

The wagon stopped before a large, rambling and rather ramshackle farmhouse in white clapboard, with a wide porch out front. Although there were lights flickering in the front window, no one came out to greet them.

Ellen slid out of the wagon uncertainly

while Jed went to get her valise.

'Should I — ?' she began but Jed just shrugged indifferently.

Gritting her teeth, Ellen marched up the porch stairs and knocked on the weathered front door.

Inside the house she heard a high pitched yelp, followed by laughter, and the scurrying of children's feet. Then nothing.

Just who was in there, Ellen wondered, and did they even know she was coming? Where was Rose, or Dyle?

'You could just go in,' Jed suggested, with the air of someone who wanted to leave as soon as possible.

Ellen threw him a dark look over her shoulder. 'Well, then, you're coming with me.'

'Me?' Jed looked horrified, and Ellen nodded grimly.

'You know these people. I don't.' She beckoned with one hand, and Jed climbed up the stairs with a martyred air.

Ellen turned the handle, and stepped into the front hall of the farmhouse. It was clean and shabby in a comfortable way, a house that seemed both much used and much loved.

There was a second of silence before a bloodcurdling cry split the air, and a boy with a mop of chestnut hair and a ferocious expression came hurtling down the stairs.

Ellen instinctively stepped backwards, jostling into Jed, who put his hands on her shoulders to steady her.

A boy skidded to a halt in front of Ellen, a ferocious expression on his little face, a wooden spoon raised threateningly over his head.

'Surrender!'

'Ppp-pardon?' Ellen stammered.

A girl about ten years old careened down the hallway. Her hair was also chestnut, a wild tangle around her face, and her wide hazel eyes were alight. She was carrying a makeshift bow and arrow.

'Got you!'

'No, you didn't!'

'Yes, I did!'

The boy made to swoop with his spoon, the girl screamed and ducked, and Jed's hand came out quick as lightning and grabbed the spoon.

'I think that's enough, Peter.' He took the spoon and tucked it into the waistband of his trousers.

'That's my tomahawk,' Peter protested, looking mutinous.

'We're playing Indians,' the girl explained, before her gaze fell on Ellen. 'But who are you? Are you the girl who's come to stay with us?'

Ellen found her voice at last. 'I suppose I am. My name is Ellen Copley.'

The girl nodded. 'Yes, Mama told us about you. She said we were to be awfully good so as not to scare you right off the island.'

Ellen swallowed a bubble of terrified laughter. 'I thought you were ill.'

'Oh, we were,' the girl assured her. 'Terribly ill, weren't we, Peter? Mama thought of calling the minister. Last rites and all that.'

'Don't be daft, Caro,' Peter rejoined irritably. 'We're not Catholic. It was just to pray, and do what ministers do.'

'But you're not ill now, it would seem,' Ellen clarified, and heard Jed's suppressed snort of disbelief.

'Oh, no,' Caro said. 'We're con . . . con — '

'Convalescing,' Ellen supplied, and the girl nodded happily.

'Yes, that's it.'

'But where's your mother?' Ellen felt sure an adult presence would have made itself known by now.

'She went to the doctor, with the baby,' Caro said. 'Andrew's still ill, and he's only little. He had a fever. Mrs Hepple was watching us, but she forgot she'd left a pie in the oven and went home to take it out. I expect she's forgotten to come back. It was awhile ago now.'

'I see.' Although Ellen didn't really see at all. How could a grown-up forget to come back? The island seemed to be filled with odd people, from the nonchalant Captain Jonah, leaving her alone in the cold and dark, to the absent Mrs Hepple. Ellen wasn't sure she liked it. In fact, she was quite sure she didn't.

'I suppose we should see about supper,' she said after a moment. 'Have you eaten?'

'No,' Peter piped up, 'and I'm hungry.'

'Show me the way to the kitchen, then,' Ellen said, and Jed shuffled towards the door.

'I'll just be off, then — '

Ellen rounded on him. 'No, you won't. You can stay till Aunt Rose comes back. I don't know the first thing about any of this.'

'You seem bossy enough to me,' Jed muttered, but he slouched into the kitchen after them.

The kitchen was a large, cheerful room in the back of the house, with an impressive blackened range and a large, square table of scrubbed pine. Ellen felt heartened by these familiar sights, and she set about pumping water into a basin and making everyone wash their hands.

An inspection of the pantry revealed a bag of potatoes, a few carrots, and half of a cold game pie. Soon Caro was setting the table,

Peter peeling potatoes, and Ellen sorting out the rest.

She leaned over the table, and her foot hit something soft underneath.

'Ouch!'

Jerking in surprise, Ellen looked down and saw two black-haired, black-eyed girls crouching underneath the table.

'Who are you?' she cried. 'And what are you doing under there?'

The girls scrambled out. One looked to be about six; the other four years old. 'We're hiding from the Indians,' the older girl said shyly. 'I'm Sarah.' Her dark hair was done in plaits, and she had a quiet, rather dreamy air about her. The other girl was quite the opposite; her hair was a riot of curls and her black eyes snapped fire, her little red mouth pursed in disapproval.

'You're not Mrs Hepple.'

'No, indeed,' Ellen replied crisply. 'My name is Ellen, and I've come to look after you.'

'Mrs Hepple said she'd bring an apple pie,' the girl said, and Sarah gave her a poke.

'Don't be rude, Ruthie.'

'Well, she did,' Ruthie said, lip jutting out, and Peter cuffed her gently on the side of the head.

'You mind Ellen,' he said, his chest swelling

104

importantly, and Ellen suppressed a smile.

'Let's sit down to supper,' she said.

Once again Jed tried to slouch off, but Ellen cornered him in the hallway. 'You can't leave me here,' she declared, to which he scowled.

'You seem to be handling all these little ones fine, Miss Bossy.'

Ellen pointed the spoon she'd been holding at him. 'You stay,' she commanded, and for a tiny second it seemed as if humour lighted Jed's grey eyes before he shrugged.

'Suit yourself. I'm hungry, anyway, and you can't have ruined the pie, at least.'

Over supper the children talked nonstop, informing Ellen of many salient facts. Peter was ten and Caro was eight, they all went to the Island School in Stella except for Ruthie and Andrew, of course, as he was just a baby. Peter had been the most ill; Papa had prayed over him with tears running down his cheeks.

'They all thought I was going to die,' Peter practically crowed.

'That's when Mama sent for the minister,' Caro added.

'Where's your papa now?' Ellen asked. 'It's too dark to be out in the fields.'

Caro shrugged. 'He forgets to come home sometimes.'

'Does he?' Ellen said, shaking her head in

disbelief. 'Just like Mrs Hepple, then.'

She saw Jed chuckle, although the laughter quickly turned into a scowl.

With a sigh she pushed herself up from the table. 'We'll all help with the dishes, and then we'll sort out baths,' she decided.

'But it's not bath night!' Peter cried, horrified.

'Perhaps not, but you're filthy.'

They only cracked two plates while washing up, and the clock in the front parlour chimed seven o'clock.

'I should go,' Jed said, looking relieved to finally be making his escape. 'Ma's expecting me.'

Ellen nodded, stiff with dignity. 'Thank you for helping. I expect Aunt Rose will be home soon.'

Jed nodded back. 'All right, then.' He sloped off to the front door, and Ellen watched him go with a strange sense of longing. As unpleasant and contrary as he could be, there was a steady sureness about Jed Lyman that she needed amidst the chaos of the McCafferty home.

Peter tugged insistently on her sleeve. 'We don't really have to take baths, do we?'

'Yes,' Ellen replied. 'You do.'

The McCafferty farmhouse didn't have running water like Aunt Ruth and Uncle

Hamish's house in Seaton, so they made do sponging down with pump water in the kitchen.

Ellen had just managed to get all three girls in their nightgowns, hair freshly plaited, with Peter hopping around and hooting like a savage in his night shirt, when the front door opened.

'Mama!'

The children rushed to her, and she awkwardly put her arms around them, a baby still cradled in the crook of one arm.

'Darling ones. I'm sorry I'm late. Did Mrs Hepple take good care of you?'

There was a moment's silence and Ellen stepped forward. 'Hello, ma'am. I'm Ellen Copley. I'm afraid Mrs Hepple left to see about a pie and didn't return.'

Rose McCafferty stared in surprise, and Ellen saw that she was a pretty woman, with sandy hair put loosely up, and faded blue eyes. There was a certain weariness to her rounded shoulders, but there was also strength and humour in her face, and she managed a little gasp of laughter now.

'Oh, my dear! How terrible for you, to be greeted with these wild ones. And you've bathed them, I see! You must be a magician.'

'No,' Peter said, 'but she's strict.'

'How delightful,' Rose murmured, giving

Ellen a sideways smile. 'Let's go into the kitchen, dear. Not you lot,' she admonished her children, 'I'm sure Ellen has had quite enough of you. Upstairs, then. You can keep out of mischief before bedtime, can't you?'

Ellen doubted that very much, but the children trooped upstairs obediently.

'Let me put Andrew in his cradle,' Rose said, 'and then we can talk properly. He's exhausted, poor lamb, but his fever's down, thank heaven.'

While Rose went upstairs, Ellen set out a plate for her, and put the kettle to boil on the range. She felt she needed to prove how useful she could be, although why, she wasn't sure.

Didn't she want to be sent back to Seaton as soon as possible? At least there she could go to school and not work like a maid.

Yet the cheerful jumble of the McCafferty house, as overwhelming as it was to a child who'd grown up in a sickroom, had a certain, odd appeal.

'There. Peace for a moment, anyway.' Rose sat down at the table, looking at the plate of pie and potatoes in surprised delight. 'You are a treasure! How did you know I'd be famished?'

Ellen shrugged, discomfited. 'It's late. Will Uncle Dyle be coming back for supper?'

Rose chuckled dryly. 'I doubt it. If he's not back now, he's found his way to the taproom.'

'I thought it closed,' Ellen said, wondering if Uncle Dyle was little better than a drunken layabout. No one seemed very concerned about his absence.

'Ours did,' Rose agreed, 'and a sad day it was. The truth is, the island can't support two taprooms. We had a hotel too, a grand place right on the lakefront, with eight bedrooms. We even served dinner. But now the shipping's changed to rail, no one wants to stay on the island. So we sold up and bought this farm, and it will give us a living, but little else.' She laughed ruefully. 'But there's still a taproom, a small one, on the other end of Stella. They only serve whiskey on Fridays, so I suspect Dyle's there.'

'Is he often there?' Ellen asked, and then bit her lip. She was far too curious.

Rose looked at her, realization dawning, and she laughed again. 'Now you think he's quite the reprobate, don't you! I assure you he's not, my dear Ellen. But he's a dreamer, and he likes to tell stories, and so he finds himself at the taproom. He does like his whiskey too, I suppose. But what he really misses is the old life, even though he's applied himself to farming as much as he can. But enough about that. Tell me about yourself.

I'm so glad Aunt Ruth let you come.'

'But I thought you asked *her* to come,' Ellen said uncertainly, and Rose gave a vigorous shake of her head.

'Certainly not. Oh, I might have suggested it, because I knew to ask you outright would set her firmly against it. But she certainly couldn't be bothered to come herself, could she? So I hoped she'd think to send you.'

Ellen digested this information silently. 'Are the children very ill, then?' she asked.

Rose gave a little laugh. 'You saw them yourself. They *were* ill, and when I wrote it seemed a good idea to mention it. And I do find it hard to cope with all of them, that I confess. But no, my dear, I didn't send for you to be our skivvy. I simply wanted to see you.' Rose sat back, smiling. 'You are quite the image of Douglas, do you know that? I do hope Ruth will let you stay through the year. You'll do well at the island school, I should think.'

'School?' Ellen repeated. 'But I thought — '

Rose laid a hand on her arm. 'I can tell what you thought, simply by all the work you've already done,' she said gently. 'But you must put those old ideas quite out of your head. You're family, Ellen, and that's why we want you here.'

Ellen sat back, stupefied, and a loud crash

sounded from upstairs.

'Ah,' Rose said cheerfully, 'they're ready for bed.'

She walked briskly out of the kitchen, and Ellen, a wondrous new hope blossoming inside her, looked around at her new home.

6

The next few weeks seemed to Ellen the loveliest she'd had since her arrival in America. Every morning she walked to school with Sarah, Caro and Peter; Jasper Lane was ablaze with changing leaves. At the end of their lane, Jed and his younger brother Lucas joined them.

Lucas was quite different from Jed, gentle, blond and bookish, while Jed carried his slate and satchel of books with a grim air.

Ellen knew Jed wanted to quit school — he made no secret of it — but his father had hopes for him to go to Glebe Collegiate in Kingston, and then perhaps even on to Queen's University.

School for Ellen was a delight. It was a one-room house on the edge of Stella, and the teacher was young and pretty. Jed and Ellen were the oldest pupils, for all the other children their age had either quit school or gone to board in Kingston for high school.

When Ellen confessed her arithmetic was quite poor, Miss Gardiner merely shrugged gaily and said, 'I shall have to find time to get you up to scratch, then. And you can help teach the little ones to read, if you'd like to. Your voice is so pretty, and you read so very well.'

Ellen flushed with pleasure, and soon she was spending the mornings with Sarah and three other little children, primers on their knees as they stiltedly sounded out letters by the wood stove.

Life at the McCafferty farm had its own challenges, including the daily chaos she found herself plunged into. Dyle, she discovered, was a cheerful, friendly man, with the same black eyes and hair as his two youngest daughters. But as Rose had said, he was quite a dreamer, and although he managed the farm reasonably well, he often forgot the simplest things, from putting on his coat to coming home for dinner.

The children, Ellen soon learned, were acknowledged to be the wildest on the whole island, but they had good hearts, and so people put up with them. While Rose managed her household with a practical grace, she was as much of a dreamer as Dyle in her own way, and often left dinner to make itself, or the clothes unironed.

Despite Rose's assurances that she was there as part of the family, Ellen set about making herself useful. She found she enjoyed keeping the household on an even keel, and

Rose was grateful when she ironed or cleaned or cooked, or simply took the children off her hands for a few hours.

One evening in early October Rose asked Ellen to deliver a chicken pie to the Lymans' farm.

'Poor Nellie is poorly again,' Rose said with a sorrowful shake of her head. 'She was never strong, and when the cold weather comes it always seems to go straight to her chest. Bringing a bit of dinner is the least we can do.'

Outside, twilight had fallen quickly, leaving the fields cloaked in a soft, purple light. Ellen could hear the baleful lowing of the cattle in a distant field, although in the oncoming darkness she couldn't see them. She hadn't told anyone she was a bit nervous of cows — afraid, she decided, was too strong a word. Still she picked her way across the fields with some care, making sure to keep a good distance from that mournful sound.

The Lymans' farm was a tidy-looking place, with several outbuildings and a large, neat house in a cheerful yellow clapboard.

Mr Lyman answered the door, still wearing his muddy farm boots, the greying stubble visible on his chin. He looked tired, Ellen thought, and supposed that taking care of a farm and a sickly wife was hard on a man.

She left the pie in the kitchen and, as Rose had requested, she asked to pay her regards to Mrs Lyman.

'I'm sure she'll be glad for your company,' Mr Lyman said, and led her upstairs to a room full of dark, heavy furniture, the curtains drawn against the night. Mrs Lyman lay in bed, her slight form covered with a quilt, her face as pale as the sheet covering her except for a hectic spot of colour on each cheek.

'Ellen, child,' she said, her voice raspy. 'It's good of you to come. Rose always seems to know when I've taken a turn.'

'Is there anything else we can do?' Ellen asked. The antiseptic smell of the sickroom and the wheezy sound of Mrs Lyman's breathing made her think painfully of another sickroom, and another woman's frail form and weak smile. Standing there, Ellen felt as if all she needed to do was close her eyes and she would be back in the smoky kitchen in Springburn with Mam. Her throat suddenly felt tight, and a wave of homesickness rolled over her, catching her by surprise.

She didn't want to miss Mam, or Da, or her old life. She was happy here on the island, with the McCaffertys. She felt like she finally fit in, and she wanted to cherish that. Yet for a moment, standing there with Mrs Lyman smiling wanly up at her, she wanted nothing more than the familiarity of her own family, her own life.

Yet that, Ellen knew, was gone forever.

She said her goodbyes to Mr and Mrs Lyman, and left by the back door. Lucas was coming in from his chores in the barn, and he glanced at Ellen in happy surprise.

'Hallo, Ellen! What are you doing here?'

'Visiting your mam,' Ellen said, and Lucas's smile faltered.

'That's good of you.'

Ellen ducked her head. 'It's no trouble.'

Suddenly she heard a low, long, keening wail from the direction of the barn. It was such a miserable sound, it set the hairs on her arms and the back of her neck prickling, and Ellen suppressed a shiver.

'What was that?'

'That was Maggie.' Lucas shoved his hands in his pockets. 'Jed's hunting dog. She tangled with a raccoon and came out the worse for wear.'

From upstairs a fit of coughing could be heard, and then the heavy tread of Mr Lyman on the stairs.

'Lucas! You're needed!' Mr Lyman shouted from the hall, and then came into the kitchen, ducking his head when he saw Ellen. 'Thank you kindly, Ellen Copley, for your visit . . . and thank Rose for the pie.'

116

It was a dismissal, Ellen knew, and she understood. There was something hard and humiliating about outsiders witnessing your weakness, and the Lymans, with their prosperous farm and well-tilled fields, wouldn't want her seeing the underbelly, the illness.

'Yes, sir,' Ellen said and, bobbing a half-curtsey, she let herself out the back into the kitchen yard.

Another wail, almost ghostly in its sound, rose up from the barn, now shrouded in darkness. Ellen hesitated, and then, without thinking too much about what she was doing or why, she crossed the dirt-pecked yard and slipped into the shadowy barn.

It took a moment for her eyes to adjust to the soft, sweet-smelling darkness; barns had a smell Ellen liked, hay and animal and old leather.

Ellen turned a corner and saw Jed kneeling by his dog, the glow of a lantern creating a halo of light around the pathetic scene.

Ellen hesitated, feeling as if she was intruding as much, or more, as she had been in the farmhouse. She was tempted to leave before Jed could see her, and had already half-turned away when he lifted his head.

'What are you doing here?' Jed's voice was surly, and Ellen twisted her hands in her apron.

'I . . . I heard — '

He shrugged away her words, one hand reaching down to stroke Maggie's matted coat. The dog thumped her tail once and whined, a terrible, tiny sound, Ellen thought. It was a plea of mercy. 'Raccoon ripped her belly open,' Jed said in a low voice. 'Pa says she won't last the night.' For a moment his features twisted with grief, and Ellen's eyes stung.

'Oh, Jed, I'm sorry.'

He shrugged again, his face hard and almost indifferent once more. 'It's the way things are,' he said. He paused, and stroked her again. 'But she was — is — a good dog.' The silence stretched on as Ellen searched for something to say, yet any words of sympathy seemed ineffectual and inane.

Then Jed looked up suddenly, and Ellen saw a spark of anger in his eyes. 'What are you doing here, anyway?' he demanded. 'Aren't you needed somewhere . . . back where you belong, Miss Nosy?'

Stung, Ellen took a step back. 'I was just — ' she began, but Jed had already turned back to his dog, and feeling both hurt and sad, Ellen turned and ran out of the barn.

By the time she reached the McCafferty farm, the moon was a lonely crescent in an inky sky, and the lights twinkling from the farmhouse windows were a welcome sight.

Ellen pushed her jumbled thoughts about Jed to the back of her mind and, as she entered the comforting chaos of the McCafferty kitchen, with several children eagerly pulling on her sleeve, she forgot about him completely — almost.

★ ★ ★

One afternoon at the end of October, Ellen took the children for a tramp through the woods, down to the pond that separated the McCafferty land from the Lymans'. It was a cool, clear day, with the leaves in full crimson and gold glory, just beginning to drift lazily down.

Ellen tucked her sketchbook and pencils under one arm. She'd been so busy settling in to her new life, dealing with children and school and the unfamiliar bustle of a family life, that she had yet to set pencil to paper, and she ached to draw the many scenes dancing through her head, from her first glimpse of wild-eyed Peter to the sunlight glinting off the lake.

The children danced around her as they made their way across the fields to the woods, the leaves crunching under their feet, the sunlight filtering through the branches and filling the forest with a hazy light.

Ellen watched them with a strange sense of satisfaction, as if she were somehow responsible for this happy little troop. Peter forged ahead, batting back saplings and brush with a switch he'd made from a fallen hickory stick. Caro was determined both to catch up and not to care when she couldn't. Behind Ellen, Sarah was wandering slowly through the long grass, weaving a wreath of yellow birch leaves.

A small hand slipped into Ellen's, and she gazed down at Ruthie's bright, button-like eyes. The little girl leaned her silky head against Ellen, and something in her heart filled and swelled.

She was happy, she realized. Happy. More than surviving, more than content, even. Happy. The thought made her smile, and then she even laughed aloud.

Ruthie glanced up at her, her little forehead furrowed. 'What is so funny, Ellen?' she asked.

Ellen smiled and shook her head. 'Nothing,' she said, 'and everything.'

They were soon settled by the bank of the little pond, with Peter and Caro setting about making a den out of some fallen evergreen boughs. Sarah and Ruthie were given the chore of collecting leaves and twigs for a make-believe dinner, and Andrew tottered after them on chubby legs.

Ellen leaned back against a clump of birch trees, their pale yellow leaves casting a golden shade, and smiled in satisfaction. The sunlight was warm on her face, and after a moment of simply enjoying the moment she turned to her sketchbook.

The cover of the sketchbook was thick and stiff, the pages creamy and blank. Uncle Hamish had given her a new book as a going away present, slipped to her on the sly when Aunt Ruth wasn't looking. Now Ellen ran her fingers along the first blank, perfect page and felt a small, surprising pang of homesickness for Seaton, and the life she'd known there. The pang subsided quickly, however, and without further conscious thought, Ellen began to draw. She made sure not to lose herself so completely in her work that she couldn't keep an eye on the children, and every few minutes she would look up to check that they were all playing happily in their newly constructed lodge.

Yet as soon as her head was bent once more, she lost herself in the lines upon the page, and the fire they ignited in her imagination. It felt so good to draw again, to feel the pencil firm and strong in her hand, the images that had been dancing through her mind now finally put to paper, given life.

Smiling at the thought, Ellen was unaware that anyone had approached until a shadow suddenly fell over her, and she looked up in surprise to see Jed gazing down at her.

'What have you got there?' he asked, jerking a thumb at her sketchbook. He was wearing his farm overalls, a cap jammed low on his head, his expression as surly as ever.

Ellen shielded the sketchbook with one hand. She didn't want to show her drawings to anyone yet, and certainly not to Jed, who would most likely laugh at them. She hadn't seen much of him since their brief encounter in the barn, and she was still stung by his harsh words. Of course, her common sense told her that Jed had been grieving, wanting to be alone, and certainly not wanting someone like Ellen to see him in his moment of perceived weakness. Yet her pride, and perhaps her heart, still clung to a fierce, childish hurt that she couldn't even give voice to.

Now she kept her hand over her sketches, her chin tilted proudly. 'Nothing.'

His interest now piqued, Jed leaned forward. 'Come on. Show me.'

'No,' Ellen snapped, 'why should I?' She was gratified to see Jed look surprised and even a little hurt by her tart reply, but before he could answer Lucas waded through the long grass up to them.

'What's going on?' he asked, smiling, and Jed, giving Ellen one last, sharp look, grinned back.

'Ellen's got a secret.'

'I haven't,' she protested, but she clutched the sketchbook to her chest all the same, her fingers curling around its edges.

Jed made a grab for it, as she knew he would, and Ellen scooted back, staggering to her feet before Jed pounced again and Ellen ran.

She suddenly had a horrible, lurching feeling that if Jed saw her drawings and made fun of them, nothing would be the same. She couldn't articulate the thought further than that even in her own mind, yet she knew she couldn't bear it if Jed laughed at her for drawing. He'd laughed at her for just about everything else, but her drawings were precious. Private. Sacred, even, and she wasn't ready to share them with anyone, and certainly not Jed.

They continued their mad ballet of cat and mouse, and a few pages fluttered to the ground, but they were too busy chasing each other to notice until Lucas stopped them with a simple question.

'Did you do these, Ellen?' Lucas asked in

wonder. He was crouched down, holding a quick sketch she'd done from memory of Peter, grinning broadly, his hands on his hips, every inch the triumphantly mischievous boy. 'But these are *good*.'

'Thank you,' Ellen said with a lack of grace. She felt her face redden as she held her hand out for the sketch.

Before Peter could give it to her, Jed snatched it away.

'It's *private*!' Ellen cried, and felt the beginnings of tears start in her eyes. Her hands clenched into fists at her sides, for she knew she wouldn't be able to wrest the drawings away from Jed until he was ready to give them.

His grey eyes swept over the page, his face strangely expressionless, and Ellen steeled herself to be mocked and ridiculed. She blinked back that first sting of tears, determined not to add to her humiliation by crying like a baby.

Then Jed looked up with a certain respect in his dark eyes.

'They're all right, I suppose,' he said, tossing her the sketch. 'Although I don't know why you have to hide a bunch of silly old drawings.'

Ellen felt a surge of both gratification and regret. It was more than she'd ever expected from him, and yet strangely it wasn't enough. Before Ellen could reply, however, Jed tossed a handful of leaves in her face, and she sputtered and gasped in indignation.

'Leaf fight!' Peter crowed, and the other children rushed into the fray, chortling with delight. Soon they were all engaged in a furious battle, tossing the golden and crimson and orange leaves through the air, stuffing them down each other's backs, helpless with laughter.

Ellen lay back against the grass, breathless, her apron covered with leaves and bits of grass and twigs. 'I don't know what Aunt Rose will say,' she said in as stern a tone as she could manage. 'We're all a complete mess!'

'She won't mind,' Caro said confidently. 'Mama's good that way. She likes us to play and have fun.'

Smiling a little bit, Jed disentangled a twig from Ellen's hair, and for a moment her heart seemed to stop, and then she found herself blurting, 'It's my birthday next week.'

'Is it?' Jed said, supremely indifferent, and Ellen flushed, wondering why she'd said anything at all, especially to Jed Lyman.

'I suppose I'll make myself a cake,' she said tartly, and the children scrambled towards her eagerly.

'Will you really, Ellen? Will you please make us a cake?'

* * *

Ellen's birthday dawned cold and dreary, and she lay in bed, reluctant to put her feet on the icy floorboards. In the last week, the leaves had all fallen from the trees as if plucked by a giant hand, and a thin, hard crust of snow lay over the frozen earth.

She tucked her toes firmly under the quilt, glancing over at Caro, asleep next to her. At first, the younger girl had been reluctant to share her bedroom, but soon softened, especially when Ellen proved willing to plait her hair with ribbons and talk in whispers even after the moon had risen to a luminous crescent in the sky.

As for Ellen, she found she enjoyed the younger girl's company, scatty and silly as it sometimes was. She'd never shared a bed before, and it wasn't until coming to the McCafferty Farm that she'd begun to realize just how solitary her existence had been.

She'd only been at the farm for a little over a month, and yet it seemed much longer than that. She felt at home here, an integral part of the family and of the island itself, even though her presence had been accepted for a mere matter of weeks.

Yet already Ellen realized she dreaded returning to Seaton. Her gaze slid to the letter she'd received yesterday from Aunt Ruth, the first since she'd arrived. It had been a rather terse, perfunctory note, with bits of news from Seaton that held no interest for Ellen.

The Cardles bought another cow. There was a fire in the hotel kitchen but they put it out before anyone was hurt. Artie Dole has gone up to his proper year.

The last felt like a deliberate dig, yet Ellen tried not to let it hurt. What did it matter if Artie Dole had passed by her own pathetic progress at Seaton School? Here on Amherst Island, she was accepted. She was, for the very first time, just like everybody else.

Ellen knew that in Seaton she'd always feel like a stranger, yet here she was just one more interesting person to add to the mix.

She closed her eyes briefly. She had all year, or so Aunt Rose had hoped.

'If I don't write Ruth, she won't inquire about you for awhile,' she confided, winking. 'And when she does write, I can always write back and say we can't possibly do without you for another three months at least. You are indispensable, you know.'

'Quite,' Dyle agreed, his eyes twinkling. 'You keep us clothed and fed, Ellen. We've not a prayer without you.'

Even though Dyle was stretching the truth a bit, Ellen liked it all the same. She liked to be needed, not just for the services she performed, but for herself.

Yet now that Ruth had written her, Ellen felt the tug of her aunt's expectations on her heart. She didn't need to look at the letter again to recall the postscript:

We'll see you at Christmas. The store is busy then, and we'll need your help.

Christmas was less than two months away. The thought of leaving the island so soon made Ellen's stomach clench with nerves and despair. She'd ask Aunt Rose to write today, she decided, praying that her Aunt Ruth would accept her sister-in-law's request for more time.

With a sigh, Ellen swung out of bed. Next to her, Caroline stirred sleepily and she could smell breakfast downstairs, porridge and sausages. She hadn't told anyone except for Jed about her birthday, and she knew he wouldn't say a word. It seemed a shame to suffer it in silence, but Ellen was too embarrassed to admit that it was a special day.

She'd never really celebrated her birthday with presents or cake, the way some children did. Occasionally, her father remembered to bring home a bit of barley sugar or a paper twist of humbugs, but more often than not with his long work days and the cares of a bedridden wife, the day passed by him completely. And now she didn't even know where he was, and she'd yet to hear from him.

It would have been nice, Ellen thought, for someone to say happy birthday at least, but it was clear throughout the ordinary day that no one knew it was her birthday, and Jed had obviously forgotten. He ignored her all the way to school, which wasn't all that unusual, but disappointed Ellen all the same.

He even pulled one of her plaits in a moment of boredom in class, and Ellen snapped at him.

He raised his eyebrows, his expression sardonic. 'All high and mighty *today*, aren't you?'

Miss Gardiner asked Ellen to stay behind and clean the blackboards, which seemed grossly unfair, yet she agreed to it with stiff-lipped politeness, and the McCafferty children walked home with Jed and Lucas.

By the time Ellen escaped the schoolroom, her scarf wound up to her nose, dusk was falling and she was feeling thoroughly sorry for herself.

The walk home which she usually enjoyed with the others was cold and miserable by herself, with a sharp wind blowing right in her face, and the sight of the farm house, smoke billowing from its chimney, its windows cheerfully lit, did not cheer her. She felt, for the first time since her arrival, as strange and apart as ever.

She let herself in quietly, but Rose heard her and called from the parlour.

'In here, Ellen, dear. I've something for you.'

Another chore perhaps, Ellen wondered sourly, and opened the door.

'Surprise!'

Over a dozen faces grinned at her, all the McCaffertys and the Lymans as well, and some others from school. Even Captain Jonah was there.

Ellen was so shocked she stumbled backwards and shut the door on the room. There was a moment of stunned silence, and then laughter erupted from the parlour.

'Come back in, Ellen, we won't bite!'

'It's your party, you silly goose!'

Blushing madly, Ellen opened the door. 'You surprised me.'

Jed guffawed. 'So it seems. You're the daftest person I know.'

'And you're the rudest,' Ellen shot back, but she was grinning, for she realized that the only way the McCaffertys would have known it was her birthday was if Jed had told them. Her exchange with Jed was lost in a flurry of greetings, cake and presents, and Ellen put Jed firmly out of her head.

There was a new sketchbook and fresh pencils from Dyle, who winked knowingly, even though Ellen had never told him about her drawing. There was an apron with lace edging from Rose, and silk hair ribbons from Caro and Ruthie, and a big bag of mint humbugs from Peter who asked hopefully if she would share.

'And there's something in the kitchen,' Rose said, her eyes glinting. 'And I think I can hear it!'

Mystified, Ellen went to the kitchen. The door was closed, and she heard a scratching sound, followed by a faint whining.

Puzzled and a bit alarmed, she opened the door and a black, long-eared puppy fell upon her with velvet paws.

'A dog!' she exclaimed, caressing the silky head. 'But how — ?'

Everyone had followed her out into the hall, and Rose clapped her hands in delight.

131

'Jed thought of it. His hunting dog, Maggie, had pups in the summer, and they're old enough to give away now.'

Ellen searched Jed out, and found him loitering by the kitchen door, hands thrust in his pockets, scuffing his boots against the door frame. Her throat was suddenly tight, for she knew Maggie had died that night she'd seen Jed in the barn. And yet she'd had puppies, and now this lovely creature was hers.

She gathered the puppy up in her arms, burying her face in the silky fur for a moment before she looked up again. 'Thank you Jed,' she said sincerely, and was rewarded with an indifferent shrug. An alarming, new thought occurred to her and she held the puppy tighter. 'But I won't be here, after this year! And I don't think Aunt Ruth and Uncle Hamish will look kindly upon a dog.'

'So they won't,' Rose agreed cheerfully, 'but we can keep it for you, Ellen. Besides, you'll be back. We'll all make sure of that.'

Ellen could only nod, her throat suddenly tight, her eyes stinging. Everyone had been so kind, so freely loving, and she didn't know how to accept such solicitude, not when her heart felt full to overflowing.

'Thank you,' she said again, her voice little more than a whisper, and she meant it with every fibre of her being.

7

By the last day of school before Christmas, the snow was knee deep and still falling thickly. This was unusual for the island, which generally enjoyed milder temperatures than the mainland.

Ellen, however, loved the snow. She loved the way it cloaked the island, so the trees and bushes and fences were just soft shapes under the whiteness. She loved the ice-encased branches silhouetted against a bright, blue sky and the way the lake became a flat, endless stretch of snow.

She spent hours at her window with her sketchbook, her pencil racing across the page, as she struggled to capture a world made beautiful by cold.

Rose had written Ruth as promised, and there hadn't been a reply yet, which had left Ellen feeling alarmed but Rose had merely shrugged. 'Silence is as good as a yes,' she said with a wink. 'And we've got you now, so you're staying.'

Ellen was greatly looking forward to Christmas. Back in Springburn, Christmas had just been another day in the year; Da might have managed to bring home some sweets but not much else. Somehow Ellen doubted that Christmas in Seaton would be much of a celebration, but at the McCafferty Farm it was an eagerly anticipated event.

There were pies and presents and a huge Christmas tree that they'd cut down themselves, bringing it home on the big sledge; there was a great, fat goose for Christmas dinner, currently residing in the ice house, waiting to be trussed; there were Christmas crackers for the table, and bowls full of oranges stuck with cloves that filled the house with a warm, spicy scent.

Now, as school let out for a fortnight, there were whoops of joy as children poured from the little building into Stella's Front Street, several boys with skates tossed over their shoulder, eager to try their blades on the cleared space on the shallow inlets of the lake, which had frozen hard last week.

Ellen walked slowly home with the McCaffertys and Lymans, as had become their habit. Jed almost lazily threw a snowball at Lucas, who only just managed to dodge. He threw one back, half-heartedly, as he wasn't one for foolery the way Jed was.

'What are you getting in your stocking then, Ellen?' Jed called. 'A broom and dust pan?'

'And you'll be getting a lump of coal,' Ellen returned. She knew Jed liked to tease her about being the McCaffertys' little maid. It didn't bother her now, because she knew she was so much more.

A boy whose mother worked in the postal office came running up to them, his face red with cold. 'A telegram's come,' he announced breathlessly. 'For the McCafferty farm. Ma said to give it to you before you got halfway to home.'

Ellen thanked him, trepidation flooding her happy heart, turning it to ice. Her breath came in frosty puffs as she stared down at the single sheet of paper.

Train fare to be reimbursed. Stop. Ellen to come home by Christmas.

Ellen looked up, her face pale. A telegram! Ruth must really want her home . . . except Seaton wasn't home, and never would be. This was.

'What is it, Ellen?' Caro demanded, pushing her way towards her. She read the telegram, her mouth forming the words soundlessly. 'But you can't leave! Not before Christmas!'

Ellen clutched the telegram in her mittened fist. 'We'll see what happens,' she said, her voice amazingly calm considering the turmoil within her.

She'd no doubt Rose had a few tricks up her sleeve to keep Ellen with the McCaffertys for awhile, but there could be no doubting the cold, hard truth that faced her with that abrupt message.

Time was running out.

For the next week, Ellen pushed the thought of returning to Seaton out of her mind. Rose had sent a telegram to Ruth, insisting she could not part with Ellen till after the syruping, in April.

'Three more months, then,' she told Ellen cheerfully, and with the snow knee-deep and all of the Christmas festivities to look forward to, three months seemed like a lifetime.

Christmas was everything Ellen had hoped it would be. Caro nudged her out of bed while it was still dark, and the floor boards were freezing. Wrapped up in their dressing gowns and slippers, everyone tumbled downstairs to open their stockings; Ellen was delighted with the little treats in hers. There was a new box of pencils, a bag of lemon drops — her favourite — and in the stocking's toe, a whole orange.

After stockings, there was a special breakfast to be had: cinnamon buns and scrambled eggs and toast, and then there were even more presents under the tree. Ellen received a dress, cut down from one of Rose's but as good as new; three new hair ribbons, in different shades of green, and best of all, a pair of ice skates which she was desperate to try out.

That afternoon everyone piled into the sledge and, pulled by the McCaffertys' two bays, they headed for the lake. A large rink had been cleared by Stella's front, and it seemed as if half the island was there on Christmas Day, trying out their new skates.

Although the lake did not freeze from shore to shore in the course of a normal winter, the shallow inlets and bays froze hard enough for skaters to enjoy themselves without fear.

'It looks like we bought out Sears Roebuck's catalogue with the skates!' Dyle said with a wink, and then made a big show of bumbling all over the ice, even though everyone knew he was one of the best skaters there.

Ellen stood by one of the braziers set up along the perimeter of the rink, warming her hands.

Jed skated by, stopping neatly with a spray of ice. 'Cold, Ellen?' he said, his eyes glinting. 'Or just cold feet?'

Ellen lifted her chin. 'It's true I've never skated before,' she replied, 'but I'm willing to try.'

'Let's see, then,' Jed dared her, and Ellen swallowed nervously. The last thing she wanted was to skate for the first time with Jed Lyman looking on, but it seemed as if she had no choice . . . not if she wanted to keep her dignity.

Ellen acknowledged glumly that her dignity would suffer if she fell flat on her face, which, gazing down at the slick ice, seemed perfectly possible.

'Well, Ellen?' Jed stood a few feet away, hands on his hips, as comfortable on skates as if he'd been born wearing them. Ellen hesitated, and Jed held out his hand. 'You can skate right to me. I'll catch you.'

'Sure you will,' Ellen retorted, and Jed looked almost hurt.

'I mean what I say.'

They'd gathered a little knot of spectators now, mostly children, watching with an open curiosity that made Ellen's stomach plummet sickeningly. She couldn't back out now.

'Fine,' she said and pushed off. The first step she took was easy. Her skate cut neatly through the ice and she sailed in a perfect line towards Jed. She heard Caro cheer and Sarah clap, and she gave Jed a dazzling, triumphant smile.

Then she put her other foot down, meaning to push off again, but somehow the movement upset her balance and she began to wobble. She flung her arms out as her heart leapt into her throat and then she made the mistake of looking down. The ice looked very hard and far away. She pushed her skate forward again, still wobbling, and Jed reached forward to catch her before she hit the ice face first.

Ellen felt his arms close around her shoulders and slowly he righted her. Her face flamed, bracing herself for Jed's mockery. But to her surprise, he merely murmured in her ear, 'Not bad, Miss Bossy.'

Ellen straightened and stepped away, wobbling once more before she finally righted herself. 'I suppose I need a bit more practice,' she said, keeping her head high, and Caro skated up to her, lacing her arm with Ellen's.

'Of course you do, Ellen,' she said loyally, 'we all do. But that was brilliant.'

Not quite looking at Jed, Ellen let Caro lead her away.

*   *   *

Christmas ended, the snow melted into a January thaw, and soon Ellen realized the three months which had glistened so promisingly ahead of her were now slipping away. Every day seemed so sweet, so short,

139

and she found herself perched on her windowsill each evening, watching the sun slip towards the lake and lamenting the end of the day.

'Why can't you stay longer?' Caro demanded one day as they helped Rose and Dyle empty the sap pails in the woods behind the farm.

Ellen had never been part of a syruping before, and she was fascinated with the process; she loved the gentle plink-plink of the sap as it dripped into the tin buckets, the frothy foam that came to the top of the pan as it boiled; and best of all, the finished syrup, thick and brown and sweet, which they poured directly on to the snow from a ladle, and let it harden into swirls and designs that they could then break off and eat.

Now she sucked thoughtfully on a piece of the maple candy and shook her head. 'I wish I could,' she told Caro, 'but Aunt Ruth and Uncle Hamish want me back. I've been gone half the year.'

'So?' Caro pouted, hands on hips. 'They didn't want you in the first place, did they?'

Ellen winced at Caro's blunt speaking, even though she wondered herself if it was true. Aunt Ruth had written diligently every month, and Ellen had always responded. The letters had exchanged a variety of news without holding any true affection or warmth.

'Maybe so,' she said at last, 'but Aunt Ruth has bid me home, and she's even sent the train fare.' It had arrived last week, and the tickets lay in a brown envelope on the parlour mantle. Ellen could not shake a vague feeling of guilt when it came to Aunt Ruth and Uncle Hamish, as if she'd disappointed them somehow. And perhaps she had; she hadn't been what they wanted, although she didn't know what that girl would look like.

Caro suddenly threw her arms around Ellen. 'Well, I don't want you to go,' she said, and Ellen returned the rather sticky hug with a smile.

'I don't want to go, either,' she said. 'But we must do what — '

'Will you be back?' Caro interrupted. 'Will you come back soon?'

'I hope so,' Ellen replied, but in truth she did not know the answer.

★ ★ ★

The cherry trees were just beginning to bud, the wind off the lake still chilly when Ellen took the ferry back to mainland with Captain Jonah in late April.

In the end, Rose had been able to convince Ruth and Hamish that she could not part with Ellen until after the syruping, and so

141

Ellen had had an extra three months on the island.

'You stayed here a good part of the year,' Captain Jonah said with philosophical good cheer, for like most islanders he considered returning to the mainland something best avoided.

Ellen merely smiled in reply, for her mind was churning with thoughts and memories, fears and anxieties. There was so much she would miss about her island life, she knew. Her island *home*, for life with the McCaffertys on Amherst Island felt much more like a real home than Ellen feared her place in Seaton with Aunt Ruth and Uncle Hamish ever would.

She would miss the warm, lighted kitchen at the end of Jasper Lane, everyone gathered around the long pine table, the puppy, Boots, at Ellen's knee, begging for scraps. She'd miss the walks to school, the snug warmth of the schoolhouse, wrestling through her arithmetic with Miss Gardiner, or teaching the little ones their letters, slates on their laps.

She'd miss the lake, having captured its many moods on paper, from the dazzling blue-green of morning to the golden sheen of sunset.

And she'd miss the people: Dyle, spinning stories by the fire, always good-natured and forgetful; Rose, practical and full of humour; the children, who buzzed around her like happy bees; and Lucas, who shyly asked to see her drawings and lent her his favourite books.

And Jed. This gave Ellen a little jolt, for what was there to miss about Jed? He was sullen and unpleasant and lost no opportunity to tease her. And yet . . . he'd given her a puppy, and he made sure no one *else* teased her, and, well, Ellen realized, she would miss him too.

'Almost there,' Captain Jonah called, and Ellen saw that the faint, dark line on the horizon had become a bustling town, boats bobbing in the harbour, smoke unfurling into the blue sky.

She thought of the long train ride ahead, the night spent in an unfamiliar boarding house, and at the end of it, her life back in Seaton.

Seaton, with Uncle Hamish and Aunt Ruth, who both seemed as pale and insubstantial as ghosts, yet would be very real and present in just another day.

Taking a breath and squaring her shoulders, Ellen smiled at Captain Jonah. Things would be different now, she told herself, because *she* was different.

She had to believe that, to cling to it, for

otherwise the future in Seaton looked far too bleak to endure.

Captain Jonah watched her with a certain understanding, and smiled in approval. 'That's my girl,' he said. 'You'll be back soon enough.'

Ellen nodded. Rose had promised she could come back in the summer, but who could tell what Aunt Ruth would say? Somehow Ellen knew instinctively that her aunt would balk at letting her traipse merrily between Seaton and Stella.

Soon enough the train from Rouse's Point was rolling into Seaton, and Ellen peered out the window at a town which had become both familiar and strange.

'Why, is it Ellen Copley?' The Seaton stationmaster started forward as Ellen came off the train. 'Ruth said something, but you have grown a bit. I scarcely recognized you.'

'It's been some time,' Ellen allowed. 'Is Aunt Ruth here? Or Uncle Hamish?' She pushed her hair off her face as she scanned the empty station platform. 'I wrote them with the train times.'

There was an uncomfortable pause, and then the stationmaster said, 'You know how they are about minding the store. I expect Hamish will be along soon.'

Ellen nodded, suppressing the twinge of

disappointment and even hurt she felt at her relatives' absence. She seemed destined to be unmet at stations. 'I know the way,' she said after a moment. 'I think I'll walk to the store. Uncle Hamish can retrieve my valise later.'

'Walk? But — '

'I'll be fine,' Ellen said firmly, and set off towards Seaton's main street. There was a light breeze, and fleecy clouds scudded across a pale blue sky. The trees were farther along here than on the island, she noted, and smiled at the cherry blossoms just beginning to open, committing them to memory to draw later.

As Ellen entered the town proper, several people narrowed their eyes in speculative curiosity.

They don't recognize me, Ellen realized in surprise. *I must have grown. I must have changed*.

She *felt* changed, taller, prouder, more certain of who she was, even if the rest of this town had no idea.

Seaton's General Store looked the same, barrels of pickles and nails and bins of fresh vegetables lining the wide front porch.

A few people were in the store, browsing the aisles or chatting at the high marble counter with Uncle Hamish. He glanced her way and his mouth dropped open.

'*Ellen?*'

'Hello, Uncle Hamish.'

'But you've . . . we didn't — ' He tugged at his collar, his smile genuine if a bit awkward. 'Welcome home, Ellen.'

'Thank you.'

Aunt Ruth came bustling out of the store room, also stopping short when she saw Ellen. Something flickered in her eyes and then her mouth tightened.

'So, you're back.'

'I did write,' Ellen said quietly.

'Trains aren't reliable,' Aunt Ruth dismissed. 'I wondered if Rose would manage to get you on the train at all, after all that nonsense about needing you with the syruping! You've never syruped in your life.'

Ellen inclined her head in acceptance, but there was something graceful about her silence that seemed to unnerve Ruth. She frowned.

'What's that dress you're wearing?'

'It's one of Aunt Rose's. I grew out of the blue muslin before Christmas.'

The few people in the store were still staring, and Aunt Ruth seemed to notice the minor spectacle they were creating, for she lifted her chin and walked over to Ellen.

'Come back to the house. You must be

hungry. No one ever gets a proper meal on trains.'

Obediently, Ellen followed her aunt back to the house. Everything seemed just the same, and she had the curious feeling that while her own life had grown and changed, Seaton and all of its residents had remained exactly as they had been the day she left last September.

She stood by the kitchen table while Ruth moved around, fixing a thick slice of bread richly slathered in butter, some leftover ham and a good wedge of cheese on a plate.

She pushed it on the table in front of Ellen, who set to it with a surprising hunger.

'You liked Amherst Island, then?' Aunt Ruth said after a moment.

Ellen looked up curiously. She swallowed her lump of cheese and bread and asked, 'Why do you say that?'

'Rose wouldn't have wanted to keep you if you were miserable, would she?' Ruth plucked at a loose thread on her perfectly starched apron. 'You were a credit to us, I suppose.'

'I hope so.'

'They're a ragamuffin sort of family anyway. Not a penny to their name, and lacking in common sense, as well. I remember Dyle from Rose's wedding.'

'Have you not seen him since then?'

Ruth's expression hardened. 'I doubt he's changed.'

'No one seems to change around here,' Ellen replied, and although her tone was mild there was a certain sharpness to her words. 'I've been gone eight months and everyone seems exactly the same.'

'Which is as it should be,' Ruth returned. 'I suppose you'll be wanting to go back to school? Finish the year?'

Despite the surprise that rippled through her, Ellen forced herself to meet Ruth's gaze directly. She'd thought long and hard about her schooling on the train, for she remembered her aunt's assumption that she would not finish school, since she'd no need to.

Ellen knew she wanted to finish school. She didn't particularly care to endure Mr Phillips's barely concealed contempt, but she wanted to know things. Do things. Perhaps be a teacher one day, or even something else. Professions were slowly opening to women, although perhaps not in places like Seaton.

'Do you need me in the store?' she asked, keeping her tone neutral, and Ruth looked at her in suspicion.

'We can always use help.'

'I would like to finish this year, if I may,' Ellen continued. 'And perhaps even go to high school.'

Ruth's mouth dropped open before pinching closed once more. 'High school! Whatever for?'

Ellen shrugged. 'One day I'll need to make my way in this world. An education would help.'

Ruth looked like she wanted to argue, but after a moment she shrugged as well. 'We'll see about that. High school is expensive.'

This last sentiment was heavy with emphasis, and Ellen went cold. 'What do you mean? Isn't my father — ?' She trailed off, suddenly filled with uncertainty. She'd always assumed her father would send money from the railway, money to keep her from being dependent on charity. Yet now she wondered if he was. Was that why Ruth had been so eager to send her to Amherst Island, because she was expensive to keep?

Ruth gave a cold, little smile. 'Ah, your father. You hadn't asked about him. A letter came for you, around Christmastime.'

She rifled in the dresser, and then handed Ellen a creased envelope.

She saw it had already been opened, despite it being addressed to her, and she bit her lip. A letter from Da.

Dear Ellen, I've arrived in Santa Fe and am at work laying the rails straight down

149

to Mexico. It's not my usual work, but I've come to like it and nothing beats sleeping under the stars of a night. They say it'll take another six months to reach the border. Keep well. Da.

Ellen read the letter through twice before laying it on the table. It had been so short, so uninformative, the letter of a stranger or at best an acquaintance. There had been no word of returning home, no apology for skipping out without a goodbye. She hadn't expected either, Ellen realized, and the thought made her sad. She'd given up on her Da and she hadn't realized it until this moment. She looked up at her aunt.

'He seems well.'

Aunt Ruth stared at her for a moment, and Ellen saw a softening of her features.

'I sent you to Rose because I could tell you were miserable here,' Ruth said abruptly. 'I thought the other children might be good for you.'

Ellen could only stare, her wits too scattered to form a reply, and Aunt Ruth swooped down to take her plate, her face averted. 'Now, you need to wash your face. There's coal dust smudged on your cheek. You look like a navvy! And I suppose we'll have to see about fetching your valise from the station. You left it there for us to fetch, I presume?'

Ellen blinked. This was the Aunt Ruth she knew. For a moment, she'd seemed like someone else entirely.

8

Returning to Seaton had at least two surprises for Ellen. One was that she was moved from Mr Phillips's class to Miss Evans's. Mr Phillips had her tested, and grudgingly admitted that she could probably scrape by in the older class. Ellen took her seat among the pupils her own age with a grateful little sigh.

The other surprise was Louisa Hopper. Louisa had moved to Seaton with her family just a few weeks before Ellen returned. Her father had transferred from Rutland to run the Vermont National Bank branch in Seaton, and such a position came with a fair amount of prestige. The Hoppers awed even the snobbiest of Seaton, with their fancy clothes, gleaming motor car, and the large, gracious home Mr Hopper had built on the corner of Maple and Water Streets.

Louisa could have been friends with any girl in Seaton, yet she picked Ellen to be her best friend.

'You're the only one who isn't toadying to me,' she confided, linking arms with a surprised Ellen one May morning in the schoolyard and bending her head with its glossy, coppery curls towards Ellen's. 'I think I'll have you for my best friend.'

'I didn't realize you chose friends like that,' Ellen replied, laughter lacing her words, and Louisa wrinkled her nose.

'Oh, do you mean I should ask you first? You don't mind, do you?'

'I suppose not,' Ellen said, for Louisa was fairly pulling her along as they walked the perimeter of the schoolyard, heads still bent together.

'Good! Now why weren't you here when I arrived? Have you been somewhere exciting? Have you had scarlet fever?'

'No,' Ellen laughed, 'but my cousins did. I've been in Ontario, on Amherst Island all winter, helping them.'

'Amherst Island! It sounds wonderful, like a jewel! A jewel on the sea. Tell me all about it, do.'

So Ellen did, describing the lake and the little town, and of course all the people, from Captain Jonah to Miss Gardiner to funny little Ruthie, with her snapping eyes and head of black curls. For some reason she couldn't fathom, she didn't mention Jed.

'What a funny place,' Louisa sighed when she'd finished. 'It sounds positively magical. You'll take me there one day, won't you?' She turned wide brown eyes appealingly towards Ellen, who laughed at her new friend's rather obvious theatrics.

'I don't even know if I'm going back myself,' she said.

'Really? But why not? It sounds much more interesting than stuffy old Seaton.'

'It is, in its own way,' Ellen said quietly. She felt a sharp pang of loss at the thought of the island, nestled among the blue-green waters of Lake Ontario, waiting for her. It was, as Louisa had said, a jewel in the sea. 'However,' she added, her tone firmly final, 'Seaton is my home.' Even if the island felt far more welcoming. She belonged here, by Ruth and Hamish's decision, and so here she would stay.

It was inevitable, once Louisa and Ellen's friendship was established, that Aunt Ruth would take a hand in matters. The fact that she approved of Ellen's friendship with Seaton's newest prominent member of society was shown with a supercilious sniff one morning at breakfast, and her aunt's curt announcement that she'd invited the Hoppers to tea that afternoon.

'Tea?' Ellen looked up from her oatmeal. For a brief moment she pictured the old, dented kettle in the flat at Springburn, the sweet, black tea Da liked, and felt a sharp

154

pang of homesickness for that old, familiar life, stifling as it had been. These flashes of longing for the past were rare, yet they still assailed her with a sharp and unexpected pain. Ellen wondered if they would ever stop.

'Yes, tea,' Aunt Ruth replied. 'Earl Grey, scones, and lemon tart. I'll make some cucumber sandwiches as well.'

Ellen nodded. A fancy tea, to impress the Hoppers, she surmised. The lemon tart had come from the Pyles' farm only yesterday, and Ruth had laid it on the pantry shelf, her forbidding expression daring anyone to cut into its pristine surface without permission.

'I'm sure that will be lovely,' Ellen said in the cool, polite voice she found she reserved for her aunt. 'May I help?'

'You can lay the table,' Ruth replied, 'and keep your pinafore clean! Louisa might have chosen you for a friend, but I don't know what her mother or father think on the matter.'

This barb seemed most unjust, as Ellen had comported herself with grace and distinction in the weeks since she'd been home. She feared that for Aunt Ruth, as well as many others in Seaton, the stink and coal dust of Springburn hadn't washed off her completely, even though she'd been in America for almost a year.

'I will do my best, Aunt Ruth,' Ellen said meekly, and was somewhat gratified to see Uncle Hamish wink at her.

Louisa was delighted to be invited for tea, and as the days passed Ellen realized she was not quite as delighted herself. At first, she'd been bemused and perhaps even a little pleased by Louisa's attention. She'd been a solitary presence in the school yard for so long that it made a pleasant change to have someone to eat lunch with and a bench mate in the classroom.

It didn't take long, however, for Ellen to realize that Louisa seemed to have only one true friend, and that was herself. Ellen she merely saw as a prop — or perhaps a mirror — to reflect her own beauty and wit.

That wit, Ellen found too soon, could also be unkind. A week after Louisa had decided to be Ellen's best friend, her eye turned to the unlucky Hope Cardle. Hope hadn't changed much during Ellen's time away; her face was still scrubbed pink, her hair kept in two stiff, yellow plaits, and the choice of colour for her dresses unfortunate.

Worse still, she was habitually clumsy, and even the gentle Miss Evans had trouble keeping hold of her patience when Hope broke another slate, or knocked over her lunch pail in the middle of lessons.

They were out in the schoolyard one afternoon after lunch, and Louisa was, as had become usual, holding court among the girls of Miss Evans's class. Ellen stood to her side, bemused and silent. Tentatively, Hope joined the group; she'd been kept inside cleaning the blackboards. Louisa's gaze flicked to her and Ellen had a sudden wave of foreboding as her new friend's eyes brightened with obvious malice.

'Just look at the state of your pinafore, Hope Cardle!' Louisa chortled, and several girls followed suit. Ellen glanced at Hope; there was a long chalk streak down the front of her already dirty pinafore.

'You look worse than a skivvy,' Louisa said with a malicious satisfaction. 'We might as well use you as an eraser, since you attract all the dirt!' Leaning forward, Louisa picked at one stiff plait as if she meant to use it as a scrub brush.

Hope's already pink face had turned scarlet, and tears of mortification brightened her eyes as the rest of the girls giggled, albeit some of them uneasily.

'Don't, Louisa,' Ellen said in a low voice. She knew too well what it felt like to be in Hope's place. 'It's not her fault her pinafore's dirty. I dare say any of us would look the same if we'd been cleaning the blackboard.'

Louisa turned, and Ellen steeled herself to be the new target of teasing, but after a moment Louisa only smiled and tossed her head.

'The only reason Hope was cleaning blackboards is because she broke another slate! I wonder, is there a dish left in your house, Hope? Or have you broken them all?'

'Louisa — ' Ellen tried again, desperately, and was cut off.

'And you, Ellen Copley, shut your mouth,' she hissed. 'I thought you were my friend.'

Ellen opened her mouth, but nothing came out for Louisa had already flounced away.

Ellen thought, and even hoped, that might be the end of her association with Louisa. She thought she preferred her own company to that of the spoiled girl's, but Louisa, it seemed, had other ideas, and was cloyingly sweet to her that afternoon. Even Louisa's kindness, Ellen reflected, made her uneasy.

The day Louisa was to come to tea, she kept up a steady stream of questions and observations throughout lunch in the school-yard, so much so that Ellen was not able to get a word in edgewise.

'Seaton is so much smaller and drearier than Rutland,' Louisa said as they washed their lunch pails in the creek that flowed behind the schoolhouse. 'I aim to ask your aunt if I can go with you to your lovely little island this summer.'

'What!' Ellen sat back on her heels, her hands red and numb from the creek water. 'Louisa, you wouldn't.'

'Why not?' Louisa tossed her head of burnished curls, her hazel eyes glinting with a cool challenge that Ellen had come to dread. 'I'm bored here and I'd like to see all the funny characters on this island of yours.'

'It's not my island,' Ellen replied, her lips compressed. 'And I don't think they'd like being thought of as funny characters.'

'Don't become all prim on me.' Louisa's eyes widened. 'Don't you *want* me to go with you?'

Ellen gazed at her friend, suddenly realizing that Louisa had chosen her as a best friend for shallow reasons at best, and manipulative ones at worst. Did she think she could control her so easily?

'No, I don't,' Ellen said after a moment. 'Louisa, if you think Seaton is dull, you'd find Amherst Island far, far duller. There are no shops except for a little store that's barely the size of my uncle's broom cupboard, and the school is just one room that's freezing in the winter. We take turns about who can sit closest to the wood stove.'

'Well, I won't be there in winter.'

159

'Why do you want to go?' Ellen asked, desperation edging her voice, for she had a terrible feeling that Louisa Hopper would not take to Amherst Island at all, and the islanders wouldn't take to her. Her summer would be quite ruined.

'Why *don't* you want me to go?' Louisa challenged, eyes snapping. 'I'll like it, I know I would.'

Ellen just shook her head. There was no point continuing this conversation, and besides she suspected that Louisa's parents would not allow her to travel all day and night by train, to stay with relatives Aunt Ruth had made no secret of thinking questionable.

Still, the whole question of Louisa's friendship tugged irritably at Ellen's mind as she set the table that afternoon, in preparation for the Hoppers' visit.

Louisa was just spoiled, she told herself, not mean. At least not too mean. She'd teased Hope, but she'd made up with her afterwards and seemed genuinely sorry. She was impulsive, Ellen decided, and she liked to be entertained, for things to be jolly and fun. There wasn't any harm in that, surely.

'I'm just a novelty to her,' Ellen murmured to herself as she laid the last crisply starched napkin on Aunt Ruth's polished dining room table. 'She'll tire of me soon, and move on to someone else.' Preferably before the summer arrived, and Ellen's plans to return to the island were discussed.

The thought of Louisa abandoning their friendship brought a certain amount of relief, coupled with a twinge of disappointment. As silly and vain as she might be, Louisa was the only friend she had at school.

Her eight months away, Ellen realized, had made her more of a stranger to Seaton than ever.

Aunt Ruth came into the dining room in her second-best dress, her silvery blonde hair swept up in a loose style recently made fashionable by the drawing of a Gibson Girl in Scribner's.

'Haven't you finished?' she asked, clucking her tongue.

'I have,' Ellen replied, and Aunt Ruth moved a napkin an inch to the left, frowning slightly.

'There.'

There was a knock at the front door, and Aunt Ruth swept out of the room again.

'Hamish, they're here!'

Uncle Hamish came downstairs, having changed his collar and tie, his face shiny, red, and affable as always. Ellen felt a flutter of nervousness and wasn't even sure why. She didn't care about impressing the Hoppers.

She suspected they were the sort of people who couldn't be impressed, and yet . . .

She had a bad feeling that if anything — *anything* — went wrong this afternoon, the blame would fall squarely on her shoulders.

With a sigh she went to greet her aunt's guests.

The first half hour of the visit went smoothly enough. Aunt Ruth led the Hoppers into the sitting room and they made polite, rather dull conversation while Louisa kicked her feet in a fit of obvious boredom and Ellen sat as straight and quietly as she could.

Mr Hopper was a dapper man, his hair and the ends of his moustache slicked back with pomade, his suit the latest style. Mrs Hopper looked much like Louisa, with her hazel and chestnut colouring, a great deal of powder on her nose to conceal what could only be described as freckles.

She smiled indulgently at her daughter, and then suggested in a sweet, girlish voice, 'Why don't the two young ones go out and play? Such talk as ours is sure to be deadly dull.'

'It is,' Louisa said sullenly, and Ruth's lips compressed, her nostrils flaring in disapproval of such bad manners.

'Of course,' she said after a tiny pause. 'Ellen, you may show Louisa your bedroom.'

There was nothing of interest to Louisa in that spartan chamber, Ellen was quite certain, but she rose from her place on the hard piano bench and led Louisa out of the sitting room.

'Let me see your dresses,' Louisa commanded when they were in her bedroom.

'I've only three,' Ellen replied nervously. She was wearing her Sunday dress, another cut down from Rose's, and the other two were plain and serviceable, having been worn many times to school.

'Is that all?' Louisa said incredulously, and favoured Ellen with a look of real pity. 'Your aunt's so keen to impress us, I thought she'd have bought you five or six at least. She can get them right from the store, can't she?' Louisa tossed her head. 'Of course, I wouldn't buy a store-bought dress like that. Mama has my dresses made up by a seamstress, you know. She copies the styles from Paris and London.'

'You're very fortunate.' There was much more Ellen would like to say, in surprising defence of Ruth, but she knew that to irritate Louisa now, with her parents downstairs and Aunt Ruth, as Louisa had rudely pointed out, so keen to impress them, would create a disaster.

'I am,' Louisa agreed with a certain

placidity. She leapt off the bed and went out into the hallway.

'Where are you going?' Ellen asked, trying not to sound too anxious, as Louisa marched downstairs again.

'They're still talking,' she whispered, rolling her eyes, and disappeared into the kitchen.

Aunt Ruth had laid the tea things out on the kitchen table, to be brought in with suitable pomp and formality, and Louisa surveyed them with a speculative air.

Ellen's breath caught, and her pulse beat in her throat. 'Louisa — '

With wide, horrified eyes she watched as Louisa plunged her finger into the middle of the lemon tart, its smooth, yellow surface now marred by a gaping, finger-shaped hole.

She licked her finger, grinning. 'Mmm. Delicious.'

'Louisa!' Ellen hissed. She was so angry, she was shaking. 'How could you! You know that tart's for tea!'

Louisa shrugged. 'I'd like to see Aunt Ruth's face when she sees that tart,' she said with a sharp little giggle.

'You will see it,' Ellen replied grimly. 'Honestly, how could you be so selfish!' She looked up, disgusted with Louisa's purposeful malice. 'So *stupid!*'

There was a terrible silence as Louisa's

face went white, then red with rage. 'You'll regret speaking to me like that!' she hissed. 'You're such a prim and proper little miss, aren't you, Ellen Copley! Everyone told me you came here dressed like something from the rag basket with an accent so thick you could spread it on bread! You were worse than one of the Irish mill girls, and *I* made you my friend!'

'I'm not likely to thank you for that privilege,' Ellen snapped back. 'And at least I didn't arrive in this town with my nose so high in the air I'd trip every time I took a step! You're nothing more than a selfish, spoiled, vain little *brat*!'

Louisa gasped in shock, then did something Ellen realized was quite possibly the worst thing that could have happened. She burst into noisy tears.

There was a moment of silence that seemed to reverberate throughout the whole house, pierced only by Louisa's obvious theatrics.

Then Aunt Ruth, Uncle Hamish, and both the Hoppers came hurrying into the kitchen.

'Oh, my Louisa!' Mrs Hopper cried. 'What on earth has happened? Are you hurt, my dear child?'

Louisa gulped noisily, her face streaked with tears. 'My *feelings* are,' she said in a

165

pathetic wail. 'Ellen Copley said horrible things about me! Horrible! And all because I told her not to dip her finger into Mrs Copley's beautiful lemon tart!'

Ellen choked in disbelief, Mrs Hopper gasped, Mr Hopper frowned and glanced at his pocket watch, Uncle Hamish looked troubled and unhappy, and Aunt Ruth's face was completely expressionless as she surveyed the scene, from Louisa's reddened face to the desecrated tart.

'I'm very sorry about this, Mrs Hopper,' Aunt Ruth said after a moment, her voice scrupulously polite. 'Clearly we need to teach the girl some more manners. You know we took her in when her father abandoned her, and clearly there is more work to do.' Ellen gasped aloud at this unfair statement, rage boiling thickly through her. 'I do hope Louisa won't take whatever Ellen said to heart.'

'It appears she already has,' Mrs Hopper replied in a frosty voice. 'She's very sensitive, you know, and I had my doubts about her friendship with your niece, orphaned as she is, and so new to this country.'

'I'm not an orphan,' Ellen interrupted, her voice choked, only to be swiftly silenced by a poisonous look from Aunt Ruth.

'Indeed, I fear your doubts may have had some foundation,' Aunt Ruth replied with a

166

grim courtesy. 'Although in the past Ellen has given very little reason for me to doubt her.'

'Has she? Perhaps you should pay more close attention,' Mrs Hopper retorted, and Aunt Ruth inclined her head.

'I hope you will still stay for tea. Ellen, you must of course apologize to Louisa.'

Ellen's chest felt so tight she could barely breathe. Her face had drained of colour, and she felt dizzy with the injustice of the situation, from Louisa's lies, to her aunt's assumption of the worst in her. Worst of all was Louisa's smug smile as she waited for an apology she had no right to have.

'I'm very sorry, Louisa,' she said in a cold, little voice, 'for what happened today. I realize my judgement was entirely in error.'

Louisa frowned, suspecting the apology was not quite what it should be, and even the Hoppers looked slightly taken aback.

'You will stay for tea, I hope?' Aunt Ruth asked. 'We may put this unfortunate episode behind us.'

'I think not,' Mrs Hopper replied coolly. 'Thank you for your offer, but we must return home. As you can see, Louisa is quite exhausted from such a hurtful experience.'

'Yes,' Aunt Ruth replied dryly, 'I can see that.'

A few minutes later, having gathered their

things, the Hoppers had left. Ellen stood in the hallway, the splendid tea still laid out behind her in the kitchen. Aunt Ruth stood at the door, the spring sunshine from the glass-paned door bathing her face in light, showing Ellen the fine lines of age and strain around her eyes and mouth.

There was an expression on her aunt's face that she couldn't quite fathom, one of weariness and sorrow and even regret. She ached to draw it, capture the sombre mood on paper, yet she knew there was something else to be got through first.

'I'm very sorry, Aunt Ruth,' she said quietly.

Aunt Ruth didn't look at her. 'As am I.'

'They'll come round, I'm sure,' Uncle Hamish said in a feeble attempt at cheerfulness. 'Awfully stuck-up folk if you ask me, but anyhow . . . '

Ellen took a breath. 'I didn't put my finger in that tart — ' she began, but Aunt Ruth cut her off.

'I don't care what you did or didn't do, Ellen Copley. If you'd had the sense you'd been born with, you'd have kept the Hopper girl sweet!'

'Sweet?' Ellen repeated in disbelief. 'But she's horrible!'

'Go to your room.' Aunt Ruth sounded

almost tired. 'Go to your room and you can stay there till bedtime. There will be no supper for you tonight.'

Wordlessly, Ellen went upstairs. Her mind was seething with protestations she knew she could not voice. Why was Aunt Ruth so angry with her, if she knew Ellen hadn't been the one to put her finger in that awful tart?

She threw herself on her bed, taking several deep breaths to compose herself, before she reached underneath her pillow for her sketchbook and charcoal pencils. With grim determination, her fingers shaking only a little bit, she began to draw.

★   ★   ★

Hamish Copley wasn't happy. The debacle with the Hoppers had cast a pallor over his home life, with which he was normally somewhat content.

It had also fed the gossip at his own counter, with plenty of elbowing and winks — and worse, disapproving frowns and nods — as customers asked him just what the Copley girl, his brother's daughter, for heaven's sake, had done to work the entire Hopper family into such a state.

'Far too many airs, they have,' Hamish muttered to himself as he stacked cans of

Benson's Best Gravy on to the shelves. The store was blessedly silent, and unusually for him, Hamish was relieved. He needed a little peace and quiet.

He'd seen Louisa Hopper walk down the street, her nose in the air, ignoring Ellen with such pointed malice. She'd chosen another best friend, poor little Hope Cardle, who looked terrified every time the Hopper girl latched on to her.

The Hoppers were cordial to Hamish and Ruth, for in a town like Seaton the bank manager couldn't be on bad terms with the owner of Seaton's finest store. It was just bad sense.

Their cold courtesy went down hard with Hamish, though. He was used to being liked. He *liked* it.

Worst of all, however, was poor little Ellen. Although she wasn't so little anymore, growing taller and more gracious every day, just like her mother, Ann, who had always preferred silence to chatter, smiles to laughter.

Hamish had always been a bit intimidated by Ann, the way it seemed as if nothing could touch her. Ellen was the same way. And yet, beneath that cool façade, Hamish thought he saw hurt in her clear, hazel eyes.

She walked alone to school, her lunch pail

banging against her knees, and when Hamish had walked past the school to the depot, he'd sometimes seen her in the schoolyard, eating her lunch alone while children gathered in happy clusters around her.

It wasn't fair, Hamish thought, and it wasn't right. Ellen was a lovely girl, and the only reason Seaton hadn't taken to her was because her father had hightailed it out of town, and then that spoiled little Hopper girl had started making Ellen's life a misery. Coupled with this thought was an uncomfortable shaft of guilt, for Hamish knew that Ruth — and even he, himself — had not made things easier for Ellen. They hadn't, he acknowledged tiredly, taken her in like a loved daughter. Hamish had a suspicion that neither of them knew *how*.

Still, it wasn't right for Ellen to be so miserable. She deserved better.

Ruth came in from the storeroom, the account books in her arms.

'I've been thinking, Ruth,' Hamish called from behind his stacked tins, before he could lose his nerve. 'We ought to do something about Ellen.'

'And what should we do?' Ruth asked a bit sourly.

'She's not happy here,' Hamish said quietly. 'And she's not likely to be, with that

Hopper brat turning everyone against her.'

'Hamish, Ellen was the one who insulted Louisa Hopper. She made her bed, now she can —— '

'You don't honestly believe that, do you?' Hamish demanded. 'There was a bit of lemon custard on Louisa's chin! I saw it myself. That girl was lying through her lemon-stained teeth, if you ask me.'

'I'm not asking you,' Ruth replied sharply. 'And I don't care who stuck her finger in the tart. Louisa was Ellen's guest, and it was up to Ellen to keep her happy and entertained. She should have seen that Louisa would make a formidable enemy! That girl is spoiled within an inch of her life. I'd take a strap to her myself, but it isn't up to me.'

Hamish was silent for a moment, the earlier shaft of guilt deepening into a painful twist of his gut. 'No, it isn't,' he said at last, 'but Ellen's well-being is. She's not happy here, Ruth. Let's send her back to Amherst Island. She loved it there, and the children seemed to get along so well.'

Ruth stared at him in wordless surprise, her mouth hanging open for a split second before she snapped it shut. 'You want her to go?' she finally managed, her voice as crisp as ever. 'For good?'

Hamish twisted his hands in his apron, a

surprising ache of sorrow and loneliness engulfing him at the thought of Ellen leaving them once more. He'd got used to her, somehow. 'No, of course I don't. I . . . I like having her here. But I want her to be happy, and you should want that as well.'

'I'd rather she was God-fearing and obedient!' Ruth retorted acerbically. Her lips compressed into a thin line, and her gaze slid away from Hamish to rest on a distant, unseen horizon. 'Rose wrote me, asking for Ellen this summer. The whole summer! We could use her in the store, you know.'

'We don't need her labour,' Hamish replied. 'Let her go.'

Ruth's expression remained distant, her eyes shuttered. 'Next summer,' she said at last. 'In a year. She'd be going to high school then anyway.'

'She wants to go to high school?' Hamish asked in surprise.

'She said something about it. I doubt it will come to anything. She hasn't proven herself an able student.'

'She did rise a grade,' Hamish objected, his voice intentionally mild. 'So she can go for the summer then? I'll tell her.' He felt both relief and disappointment. He didn't want Ellen to leave, yet he still wanted her happiness. The two, he realized, seemed to be forever separate, and the stark realization, and what it meant about his and Ruth's own failings, made him sad. 'She'll go next summer, for who knows how long.'

Ruth glanced at him sharply. 'Not forever.'

'No,' Hamish agreed. 'Not forever.'

★   ★   ★

That evening he knocked on Ellen's bedroom door. When she bid him enter, he saw she was curled up by her window, a pad of paper across her knees.

'Uncle Hamish? Is everything all right?'

'Yes, of course, my dear.' He smiled awkwardly. 'May I sit down?'

'Of course.' Ellen put the paper aside, looking at him with bright, alert eyes and no small amount of curiosity.

'Your aunt and I have been discussing your future. It seems to us you might do better back on Amherst Island.'

Ellen's face was still, expressionless. She looked down at her lap. 'Is it because of the falling out with Louisa?'

'Partly,' Hamish admitted. 'Not that we — I — think you're to blame, Ellen. It's just . . . you're not happy, are you?'

Ellen took a deep breath. 'No,' she confessed quietly, 'I'm not.'

'You see?' Hamish sighed heavily. 'I wish . . . I wish things could be different.'

Ellen looked up at him. 'You do?'

Hamish shrugged, suddenly uncomfortable. 'We want what's best for you, Ellen. I wish it could be us.' Ellen didn't reply, and with her eyes so bright and her head cocked to one side, Hamish wondered if she believed him. He wondered if he believed himself, for he was now honest enough to sense his own relief at Ellen's departure, mixed in with the sorrow and guilt. He slapped his knees as he made to rise. 'You never know how life is going to treat you, I suppose, though your aunt would say it's more how you treat life.'

'When am I to go?' Ellen asked. Like Hamish, although she didn't realize it, she felt disappointment mixed in with the relief and excitement. Would she actually miss Seaton? Or was she just sorry to have failed Ruth and Hamish somehow, although her uncle seemed to feel that they had failed her?

'Next summer, a year from now,' Hamish replied. 'I know it seems a long time, but I thought I'd tell you now. Something to look forward to, eh? And perhaps we can all make the best of the next year.'

'Yes, I hope so.' A whole year! It seemed an eternity. Ellen realized she'd been harbouring silent, latent hopes that she might go this summer, in just another month, but now she realized how foolish that unvoiced dream had been. Ellen looked out the window, the stars pricking an indigo sky, and imagined the night settling softly on Jasper Lane, the oak trees' leaves whispering in the evening air. One more year and she would be there . . .

Hamish made to leave, and then his gaze fell on the paper next to her. 'What's that?'

'Nothing.' Before Ellen could cover it, Hamish had picked up the sheet of paper and looked in surprise at the sketch of Ruth Ellen had drawn from memory. 'I just — ' she began, but trailed off, for the drawing, with Ruth's surprisingly sad eyes, the weary set of her shoulders, seemed all too revealing. Ellen hadn't expected the drawing to turn out that way. When she thought of Ruth, she thought of a stony expression, hard eyes, determination in every taut line of her body. Yet this drawing was completely different.

'It's a good likeness,' Hamish said quietly. 'You've quite a hidden talent there, Ellen. You could go far with that.'

Ellen gathered up the other sheets of paper. 'I don't want to go anywhere with it,' she said. 'It's just something I do.'

'May I keep this?'

Ellen bit her lip. The only person she'd given a drawing to was Mam, yet she could hardly refuse her uncle. 'All right. I don't know if Aunt Ruth will like it, though!'

'I won't show it to her.' Uncle Hamish's smile was a little sad. 'It's just for me.'

After he'd left, Ellen tucked her knees up to her chest, resting her chin on top, and gazed out again at the starry night. A whole year until she was back on Amherst Island! And yet perhaps, wondrously, she might be back for good . . . forever.

'And no Louisa coming with me,' Ellen murmured with a little smile of relieved satisfaction.

Yet about that she soon discovered she was quite, quite wrong.

9

The following winter was long and cold in Seaton. Even at the beginning of April, the ground was covered with a hardened crust of snow, and the trees looked dead and black, their branches stark against a pewter sky.

Ellen had passed the months slowly, ticking each one off on the Farmer's Almanac calendar Hamish had given her from the store. There had been a few letters to liven the long, cold days: two from Da, brief and uninformative as ever. He had settled in Santa Fe, and was now working on the engines. He'd even sent a silver dollar, which seemed an astronomical amount of money, and although Ellen could think of a dozen ways to spend it, she'd dutifully handed the coin over to Aunt Ruth, knowing this was all the money her father had ever sent for her keep. Aunt Ruth had taken it with a grim little nod.

Knowing that her father had settled gave Ellen a leaden feeling in her middle, for it made it all the more certain that her father would not return. She hadn't seen him in a year and a half, and in all that time there had only been three letters, with barely enough words to fill a single sheet of paper.

Yet there had been other letters, cheerful, newsy missives that filled page after page. Rose had written, and Caro and Sarah; Lucas had written too. He was cataloguing all the plants of Amherst Island and sent Ellen pressed specimens which she kept between the pages of her rapidly filling sketchbook.

Each letter from the island was like a burst of light into Ellen's dreary existence; she sat silently through school before returning back to her aunt and uncle's to do her chores or help in the store. The evenings were spent in quiet, and usually solitary pursuits, although once in a while her uncle asked her to play draughts in the parlour, with Aunt Ruth sitting in her usual rocking chair, darning furiously, a scowl hovering around her mouth.

Ellen always obliged when her uncle asked, although these exercises seemed more aimed at assuaging his nebulous guilt than in affording either of them any true pleasure.

Louisa had been ill with scarlet fever for most of the winter, and had not been to school since November, which provided Ellen with some relief from her spiteful comments and malicious jokes. Even though she hadn't been able to find many other friends, the peace of solitude was welcome to being the butt of the schoolroom's uneasy humour.

One morning as Ellen was finishing her oatmeal in her usual silence, Aunt Ruth bustled in, hands on her hips, and announced, 'Louisa is recovering and would like visitors.'

Ellen's spoon hovered halfway to her mouth as she stared at her aunt in surprise. 'Surely you don't mean me.'

'Why else would I be telling you?' Ruth replied irritably. She moved around the kitchen, wiping the already clean counter top and moving the sugar bowl from its perfectly good place.

Ellen sat still. She could tell Ruth was bothered, and not by her own actions for once.

'She asked for me in particular?' Ellen asked and Ruth replied, 'Yes. Of course. You're to go this afternoon, and take a present. Something from the store, a hair ribbon or some such.'

Ellen nodded, her mind still whirling. Why would Louisa want to see her? Could it be just to poke fun from her sickbed? Surely not, and yet Ellen couldn't think of another reason. Louisa had not had a kind word for her in nearly a year. Had being ill changed her? Ellen felt a chill of foreboding. She

180

didn't want to see Louisa, changed or the same. She didn't want to see Louisa at all, for she knew no good could come of it.

Yet judging by Ruth's indomitable expression, her mouth set in a puckered line, Ellen knew there would be no arguing. There never was.

After school she went to the store, and asked Hamish for something for Louisa.

'Poor mite,' Hamish said affectionately, for though he'd disliked Louisa after the disastrous tea nearly a year ago, he couldn't stay angry with anyone for very long, and his memories had the habit of conveniently fading. 'We've some new hair ribbons in, striped silk. Just the thing. And what about a bag of lemon drops? They always slip down nicely.'

Dutifully, Ellen took the presents. 'I'm surprised she wants to see me,' she said after a moment, and Hamish's brow wrinkled slightly before he gave her one of his jolly smiles.

'I expect she wants to be friends again,' he said cheerfully, and Ellen found she could not quite smile back. She did not want to be friends with Louisa again, she realized, and she distrusted the very thought of Louisa announcing that she had decided to accept Ellen as her friend once more.

Straightening her spine, Ellen smiled fleetingly at Uncle Hamish before leaving the store.

The breeze blowing a few leftover leaves down Main Street was chilly, and the sky was a pale grey that couldn't make up its mind as to whether it would clear or not.

People nodded or murmured their helloes to Ellen as she walked to Water Street. Even though she still felt apart, most of Seaton seemed to have accepted her somewhat, at least enough to bid her good day when they passed her in the street. After nearly two years, it wasn't much, yet Ellen knew it was all she was likely to get.

And, Ellen acknowledged, needing to be fair, it was partly her fault. Ever since she'd learned she'd be returning to Amherst Island, her true home, she'd only been in Seaton in body rather than spirit. She didn't even try to make friends at school or church, although she was always polite and well mannered.

And now, in just two months she would be taking the train and then Captain Jonah's ferry to Amherst Island. A little shiver of anticipation ran up and down Ellen's spine as she contemplated that journey.

It was a thought which had sustained her through many cold, lonely months, a thought which held a pleasing if confusing tangle of questions and ideas. No discussion had yet been held about what Ellen would do after the summer away.

Would she return to Seaton? Go to high school in Rutland? Or do something else entirely? Ellen didn't know. She wasn't sure she wanted to know. As long as she didn't make a decision — and Aunt Ruth didn't force her to — a wealth of opportunity still awaited, possibilities brimming out of a bright future.

A vague contemplation of these possibilities occupied Ellen's mind all the way to Water Street, so that she skidded to a halt in front of the Hopper's impressive mahogany door with its bronze lion knocker and stained glass panes.

'Hello, Ellen.' Mrs Hopper herself answered Ellen's knock, her mouth tightening and nostrils flaring as she looked at her. No doubt the lemon tart incident was still fresh in Mrs Hopper's mind, as it was in Ellen's.

Ellen smiled politely. 'I've come to pay my respects to Louisa. I trust she's better?'

'Not completely,' Mrs Hopper said rather shortly. 'It has been a very difficult time for poor Louisa. She is so sensitive, and she's been greatly weakened by this trial.'

'I'm sorry to hear that.' Ellen heard the implicit warning in Mrs Hopper's words, and took it to heart. The last thing she wanted was to upset Louisa, and bring Aunt Ruth's wrath upon her once more.

Ellen followed Mrs Hopper up the thickly carpeted stairs to Louisa's room.

Louisa lay in a frilly, canopied bed, a pretty picture of an invalid. She wore a white nightgown with heavy lace on the cuffs and a pink satin ribbon threaded through the neckline. Her hair, although a bit lank and dull, lay brushed over her shoulders, and her hands were folded docilely over the coverlet.

'Ellen,' she said, 'I'm so glad you came.'

'It's good to see you, Louisa.' Awkwardly, Ellen handed over her gifts. 'Some little things from the store. I thought they might cheer you.'

'How kind,' Louisa murmured, examining the ribbon and bag of sweets as though they were precious treasures. Ellen shifted uncomfortably, not sure what to make of this subdued, well-mannered Louisa. She suspected it was just a part, perhaps one that amused her, if only for a time.

At some point the mask would slip and the spite would out. Wouldn't it?

'I'll leave you two alone for a moment,' Mrs Hopper murmured, and went out, shutting the door.

'How have you been?' Louisa asked after a

minute's uncomfortable silence. Outside, a robin chirped indignantly, the sound loud in the hushed stillness of the room.

'Well, I suppose. Busy with school and things.'

'I shall have to repeat this year, you know,' Louisa said. The mask dropped for a second, but all Ellen saw was bleakness. 'I shan't go to high school with the others.'

'Not everyone is going to high school,' Ellen said. 'Artie Dole isn't, and Bert Duncan. Hope Cardle isn't, either.'

'Hope Cardle,' Louisa dismissed. 'Silly girl. Her mother dresses her in that awful pink satin, and she looks like a boiled ham.'

'Louisa, that's unfair,' Ellen said quietly. 'Hope has been your friend since you left off with me. You chose her yourself. Besides, she's grown taller over the winter, and she has some lovely new dresses, blue to match her eyes.'

Louisa looked as if she wanted to say something spiteful, but she swallowed it down. The robin chirped again, louder, and Ellen almost asked why Louisa had invited her.

Louisa glanced down at Ellen's gifts lying on the coverlet and threaded the silk ribbon through her fingers. Her head still bowed, she said, 'I know I was awful to you.'

'Do you?' Ellen said with some surprise. 'I wondered if you had a conscience.'

'I suppose you did.' Louisa smiled faintly, which surprised Ellen even more. 'I was so angry with you for speaking to me like you did, but I suppose I deserved it.'

'Yes, you did.' Ellen knew she was treading on dangerous ground, and Louisa's temper — or tears — could burst any moment, but somehow she doubted they would. She sat hesitantly on the edge of the bed. 'Have you been very ill?'

'I don't know,' Louisa answered. 'Mother was frightened for me, but then she always is.'

'I'm sorry if you have. It's not an easy thing, to be an invalid, even if it is just for a while.'

Louisa glanced at her with bright, curious eyes. 'Have you ever been so ill, Ellen?'

'No, but my mother was.' Ellen paused, remembering Mam. She seemed so distant now, a shadowy picture from another life. Even Da, gone now nearly two years, seemed lost in faint memories.

Perhaps she was an orphan after all.

'Your mother?' Louisa repeated. 'She . . . she died, didn't she?'

'Yes, she did.' In her mind's eye Ellen saw the bed set up by the coal stove in the kitchen, her mother's pale, tired face on the

186

pillow, yet still with a smile gracing her worn features.

'I'm not going to die,' Louisa said with the firmness of someone who had recently believed she might. 'Not yet, anyway. I'm better every day. Father wants to send me somewhere warm for the summer, where I can rest and get stronger.'

'That should be lovely,' Ellen murmured. Outside the window she saw the grey sky clearing to fragile blue, and she longed suddenly to leave this stuffy sickroom for the freedom of the fresh air.

'I have just the place,' Louisa said into the silence, and Ellen saw a familiar expression of determination lighting her hazel eyes.

'Oh? Where would that be?'

'Why, your island, of course.'

There was a full minute of stunned silence while Ellen scrambled for something to say.

'You can't!' she finally blurted, only to have Louisa's expression cloud dangerously.

'You don't want me to go?'

Why would I, Ellen wanted to snap, *considering how you treated me?* She took a deep breath, willing herself to stay calm. Louisa, she knew, was just the kind of person to insist on something simply because she knew no one, including herself, wanted it.

'Of course, it could be pleasant to have you

there,' Ellen said carefully, 'but I'm thinking of you, Louisa. It's certainly not warm — it's most likely cooler than here, and it's a rough place as well. As I told you before, there are few shops and fewer entertainments. It's just a bunch of farmers. You'd find them all terribly stuffy and dull.'

Louisa's lower lip jutted out, which Ellen took to be a bad sign. 'How would you know what I find stuffy or dull?'

'You've told me yourself!' Ellen heard the edge of desperation, the bite of impatience in her own voice, and wished she could take the words back. They would only make Louisa more stubborn and difficult. 'You told me you found Seaton dull, and Seaton is a metropolis compared to Stella, I promise you! You'd get there and be bored and irritable, and have wasted your whole summer.'

Louisa folded her arms. 'You just don't want me to go.'

'No, I don't,' Ellen replied, 'and I told you why.'

'It's because you don't like me,' Louisa answered, daring Ellen to deny it.

Ellen took another deep breath. 'I don't like you,' she said. 'I'm sorry you're ill, but you've been selfish and stupid and vain since the day I met you, and nothing you've done since then has convinced me otherwise. Don't

188

burst into tears now,' she warned, 'I'll just leave anyway, and I don't care what your mother thinks of me. I'm leaving for the island in another month, and I won't be coming back here at all.'

Saying the words made it real, and Ellen felt a peculiar jolt in her midsection.

Louisa's eyes widened. 'Not ever?'

'I don't know,' Ellen allowed. 'But not for a while, at least.'

'Don't you see, Ellen?' Louisa said sadly. 'When you talk about that island, your eyes light up like you have the most wonderful secret. That's why I want to go. I want that secret too.'

Ellen leaned back against the bedpost, at a loss for words. She was afraid that Louisa was just determined enough to make her wish come true.

★　★　★

The wheels of Louisa's plan were set in motion before the week was out. Mrs Hopper called on Aunt Ruth, and Ellen didn't need to eavesdrop on their hushed conversation in the front parlour to know what they were talking about.

The blow fell at supper time, when Aunt Ruth announced, 'Louisa Hopper has taken it into her contrary head to come with you this summer to visit your cousins. Her mother was quite against it, naturally, but her father can't deny her any foolish notion and so it's agreed.'

Ellen stared at the mound of mashed potato Ruth had dolloped on to her plate. 'Doesn't Aunt Rose have any say in it?' she asked, although what she really wanted to ask was, *Don't I?*

'I'll send her a telegram, of course,' Ruth allowed. 'But I can't see as she'll mind. They've a houseful already, and the Hoppers will pay generously for Louisa's bed and board. I dare say those McCaffertys could use the extra money.'

Ellen stiffened at the implied slight. 'Don't *I* have any say in the matter?' she blurted, and Ruth's lips thinned.

'No,' she replied bluntly, and sat down to eat.

The next few weeks passed by too quickly, for although Ellen was looking forward to her return to Amherst Island, the addition of Louisa to her summer plans left her feeling quite sick with dread.

She also found she was more and more ambivalent about her departure from Ruth and Hamish's house, realizing suddenly that their little quirks and irritations had become endearing now that she did not know what the future held for any of them.

'You will have to decide what you want to do, come autumn,' Ruth warned as Ellen packed her valise. 'I know you've taken the entrance exam for Rutland High School, but it is expensive, and you'd have to find a place to board.'

'I could go to high school in Kingston,' Ellen said unexpectedly. 'With Lucas and Jed. Even Peter will be going in another year or two.'

'You haven't taken the exam for that school,' Ruth objected, her lips thinned to an unforgiving line. 'And where would you board there? The money, I'm sure, is the same.'

Ellen stared down at her neatly folded clothes. She couldn't blame Ruth for mentioning the money, not when she knew how little her father sent home. Ellen wondered just what he was doing with his wages . . . his life, even. The few letters he wrote gave little away.

'I wish I had money of my own.' Ellen didn't realize she'd said it out loud until she saw Ruth's startled look.

'That's as it may be,' Ruth said, 'but you don't. We're Christian people; we've a notion of charity.'

But charity only extended so far, and Ellen didn't want to be beholden to it. She sighed. At least with the McCaffertys she didn't feel the burden of her keep so much, yet they could hardly pay for her high school, and it seemed all too brazen to ask Aunt Rose and Uncle Dyle to pay for her board up in Canada.

All too soon, Ellen and Louisa were boarding the train to Rouse's Point, as Hamish waved cheerfully and Mrs Hopper cried noisily into her handkerchief on the station platform. Aunt Ruth hadn't come to the station; as she said, 'Someone needs to mind the store'.

The train journey was uneventful, and after the first few hours Louisa's excited chatter died away and she asked no more questions about the island. They were soon both lost in their thoughts, exhausted by the time they reached the boarding house, and then the train to Ogdensberg the next morning.

'I heard another little lady was coming,' Captain Jonah greeted Ellen as she and Louisa stepped on board the ferry to Amherst Island. 'Rose said a friend of yours was going to summer here. What's your name, missy?'

'Louisa Hopper.' Louisa looked taken aback by Captain Jonah's craggy face and toothless grin, and Ellen suppressed her own smile of amusement. Louisa had a look on her face that said she'd wished she'd lent credence to the things Ellen had warned her about.

The spray from the lake stung Ellen's face, although the wind was balmy and the blue-green waters fairly shimmered in the sunlight.

Captain Jonah chatted for a few minutes about island affairs, the money raised for a new library, the scandal caused by Mr McGuiness hiring two boys to fetch a horse from Kingston, only to have them lose the animal in the city streets for a prank.

'Was the beast hurt?' Ellen asked, and Captain Jonah spat neatly into the foaming water.

'Scairt, more like. The poor animal won't ever be the same now, and Mr McGuiness wants his money back from those boys, but he ain't getting it from the scalawags, and that's a fact.'

Louisa's eyebrows rose to her hairline at the Captain's colourful language, but Ellen just grinned. It was good to be back.

This time when Ellen came off the ferry, a wagon hitched to two horses was waiting in front of the station, and Dyle stood by it, a wide grin on his face, his dark eyes snapping with life and excitement.

'Ellen, my girl!'

Ellen ran into his arms. 'It's so good to see you,' she said, breathing in the scent of hay and cigar smoke on Dyle's coat. 'It's so good to be back.'

'It's good to have you back,' Dyle replied as he hugged her tightly. 'You need to keep us all on the straight and narrow! Now, this must be Louisa.'

Louisa nodded stiffly, and taking pity on her, Ellen pulled her forward. 'Louisa, this is my Uncle Dyle.'

'Pleased to meet you,' Louisa said in a scratchy whisper, and Dyle, taking the measure of her in one knowing gaze, smiled easily.

'And you, Miss Louisa. Climb in the wagon, girls, and I'll get your valises. Rose has made us all a slap-up meal.'

Dyle regaled them with news of all the McCaffertys and the Lymans all the way home. 'Ruthie's shot up a foot this year, Ellen, she's quite the little madam. Peter can't wait to go to Glebe, he's practising for his exams already and he's only twelve! Lucas will go up to Glebe in the fall, of course.'

'And Jed as well?' Ellen asked.

'Jed?' Dyle shook his head. 'He'll stay home and help his pa with the farm. He was never much of one for school learning.'

Ellen thought of Jed, with his almost silver eyes and scruffy dark hair, his constant scowl, and had to agree. She wasn't sure how she felt about that bit of news, especially when her own future was still undecided.

The farmhouse was awash with the last of the sun's rays as they drove up Jasper Lane with its arch of oak trees, the leaves golden in the fading sunlight, the soft summer twilight beginning to settle around them.

Rose had opened the door before Dyle even stopped the wagon, fiddling impatiently with her apron strings as she hurried to greet Ellen, the children tumbling like puppies behind her.

'Ellen, oh Ellen! It's so wonderful to have you back, child!'

'It's wonderful to be back,' Ellen replied, enveloped in Rose's warm hug, her cheek pressed against hers. She was laughing even as tears stung her eyes, and she just managed to pull away to introduce Louisa to Rose and the children.

'But of course!' Rose brushed a stray wisp of hair from her eyes, smiling as easily as Dyle had. 'We're so pleased to have you here for the summer. Any friend of Ellen's is a friend of ours!'

Louisa was looking very stiff and pinched, her face pale, and her dress of rose silk embroidered with silk french knots in darker pink seemed ridiculously fancy and inappropriate in the farmhouse's yard of pecked dirt and patchy grass.

With a pang of conscience, Ellen realized how the journey must have tired her, and how out of place and homesick she must feel.

'Louisa's been ill all winter, Aunt Rose,' she said. 'I'm sure she's quite worn out.'

'Oh, but I'm so sorry!' Rose exclaimed. 'Ellen, why don't you show Louisa her room? The back bedroom with the yellow curtains.'

Ellen took Louisa up the front stairs with their tarnished brass runner and worn carpet, down a long, narrow hallway to a bedroom at the end. The McCafferty farmhouse was large and rambling, and had no end of funny little nooks and rooms, including the small bedroom by the top of the back stairs that seemed almost an afterthought.

'This is one of my favourite rooms,' Ellen confided. 'It gets so much sunshine.' She'd sometimes come in here to draw by the window, although she didn't plan on telling Louisa that.

Whistling, Dyle came in with Louisa's valise and deposited it at the end of the bed.

Ellen drew the curtains and glanced around at the simple furnishings. There was an iron bedstead, a dresser with a wash stand,

and a few hooks for dresses, and that was all. Ellen was used to it — her room back in Seaton was nearly as spare — but she remembered Louisa's bedchamber with its canopy bed and sumptuous furnishings, and thought it must all seem rather hard.

'Will this be all right?' she asked, gently, for Louisa's face was still pinched tight and she hadn't spoken.

'You meant what you said, didn't you?' she said after a moment. She removed her straw boater with its trailing silk ribbons and put it carefully by the washstand. 'It's very different here.'

'Yes.'

Louisa nodded slowly, as if deciding something in her own mind. 'I'm very tired, as you said. I think I just might go to bed.'

'Shall I bring you up some dinner on a tray?'

Louisa paused, then shook her head. 'No . . . no. I haven't any appetite. Give my regards to everyone. I'm sorry not to say hello properly. I will tomorrow.'

'Of course.' Impulsively, Ellen squeezed Louisa's shoulder lightly on her way out. This was home to her, but she could see the spare rooms, their furnishings shabby, yet filled with noise and laughter, were strange indeed to Louisa.

Back in the farmhouse kitchen, Ellen was passed from person to person like a parcel as they examined her and exclaimed in surprised delight how much she'd grown.

'You must be a foot taller!' Dyle exclaimed and Rose chimed in, smiling, 'We'll have to cut down some more dresses for you, although I don't know how much cutting down we'll have to do!'

'I think she looks exactly the same,' Ruthie announced in a loud voice, and Ellen smiled in return.

'I feel the same,' she confided to the not-so-little girl. 'I feel exactly the same.'

Over dinner Ellen caught up on all the island news.

'The Lymans have had a hard winter,' Rose said as she served the summer's first strawberry and rhubarb pie, generously doused with fresh cream.

'How so?' Ellen asked, swallowing her bite of pie, and Dyle chipped in.

'The pond between our properties flooded from all the rain,' he explained soberly. 'The land runs downhill from here to there, and a good ten acres was covered in water. Some of his best crops.'

Ellen's eyed widened in shocked dismay. 'But that's terrible!'

'So it is,' Dyle agreed, 'but the Lymans will

198

do all right. He's got a bit put by. He can survive one bad harvest.'

'But poor Nellie Lyman hasn't been well, either,' Rose said. 'She's always been poorly, as you know, Ellen, but because of the wet her cough took a turn for the worse, and over Christmas we all thought . . . well — ' Rose's expression clouded and she shook her head. 'But she pulled through, although she's completely bedridden now, and no one knows — '

'I had no idea,' Ellen said, shocked, for Lucas hadn't mentioned any troubles in his letters. 'Perhaps I should visit them.'

'I'm sure it would do a world of good,' Rose agreed. 'Nellie doesn't see many people these days, although I always go over of a Monday to help with the washing and baking. But still, you'd be a breath of fresh air to her, Ellen.'

Ellen wasn't sure about that, but dutifully she took the lantern from its hook by the back door and walked over that very evening. Rose protested she needn't go that night, but Ellen said she was happy to. Truthfully, she didn't want to have to take Louisa with her the next day. She didn't think Louisa would do well in another's sick room, and besides, she wasn't ready to share the Lymans with Louisa, though she knew she would have to, soon enough.

It was peaceful to make her way through the copse of trees that separated the Lymans' property from the McCaffertys', and the shadows were soft and welcoming. A large, luminous moon had risen in the sky and cast a pearly glow over the pond that had flooded the previous autumn and left several fields now verdant and fallow.

As she broke through the trees, Ellen saw the welcoming yellow light of the farmhouse kitchen, and a dog — a new one, she supposed — set to barking as she crossed the kitchen yard.

The back door opened, and someone peered through the darkness before calling in delight, 'Ellen!'

'Hello, Lucas.' Ellen had just set the lantern on the porch steps when Lucas swept her up into a surprising and warm embrace. As her arms closed around him automatically, Ellen was surprised again to feel how his thin, boyish frame had filled out; a year ago Lucas had been a thirteen-year-old boy, and now he was, felt, like a man.

'It's so good to see you,' he said, releasing her and stepping back so they could both examine each other in the light cast by the lantern. Ellen smiled, seeing how familiar Lucas's hazel eyes and floppy hair were, squinting slightly as he always did because he needed spectacles yet never wore them. 'Come into the kitchen. We've just finished supper, but there's cherry pie leftover.'

'I could always make room for another piece of pie,' Ellen replied with a smile, and followed Lucas inside.

Within a few minutes she and Lucas were seated at the wide table of scrubbed pine, and he'd fetched the pie from the pantry himself and cut two generous slices.

'Jed's out in the barn, seeing to the animals,' he said after a moment, and startled, Ellen realized with a guilty flash that she'd been looking around for someone . . . and it had been Jed.

'Where's your pa?' she asked, trying not to flush, and Lucas shrugged. 'In the barn too, most like. I was seeing to Ma.'

'I was sorry to hear she'd taken poorly, Lucas,' Ellen said soberly. 'It's a hard thing.'

Lucas nodded, his eyes shadowing to a darker, deeper brown. 'It is. We didn't think she'd last the winter.'

'Why didn't you tell me in your letters?' Ellen asked. 'It must have weighed on your mind, along with all your specimens!'

'It did,' Lucas replied, and there was an understanding glint in his eyes as he added quietly, 'but I didn't want it weighing on yours. I know you've borne that burden once already, Ellen.'

Ellen nodded. Lucas's understanding and compassion, especially in light of his own current suffering, humbled her. 'I still would have gladly borne it for you, if I could,' she said quietly, and Lucas gave a smile of sorrowful speculation.

'Would you?' he asked, and Ellen had the uncomfortable feeling the question had more depth than she'd care to examine.

'Tell me about your plant specimens,' she said. 'Have you collected every variety on the island yet, do you think?'

'It's difficult to tell. Now that everything has been in bud it's easier to note the changes. Pa ordered me a big book all the way from Toronto. It's got illustrated plates of just about every plant or tree you can imagine, and in colour too!' He smiled, caught up in his own enthusiasm. 'I'm hoping to study biology at Queen's, you know, in Kingston.'

'And next year you'll go to Glebe?' Ellen asked, and heard the wistful note in her own voice.

'Yes, although Jed's staying here. And what about you, Ellen? Your aunt mentioned you might stay beyond the summer.' Now the wistful note could be heard in Lucas's voice, and for some reason it made Ellen blush.

'It's hard to say — ' she began, when the creak of the back door and the heavy tread of booted feet cut her off. She turned, and felt her heart give a funny sort of somersault before beating extra hard at the sight of Jed's tousled hair and weary expression.

His expression cleared — blanked — for a moment as he caught sight of Ellen, and then he smiled with his usual touch of mockery.

'Ellen Copley, is that your second piece of pie?'

Ellen glanced down at her plate which only sported a few crumbs. Somehow, in talking to Lucas, she'd managed to eat the large portion he'd laid out for her. 'How do you know that?' she demanded, and Jed's smile grew into a full-fledged grin.

'I saw Dyle this afternoon and he mentioned there was pie for dinner tonight.'

'Well,' Ellen said defensively, 'you can't have too much pie.'

'No,' Jed agreed, 'I reckon you can't.'

They all fell silent, yet it was a strangely expectant hush that made Ellen's heart beat all the more. She couldn't quite tear her expression from Jed, who watched her with that faint, mocking smile on his face, lighting his eyes. When she finally did drag her gaze away, she saw Lucas looking at her with a certain speculation that made her want to fidget. She stood up instead.

'I ought to go pay my respects to your Ma,' she said, and with the room still expectant and silent, she hurried out to the relative safety upstairs.

10

It took Louisa a while to 'find her feet' as Dyle said, learning everyone's names (Ruthie and Caro kept switching names, trying to confuse her) and getting used to island ways.

Ellen tried to help her as much as she could, although she soon realized that she did Louisa no favours by treating her differently.

'She's a bit snooty, isn't she?' Caro said one evening as they were washing up the supper dishes. She pumped water into the pail, the rusty squeaking of the pump keeping them from being overheard by Rose.

'She's been ill,' Ellen said, and Caro simply looked at her.

'So? She acts like a princess, excusing herself after supper without so much as taking in her plate! And when we asked her if she wanted to come berry picking, she looked as if we were telling her to scrub the outhouse! I don't like her.'

Ellen looked at Caro's mutinous face, her sturdy body, still with a childish chubbiness, in a stance of stubborn dislike, and sighed. 'Louisa is from a wealthy family, it's true,' she said, 'and she's an only child. This is all very strange for her.'

'What I want to know,' Caro asked, 'is why she wanted to come?'

Ellen shook her head. 'I honestly don't know.'

Despite Louisa's discomfort with this new world, Ellen still found time to enjoy all her old island pursuits. She took the children and her sketchbook for walks, finding a rock or grassy meadow to sit in while she sketched the many delights of the island in full summer.

Andrew, now three, running through a field as the grass tickled his face; the fat, red raspberries fairly dripping from brambles; the tumbled buildings of an old farm overlooking the placid bay. All these and more went into her sketchbooks, which Ellen showed no one, save Lucas.

Their friendship had deepened unexpectedly this summer, fed by the letters they'd exchanged over the winter. Now Ellen found she trusted Lucas's quiet, thoughtful replies, and enjoyed his soothing, steady presence. If, when at the Lyman farm, she found her gaze wandering for a familiar, solitary figure, she did not admit it even to herself. At nearly seventeen, Jed was too busy for childish pursuits. Lucas, with a glittering high school career ahead of him, was exempt from some of the more demanding farm labour, although Ellen saw plainly enough that he still pulled his weight, and was always willing to sit by his mother's bedside and read to her from the Bible or a novel taken out of Stella's small but steadily growing library.

One afternoon in late July, he and Ellen sat in the hayloft of the Lymans' barn, the bales of hay as good as any pillow, the sun streaming in from the open hatch. It had become their hiding place, by default, Ellen supposed, for they'd never discussed it.

Yet up in the hayloft they could speak with a quiet and intense honesty about their dreams: how Lucas wanted to go to Queen's to study biology and go on to explore the last untouched corners of the earth, cataloguing plants and animals. Ellen even shyly gave voice to her own dreams, vague, formless things she had not dared previously give shape to. Even in the intimacy of the hayloft she found herself shying away from admitting that she wanted more than she already had, that she, an uneducated lass from Springburn could dare to dream of a future for herself beyond what she'd been grudgingly given.

Lucas encouraged her, however, and his own quiet certainty and determination gave Ellen's imaginations wings.

'These are good,' he said quietly as they sat amidst the hay and sunshine. He was paging through her sketchbook, giving each drawing careful and intent study.

Ellen ducked her head and tucked her bare feet under her skirt. Louisa chided her for running around the island barefooted like a hoyden, but Ellen loved feeling so free.

'Thank you,' she said, 'but to tell the truth, it doesn't matter to me whether they're good or not. It's just something I need to do.'

'Which makes it all the more important,' Lucas said. 'Ellen, you could have a serious future as an artist — '

They'd had this conversation many times already, and as always Ellen shied away from Lucas's urgings.

'I wouldn't even know — '

'All the more reason to find out,' Lucas replied firmly. 'I'm going to high school to learn things, Ellen. To know things. You could, as well.'

Ellen looked away. 'High school costs money.'

Lucas was silent for a moment, and Ellen wished she hadn't said anything. She'd revealed too much, and she felt ashamed for herself as well as the McCaffertys.

'You could sell your drawings,' Lucas said at last. 'You know daytrippers come to the island in the summer, from Kingston. You could sell them at the ferry office, or even on the dockside.'

Ellen turned to him, her mouth dropping open. 'I couldn't!' The idea was both ludicrous and frightening.

'Why not?'

'Because — ' Ellen shook her head. She didn't want to explain to Lucas that the idea of nameless tourists pawing through her drawings, dismissing them out of hand, was too terrible to contemplate.

'What if it's the only way to go to high school?' Lucas persisted. 'Is your pride too high a price to pay?'

'It isn't just pride — ' Ellen began helplessly.

'And what about a book of sketches eventually? *Island Life*, you could call it. I bet it would sell in Kingston or even Ottawa. Who knows?'

'Away with you.' Ellen shook her head, trying to laugh, to dismiss it all as fanciful folly. 'I've never even taken a course, or been taught properly. I'm sure I'd be laughed out of a gallery or studio . . . I wouldn't even know — '

'You could learn,' Lucas insisted earnestly.

Ellen looked down at the sketchbook, open to a drawing of Jed tossing Ruthie into the air. She'd been proud of the way she'd captured the look in Jed's eyes, simple pleasure hidden by the usual gruffness. Something in his look made her stomach tighten, and her heart hardened with resolve.

She shook her head. 'I'm flattered you think these are worth selling, but I've no plans like that. They're really just for me. I couldn't bear to think of them being looked at and not liked, thrown away even. They mean too much.'

Lucas nodded slowly, accepting defeat. 'Sometimes,' he said quietly, 'when something — or someone — means that much, you need to take a risk.'

Ellen looked up, her breath drying in her throat, leaking out of her lungs as she took in Lucas's intent look. There was something deep and purposeful in his eyes and the set of his jaw that made her both uneasy and hopeful.

A voice from below in the Lymans' kitchen yard broke that silent, suspended moment.

'Ellen! Ellen, are you here?'

Lucas peered out of the hatch, his eyes widening in surprise. 'It's Louisa. What's she doing here?'

'Looking for me, it would seem,' Ellen said with a sigh. She'd scarpered before Louisa could latch on to her that afternoon, and now she felt guilty. Louisa was still her friend and guest, even if Ellen accepted that responsibility reluctantly. 'I'd better go down.' Brushing bits of hay from her skirt, she made for the ladder.

'Wait!' Lucas's look of surprise had turned to one of mischief. 'She doesn't know you're up here. It's a perfect opportunity.'

'Louisa's not one for jokes, Lucas.'

'Maybe that's her problem.' With a grin Lucas ducked back from the hatch and out of sight.

'Ellen?' Louisa called out uncertainly, for the yard was bare and silent save for the rustlings of the animals below. Mr Lyman was out in the fields with Jed, and Mrs Lyman lay, as usual, in her sickroom.

Suddenly Lucas made a noise — something bestial although not quite like a cow — that had even Ellen jumping in frightened surprise.

Louisa screamed.

Covering his mouth to stifle his laughter, Lucas glanced at Ellen, his hazel eyes dancing with merriment.

Ellen felt a bubble of laughter rising in her own chest.

'Ellen?' Louisa sounded frightened now. She wasn't a country girl, even after a year in Seaton. 'Are you there? Your aunt said you'd come this way — ' Her voice sounded thin and strained, and then Lucas moaned again, the animal-like noise raising the hairs on the back of Ellen's neck.

Louisa made a noise that sounded like a sob, and ran from the yard.

Lucas let out a loud guffaw of laughter. 'That should teach her.'

'Oh, Lucas, we shouldn't have,' Ellen said, regretting the whole incident now. 'Louisa is delicate, and she's not used to country ways. We've probably scared her witless.'

'She deserves it,' Lucas replied with a shrug. 'I don't like the way she treats you.'

'Me?' Ellen's eyebrows rose in surprise. 'She's my friend — '

'And she treats you like her maid. And you allow her to, Ellen. You're better than that. More important — ' His voice lowered, his gaze averted, 'to me, anyway.'

Ellen's heart skipped a beat and she made for the ladder. 'I'd better go find her, before she runs screaming all the way home.'

'I'll come with you. It was my idea, and I won't have you taking the blame.'

They didn't have far to go; halfway across the yard Jed came round the corner of the barn, his arm around a shaking Louisa, his face a mask of grim fury. Ellen faltered in her steps, but Lucas stood with his feet spread

212

apart, hands on his hips.

'Louisa heard a noise from the barn,' Jed said in a voice that was somehow more terrible by its calm and even tone. 'Said it sounded like a frightening beast.'

'More like an ailing cow,' Lucas replied. He flicked his gaze towards Louisa, who was trying to recover herself with some dignity, yet, Ellen thought cynically, still playing the frightened maiden for Jed's benefit. 'Cows won't hurt you, Louisa. They're gentle animals.'

'It wasn't a cow,' Louisa sniffed.

'And we don't have any ailing ones,' Jed cut in. His eyes narrowed. 'Not unless they're up in the hayloft.' He glanced at Ellen, and she quailed at the look of contemptuous judgement she saw in his eyes. She'd been the recipient of his scorn before, yet there had been something gentle and good-natured about it, not like this. She looked down at the ground, her cheeks flushing.

'It was you two!' Louisa exclaimed, realization dawning. 'You were up in the hayloft . . . making a fool of me!'

'It's not a difficult task,' Lucas replied coolly, 'but it was just a harmless joke, Louisa.'

'Harmless!' Louisa shrugged off Jed's arm, her eyes blazing. 'How could you treat me in

213

such a manner, Ellen? And I thought you were my friend!' Anger gave way to tears, as Ellen had known it would, and with a choked cry, Louisa whirled away, heading back to the McCafferty farmhouse.

The moment after Louisa left was taut with silence, broken only by the rustling of the animals in the barn.

'It was just a joke, Jed,' Lucas said after a moment. He shrugged, although his voice, pitched low, carried a current of intensity. 'And one you would've played yourself a year ago.'

'Maybe so,' Jed replied evenly, 'but I've had to put such things behind me, and so should you, Lucas. We're not children any more.' He turned to Ellen, and she flinched at his tone. 'None of us is,' he finished shortly, and before either of them could reply, he turned on his heel and made for the fields once more.

Ellen curled her bare toes in the dust of the farmyard. What had seemed silly and lighthearted a few moments ago now made her flush and ache with shame.

'I'm sorry, Lucas,' she said after a moment. Lucas shrugged, his jaw tight, his eyes sparking.

'I'm not. It was just a bit of fun. Jed thinks just because he's the one staying at home no one else — ' He broke off, shaking his head, and Ellen knew the argument between the brothers had been about more than just Louisa's tender feelings.

She tried to smile, her sketchbook clutched to her chest. 'I'd better go find Louisa,' she said, keeping her voice as light as she could, 'in case she runs into another cow.'

★　★　★

A few weeks later, about halfway through the summer, all of Amherst Island prepared for an exciting event — an island wedding.

Never having been present for such a ceremony, Ellen was amazed at the vast preparation the entire island set to. Everyone was invited, everyone was involved. The Presbyterian church in Stella would be overflowing; even the Methodists would grudgingly attend, and the party afterwards was to be at the bride's family farm, with the whole barnyard turned into a dance floor, and everyone on the island who played an instrument, even a tin harmonica, roped into providing music.

All the McCafferty girls were busy baking for the feast, as well as sewing new lace and ribbon on to their best dresses. Even Louisa entered into the cheerful fray, laying out her gorgeous silk and satin dresses, wondering which one to choose.

Even Caro stroked the smooth, rich fabric with a touch of envy, although Ellen knew she would never admit such a thing to Louisa.

'I'll do your hair for you if you like,' Louisa offered with a toss of her own burnished curls. 'Maybe then it won't look like such a haystack.'

Ellen forced herself to smile back. Ever since the day in the Lymans' barn yard, her friendship with Louisa had been strained. Ellen had duly sought Louisa out and apologized for the episode, and while Louisa accepted, she remained frosty and distant.

In some regards Ellen had been relieved, for a little distance from Louisa was no bad thing. Yet she also felt an uncomfortable pang of guilt, for as Jed had so coolly reminded her, Louisa was both her guest and responsibility.

When the day of the wedding finally arrived, everyone was fairly dancing with excitement, even though the music had yet to begin.

Louisa and Ellen walked with the other McCaffertys down Stella's Front Street to the church. Ellen had added lace to the cuffs and collar of her best green dress, and Louisa wore a frilly concoction of blue silk with a wide, deep sash, her hair in curls. She looked very pretty, Ellen thought, and entirely overdressed, but then all of Louisa's frocks were too fussy for island life.

Still, she tried to mend the bridges between them and offered, 'You look beautiful, Louisa.'

'Thank you.' Louisa preened a bit, but there seemed something false about both her gestures and words. Instinctively, Ellen walked more slowly so they fell behind the McCafferty children. Louisa matched her pace, and when they couldn't be overheard, she spoke.

'You were right about your island,' Louisa said in a low voice, her face averted from Ellen's. 'I was jealous of what you had, but I should've realized I could hardly snatch it for myself.'

Ellen looked at her uncertainly. 'What do you mean?'

'That secret you have? The way you love this island and it loves you? That's yours.' Louisa shook her head, bitterness spiking her words, her hands clenched on the shiny taffeta of her dress. 'It will never be mine.'

Ellen was silent for a moment. She knew what Louisa meant. Before coming to Amherst Island, she had never felt like she belonged. Even back in Springburn, she'd been a stranger, set apart, spending most of

217

her days in the sick room with Mam.

She'd just never thought Louisa, with all her pampered privileges, might feel the same way.

'You've made friends here — ' she began, but Louisa just laughed sharply.

'Friends? Like Lucas, who thinks I'm no more than a spoiled brat? Or Caro, who says so to my face?' She turned to Ellen, her face hard despite the vulnerability and hurt lurking in her eyes. 'Do you think I don't notice the way you all look at me, Ellen? Do you think I can't hear the whispers?' She shook her head. 'I see it all. I hear it all.' She paused, her face averted once more. 'I feel it all.'

'Louisa — ' Ellen began, helplessly, for she didn't know what comfort she could offer.

'I know it's my own fault,' Louisa continued. 'I should try to fit in, to make myself useful and liked, but I can't.' Her hands clenched once more on her dress. 'I've never had to before, and I won't start now.'

Ellen's sympathy lessened a bit at this willful remark. 'You're just stubborn, then,' she said bluntly. 'And it's worse because you know it! If you just helped out a bit, Louisa, dirtied your hands or your apron and didn't turn your nose up at island ways — '

'It's not quite so easy, Ellen Copley,'

Louisa snapped. 'You can't change the way you think just like that.'

Ellen sighed. They were well behind the others now, and they would have to hurry to catch up. 'You're right,' she said quietly. 'I'm sorry, Louisa. I did warn you.'

'Oh, don't say that!' Louisa cut her off. ' 'I told you so!' I know you want to gloat, Ellen, but don't do it in my presence.'

'I'm not gloating,' Ellen protested, thinking this very unfair.

'Aren't you?' Louisa replied a little shrewdly. 'You were worried I'd steal this island from under your nose, and I haven't. It's still yours.'

Ellen had a prickling awareness of Louisa's meaning. It was a competition, a contest, in her mind, between the two of them. There could only be one winner, and Ellen knew Louisa well enough to understand that she would not give up so easily. 'Well,' Ellen said finally, 'you'll just have to find your own island, then.'

'Yes,' Louisa agreed, her face hardening, 'I will.'

The wedding was lovely, with the church crowded and Captain Jonah blowing his nose loudly on his old spotted handkerchief right in the middle of the service.

The party afterwards was every bit as jolly

an affair as Ellen had hoped. Long wooden trestle tables fairly sagged under the weight of food, plates of ham and biscuits, pies of every berry and fruit, bowls of punch and lemonade.

The band, twelve strong and playing a merry tune, struck up after the eating was done and just about everyone took to the floor. Ellen stood uncertainly on the side of the swept yard, watching the ladies' skirts swirling up clouds of dust as her own foot tapped a happy rhythm.

'Do you think anyone will ask you to dance?' Louisa asked, her eyes narrowed speculatively as she searched the crowd for a prospective partner.

'I don't know. I haven't danced much before.' Ellen fiddled with the lace at her cuffs. She wasn't quite ready to admit even to herself how much she wanted to dance.

'You could always dance with Peter, I suppose,' Louisa said, and Ellen bit back her sharp reply. Dancing with Peter would be a laugh, but he was still a full head shorter than her and not the kind of partner she had in mind.

Just then she saw Jed walking towards her, scuffing his feet and looking both determined and just a little bit uncertain. Her heart lurched at the sight of his hair, usually so scruffy, now brushed back from his forehead. His eyes looked almost silver and he held his hat in his hands.

Ellen's breath nearly stopped as he came to stand in front of her, ducking his head a bit as he asked, 'Would you have this dance — '

'Yes — ' Ellen began in shy pleasure, only to have Jed finish,

' — Louisa?'

'Oh.' Ellen cheeks burned and she took a step backwards as if to distance herself from her terrible gaffe, while Louisa purred, 'I certainly would, Jed Lyman. Thank you for asking me.' Taking his extended hand as elegantly as a ballerina, Louisa sashayed to the dance floor, tossing Ellen one triumphant look over her shoulder.

Ellen could feel her face flame. Why had she assumed Jed was asking her? He'd been so cross with her over the stupid joke with Lucas, and they hadn't spoken since. She could hardly expect him to ask her to dance. Yet she was angry, and hurt even, not just because he hadn't asked her, but because he *had* asked Louisa.

She didn't even like Jed.

'If he was going to ask Louisa, he should've stood in front of *her*,' Ellen muttered, only to have a voice behind her say,

'Ellen?'

'Lucas!' Ellen smiled in relief. It was good to see a friend.

'Will you dance with me?'

'Of course.' She took his hand easily, warning him, 'I'm not much of a dancer, you know.'

'Neither am I. I'm glad you're wearing sturdy shoes.'

Ellen thought of Louisa's silk slippers, dyed to match her dress, and grimaced inwardly. She wondered if Jed was a good dancer. No doubt he'd step all over Louisa's poor feet. The thought, childishly, made her smile.

Lucas was a better dancer than he'd said, and Ellen found that after the first few stumbling steps they could both move quite easily around the makeshift dance floor. Lucas smiled down at her, his hazel eyes glinting.

'You're good.'

'Only because I'm letting you lead,' Ellen said with a little laugh.

'It would look rather strange if you led,' Lucas observed, and Ellen smiled.

'I suppose it would.' Somehow she found her gaze moving from Lucas's smiling face to the couple just over his shoulder.

Lucas, seeing her gaze, glanced back, his mouth hardening a bit. 'Jed shouldn't dance in his work boots,' he said after a moment.

'He'll wreck Louisa's feet.'

'I was just thinking the same thing,' Ellen laughed, although she noticed that although Jed was not precisely a graceful dancer, he was not stomping around the dance floor either.

'I don't know what he sees in Louisa,' Lucas remarked. 'She's such a spoiled, vain creature. Hardly the kind of girl for Jed.'

Alarm leapt in Ellen's chest and she strove to keep her voice casual. 'Does he really like her, then?'

Lucas shrugged. 'Who knows? But Jed doesn't ask anybody to dance.'

There was no reason for Ellen's spirits to sink, especially as she found herself never short of a dance partner. After the dance with Lucas, there was always another island boy eager for her hand.

Several hours later, with dusk settling over the farmyard, the lanterns lit and the music still going strong, Ellen found herself in front of Jed.

She stiffened, remembering her embarrassment, and he smiled. 'You're not cross at me, are you?'

'I thought you were cross at me,' Ellen admitted. 'Because of that silly joke about the cow.'

The corner of Jed's mouth quirked in a tiny

grin. 'I couldn't stay mad about that for long,' he told her, and Ellen's heart swelled.

Another tune started up, and she slapped a mosquito away from her arm. Jed held his arms out with a shrug.

'We might as well dance.'

It was so far from a proper invitation that Ellen was stung to reply, 'Not if you'd rather dance with Louisa.'

Jed looked at her in surprise. 'Ellen Copley, are you jealous?' He sounded so smug and gloating that Ellen decided right there she was certainly not jealous.

She fixed him with her haughtiest look — borrowed straight from Louisa — and said, 'What do you think?'

Jed deflated slightly even though he was still smiling. 'You couldn't be jealous,' he said, and reached for her hand. 'Now let's dance before this number's over.'

It felt strange to be so close to Jed, one hand, warm and dry, clasping hers, the other lightly touching her waist. She was eye level with his chin, and could see the dark stubble glinting there, and the strong pulse in his throat. Jed was surprisingly light on his feet, and Ellen prayed she wouldn't stumble.

'You couldn't be jealous,' Jed resumed, his voice pitched low for only her ears, 'because you don't even like me.'

Ellen glanced up, surprised. 'That's not true.'

Jed raised one eyebrow in blatant scepticism. 'Really, Miss Bossy?'

Ellen gave a little smile. 'You might have been the most ill-tempered boy when I first met you, but you've improved a little.'

Jed laughed and twirled her round. 'So have you,' he said, leaving Ellen breathless. 'A little.'

The party lasted well into evening, with the moon high and yellow in the sky, and the crickets chirping a loud evening chorus. The bride and groom were finally run off with many cheers and bawdy jokes, and the McCaffertys began to pile into the wagon, Andrew asleep in Rose's arms, and Ruthie trying to stay awake as she leaned against Ellen's shoulder.

'That was wonderful,' Louisa said to Ellen as they began the bumpy ride back to Jasper Lane. A silk ribbon had fallen from her hair and she twisted it dreamily through her fingers. 'I reckon I could make him fall in love with me.'

Ellen looked at her in surprise. 'Who?'

Louisa's smile was that of a cat, smugly contented. 'Why, Jed, of course.'

Ellen felt as if her stomach had been dipped in ice. 'I can't imagine Jed in love with anyone,' she said after a moment, and Louisa chuckled.

'I can. I'd almost think you were jealous, Ellen, but you can't be, not with the way Lucas makes calf eyes at you.'

'Lucas?' Ellen shook her head. 'Good gracious, Louisa, you see stars in everyone's eyes! We're only fifteen, after all. I don't want to fall in love with anyone just yet.'

Louisa's reply was only another chuckle, and Ellen leaned against the side of the wagon, a vague feeling of foreboding disturbing her enjoyment of the still, balmy night.

11

The summer came to an end all too quickly. It seemed to Ellen that one moment it was hot and drowsy, the raspberries dripping fatly from bushes, the evenings long and lazy and warm. Then, suddenly, the air was crisp and the oak leaves tinged with yellow, and the postman brought a letter from Seaton that had dread curdling in the pit of Ellen's stomach.

She read it on the front porch, where she'd been sitting with Rose, shelling peas and enjoying the late summer sunshine.

'And what does Ruth say now?' Rose asked, one eyebrow raised, and Ellen tried to smile.

'She wants to know what I'm doing,' Ellen said, and something caught in her chest as she scanned the lines.

> *If you would still like to go to high school, we can make arrangements here. You may take a test in the autumn and board in Rutland.*

It almost sounded, Ellen thought, as if

Ruth wanted her back. Except why should she? It would be more expense, and Ellen wouldn't even be in Seaton. No doubt her aunt was just doing her Christian duty, dispensed with a grim smile as always. Yet still Ellen felt a surprising pang of something that was almost — almost — homesickness for Seaton, for Ruth and Hamish.

Rose put down the bowl of peas and gave Ellen a level look. 'And what are your plans, Ellen? Will you stay on the island with us? You know you're more than welcome, although the way the island closes down in winter might be a bit hard for you.'

'It might be,' Ellen allowed, 'but I don't think so.' She let out a little sigh. She'd shied away from any thoughts for her future all summer, wanting only to savour the long, lazy days. Even her chats with Lucas had always held an aura of unreality, as if the dreams and plans they voiced would never truly come to pass.

And perhaps they wouldn't — they certainly would have no opportunity if she continued to dally and dither!

'I don't want to go to high school,' she told Rose at last. 'I've decided against that.'

'Have you?' Rose raised her eyebrows. 'I always thought you were clever enough, certainly.'

Ellen glanced away. Sunlight slanted across the wooden floor of the porch, and she could hear the distant sound of the children's laughter ringing from the meadow.

'It's not that,' she said, taking another handful of fat pea pods. 'I just don't want to.' That wasn't strictly the truth, but she wasn't going to admit that she didn't want to burden anyone with the cost of her education.

'Then what shall you do?' Rose asked.

'I've thought about going to nursing school,' Ellen admitted quietly. 'I know there's a fine one in Kingston.'

'Nursing school!' Rose exclaimed. 'I had no idea.'

Ellen ducked her head. 'I've had some experience, nursing my mam.'

Rose was a silent for a moment, her face softened with a tenderness Ellen couldn't quite understand. 'Of course you have.' She turned back to the peas, her movements brisk. 'I believe you need to be eighteen to go to nursing school. What if you stayed here till then? Dr Bandler is the island's only doctor, and I know for a fact he needs help. You could work with him and gain a bit more practical experience before heading off to Kingston.'

Ellen sat back, startled by the sudden, specific direction her life seemed to be taking.

'I suppose I could,' she said slowly.

Rose smiled. 'Why don't you think about it for a few days? I need to get supper started. Will you bring in the children?'

Ellen nodded, her mind whirling with a strange and inexplicable mixture of hope — and disappointment.

At least, she supposed, before her future had been decided, anything had been possible. Yet now once a road had been taken, she found herself thinking of the other nameless opportunities. High school, art . . .

She was as dreamy as Lucas, she chided herself, with her head in the clouds. A nurse was a practical and sensible occupation for a young woman such as herself, and she would count her blessings if Dr Bandler took her.

* * *

Rose took Ellen to see Dr Bandler the very next day. He had a surgery on the main street of Stella, a stone's throw from the ferry office where Ellen had first waited that September nearly two years ago.

She'd met Dr Bandler before, of course; he'd made a handful of house visits to Jasper Lane, and she'd seen him at church and various island functions. Yet she'd never needed to visit his surgery herself, and now she found herself gazing round at the shiny, metal instruments and the pamphlets about eating green vegetables and drinking milk with an air of uneasy awe.

'Ellen Copley?' he barked, looking up from his desk, his bright blue eyes peering at her from behind small, round spectacles.

Ellen swallowed nervously. 'Yes, sir.'

'Are you ill?' he demanded, and she took an inadvertent step back. 'No! That is — '

'Then why are you here?'

Ellen felt herself flushing. 'My aunt, Rose McCafferty, thought I might be of help . . . somehow — ' She realized she was mumbling, and her face reddened all the more.

Dr. Bandler smiled. 'That's all right, my dear, I know why you're here. But I can't have a high-strung miss in my surgery, you understand, not when a man might be dying.' Ellen's eyes widened and the doctor hastened to add, 'Not to say there *will* be a man dying in here. But just in case. Just in case.'

'I see,' Ellen managed, and he indicated she take a seat in front of his desk. Ellen sank down gratefully as Dr Bandler folded his hands on top of his desk and surveyed her with a more kindly air.

'Your aunt said you are considering nursing?' he asked. Ellen nodded.

'Yes. I'd like to. I have a small amount of experience nursing my ma — mother. She was ill for many years.'

'I'm sorry to hear that,' Dr Bandler said, and Ellen felt he meant it. 'You do realize, however, that nursing encompasses much more than sitting by a bedside, bathing a forehead or making tea?'

'Yes — '

'Not,' Dr Bandler cut her off, the speed of his thoughts making Ellen's head spin, 'that that was all you were doing. But in a doctor's surgery, you'll find you come across all sorts of patient — expecting mothers, farmhands with injuries, children with scarlet fever.' He smiled wryly, and Ellen knew he was recalling the McCaffertys' experience with that illness, when she'd first arrived.

'All those different situations should be good experience,' Ellen said, and Dr Bandler nodded in approval.

'Indeed. I'm afraid I can't offer you much in the way of recompense.'

'Oh, that's not necessary,' Ellen interjected, and Dr Bandler smiled, tilting his head to one side.

'Surely a little is deserved?' he asked lightly. 'We'll see what I can manage. Can you start the first of September?'

Ellen could hardly believe the interview

had been conducted with such alacrity. 'Really?' she asked. 'I mean, that's . . . it?'

'That's it,' Dr Bandler agreed cheerfully. He stood up, and so did Ellen. 'So I take it you're to stay on the island with us, Miss Copley? No going back to the States?'

For some reason his words gave her a pang. She thought of Ruth and Hamish, waiting for her response. 'No going back,' she answered, 'for a while, at least.'

'We're glad to have you.' Dr Bandler shook her hand, his grip sure and firm. 'I'll see you on the first of September!'

★ ★ ★

That night, curled up by the window of her bedroom, her pen tapping her teeth, Ellen gazed at the nearly blank page on her lap.

Dear Aunt Ruth and Uncle Hamish . . .

She hadn't written anything else. She didn't know what to write, how to explain her choice to stay on the island when her aunt and uncle had as good as offered her a place at the high school in Rutland, an opportunity unsurpassed here.

She felt, somehow, by staying, she was betraying them. She closed her eyes, conjuring Ruth's face, the stern line of her mouth, the flintiness of her eyes, but for some reason all she could see in her mind's eye was Ruth as she'd drawn her, her expression resolute but weary, a certain vulnerability in the curve of her cheek and rounded slump of her shoulder.

And Uncle Hamish, with his slipped sweets and jolly smiles. Ellen had long ago recognized her uncle's gentle ineffectualness, but he had a good heart, and she knew he loved her.

Did he want her back? Did Aunt Ruth? Would she be disappointing them both by staying? Sighing, Ellen put the paper aside. She was an artist, not a writer, and tonight it seemed the words wouldn't come.

A knock sounded on the door, and then Louisa peeked her head around the corner. 'May I come in?'

'Of course.' Ellen tucked her pen and paper away, out of sight.

'Aunt Rose told me you're staying on the island,' Louisa said. She leaned against the door and watched Ellen speculatively.

'Yes, I am. I'm sorry I didn't tell you, Louisa. It has all happened so quickly.'

'I'm sure.' Louisa's smile was a little twisted. 'I suppose you'll have a grand time. This is home to you, isn't it?'

Ellen's glance slid inadvertently to the unfinished — un*started* — letter. 'Yes,' she admitted quietly, 'it is.'

Louisa sighed. 'I wish it were for me,' she said, and Ellen almost felt sorry for her, until she added, 'perhaps it will be one day.'

A strange prickling crept down Ellen's spine. 'What do you mean, Louisa?'

Louisa shrugged. 'Aunt Rose invited me for next summer. I thought I'd accept.'

Aunt Rose, not Mrs McCafferty, Ellen noticed. Somehow Louisa Hopper, with her snooty ways and snobbish air, had weaseled her way into the McCaffertys' affections. And, Ellen considered darkly, perhaps others' affections as well.

She knew she was being unfair. Worse, she knew she felt jealous, and she wasn't sure why. The McCaffertys loved her; she had never felt slighted in the least.

And yet, just as Louisa had observed, the island was hers. The people were hers. She didn't want to share them.

'That will be nice,' she finally said, realizing the silence between them had stretched on too long. Louisa just laughed.

'It's gracious of you to say so,' she replied, 'even if you don't feel it. I know this island is yours, Ellen, but I want my own little piece of it.' Her smile was almost compassionate as she added, 'It shouldn't bother you too much, should it?'

Ellen smiled stiffly. 'It's not a competition, Louisa.'

'Maybe not,' Louisa agreed, 'although, after all, there is only one island.'

Louisa left a week later. The wind off the lake was chilly, blowing up white caps, and the leaves were more than just touched with crimson and gold. Ellen saw her off, her shawl wrapped tightly around her shoulders.

'Godspeed, Louisa,' she told her, and leaned forward to kiss her cold cheek.

Louisa's eyes were bright and her smile a bit twisted as she gave Ellen a quick, tight embrace. 'Goodbye, Ellen. Who knows, perhaps I'll see you again . . . sooner than you think.'

The possibility seemed so remote, and her own future still gleaming with possibility and promise, that Ellen was able to smile easily. 'I hope so, Louisa.'

Behind them, Jed shifted his weight with awkward irritability, and Louisa smiled prettily at him.

'Thank you for driving me to the ferry, Jed,' she said, and he nodded, tipping the brim of his hat at her. It was, Ellen thought, a touching farewell for Jed.

She stayed at the ferry until Captain Jonah's little boat was a speck on the water, and then it was lost to the horizon and all

236

Ellen could see was the shining lake in every direction.

'You ready to get back?' Jed asked, and Ellen turned. Jed was looking as surly as ever, his hat pulled low so she could barely see his eyes. Yet even so Ellen felt a little bubble of happiness. She was here; she was actually going to stay on the island all year!

Despite her misgivings about Aunt Ruth and Uncle Hamish, despite her fears and nervousness for the year ahead with Dr Bandler, she was happy. She grinned up at Jed, who looked slightly taken aback.

'Yes, I'm ready.'

He helped her into the wagon, and they sat in companionable silence almost all the way to Jasper Lane.

Jed slowed the horses by the lane's old gate, half hanging off its hinges and needing to be painted. Between the arch of oaks, their leaves now solid yellow, Ellen could only just glimpse the farmhouse.

'So it seems you're staying with us this year,' Jed said, his hands loose on the reins.

'Yes, I am.'

'You fancy yourself a nurse?' He quirked one eyebrow in mockery, although his voice was gentle enough for Ellen not to take offence.

'Not yet. I still need to go to nursing school,' she said.

'Big dreams, then.'

'I'd say they were medium-sized,' Ellen replied, and Jed smiled, little more than a flicker of emotion. 'And what about you, Jed?' she asked impulsively. 'Have you got big dreams?'

Jed gazed off in the distance, his hands still on the reins. 'Me?' he finally answered after a long moment. 'I reckon I've got everything I need right here.' His gaze turned back to Ellen and rested on her for a long moment, long enough for her cheeks to warm, before he clucked to the horses and the wagon turned up the lane.

12

Three years later

The birch trees by the pond were tinged with yellow as Ellen sat with her sketchbook on her knees. It was late August, and there was a crispness to the air that hadn't been there a week or even a few days ago.

She leaned her head against the oak tree behind her and closed her eyes. This last summer at Jasper Lane had been a golden one, full of happy memories, days tending the garden or playing with the children, evenings telling stories by the fire. Berry picking and jam making, the McAllister wedding (Captain Jonah had too much to drink and serenaded the bride!) and long, lazy days on the shore, paddling in the lake or looking for shells.

And it was all about to change. Ellen opened her eyes, shielding them from the sun as she gazed out at the fields that seemed to roll right into the blue-green waters of Lake Ontario.

Dyle and Peter were tending the harvest, and she could see on the other side of the pond Jed and Lucas were hard at work with their father. Ellen, Rose, Caro, and Sarah had all taken turns bringing in the wheat, and they jealously tended the McCafferty kitchen garden with its fat tomatoes and waxy yellow beans. The groundhog had eaten all the peas — Rose had been pragmatic about it.

'I never liked them anyway,' she said as she inspected a stripped plant. 'So much fuss and bother for such a few little peas!'

One more week of harvesting, and then everyone would be going their separate ways. Ellen thrilled to think of it, even as she felt a shudder of trepidation reverberate through her very bones.

In the spring she'd been accepted to Kingston General Hospital's nursing school, and she would be leaving on Captain Jonah's ferry that Tuesday. Peter would be joining her in Kingston, to go to high school, and so would Lucas, about to start his first year at Queen's College.

It seemed incredible that it was all about to begin, the adventure she'd been waiting for the last three years to start.

Not, Ellen acknowledged wryly, that those three years had been interminable. On the contrary, they'd been wonderful, full of friendship, laughter, and happiness, living with the McCaffertys and assisting the island doctor, Dr Bandler, in his many duties.

Ellen was grateful for the medical knowledge she'd learned in the last three years, from dressing a wound, to instructing someone how to prepare a mustard plaster, to soothing an anxious father as his wife prepared to give birth.

There had been the minor tragedies that peppered life, of course — a bad harvest, a long illness of Sarah's which had left her a bit fragile.

Nellie Lyman had also continued her downward spiral of health, and although she continued to be bedridden, she still clung tenaciously to life. Yet it made Ellen ache to see Jed reading to her when she came to visit, as she often did, with a pie or bunch of flowers. She'd catch Jed sitting by the bed, his head bent over a book as he carefully read from the Bible.

Mrs Lyman leaned against the pillows, her face pale but composed, a slight smile softening her features.

Perhaps saddest of all in the last three years had been the death of her beloved dog, Boots, the winter before last. She'd caught cold and simply hadn't recovered. For her seventeenth birthday, Jed had got her another puppy, this one buttery yellow with long silky ears. She called him Pat, because curled up in front of the coal stove he looked

241

just like a pat of golden butter.

'Penny for your thoughts, lazybones.'

Ellen looked up in surprise to see Jed striding in his easy, long-limbed way towards her. His hat was in his hand and he raked his fingers through his sweaty hair.

'I'm having a well-earned rest,' Ellen replied pertly. 'I've been in the kitchen all morning, canning tomatoes, and Rose practically chased me out. What's your excuse?'

'It's almost dinner, or hadn't you noticed? How long have you been out here, Ellen Copley?'

There was something about the way Jed said her name, how it rolled off his tongue with such laughing ease, that made Ellen feel as if she wanted to shiver.

She looked at him, giving her his usual smile that was teasing and friendly and just a tiny bit mocking, and smiled back.

'When I draw, I lose track of time,' she confessed.

Jed stretched out next to her and before Ellen could say a word, he reached for her sketchbook. 'Let's have a look, then.'

'Jed!' Ellen tried to grab the book back. 'They're private.'

He looked at her, his gaze heavy-lidded. 'You let Lucas look at them.'

'That's different — '

'Oh? How so?'

Ellen bit her lip, unsure if she could explain. Unsure if she even knew. 'It just is.'

'I won't laugh, if that's what you're afraid of.'

'You will so laugh!' Ellen retorted. 'When have you missed an opportunity to tease me?'

'Rarely, it's true.' Jed grinned and slowly crossed his heart. 'Promise, though.' He paused, his hand on the sketchbook. 'May I?'

'All right.' Ellen found her heart was thudding with a strange, new, thrilling anxiety as Jed slowly turned the pages. There were several months of sketches in there — she usually filled a book quite quickly, and Mrs Smeaton at the general store laughed that Ellen kept them in business just with the paper she bought.

He gazed at each sketch silently, his expression unfathomable. Ellen sat with her hands clenched in her lap, watching as the sketches went by under his fingers. There was a chipmunk peeking out from a pile of logs, the birch trees with a few leaves beginning to flutter down, Rose caught in an unguarded moment, leaning against the kitchen table, her eyes thoughtful and a bit weary.

And then there was Jed. Ellen bit her lip; she'd forgotten that particular sketch was in the book. She'd drawn Jed from memory, putting him in a setting she'd never actually seen. He leaned against a fence post, hands shoved in his pockets, his gaze faraway and wistful. It was an intimate sketch, showing a vulnerability that Ellen hadn't fully realized was there until they were both sitting there staring at it.

She felt as if that sketch revealed something about Jed, but even more so it revealed something about her. She felt her cheeks warm and she looked away, studied a distant birch tree with desperate concentration even as she waited for Jed to finish, to say something.

After a long, silent moment, Jed turned the page. He finished looking at the sketches, then handed back the book.

'Thank you,' Ellen murmured. She found she still couldn't quite meet his eyes.

'I suppose no one is safe from your pencil,' Jed said lightly, and Ellen felt both relieved and disappointed that he was going to dismiss the sketch, and that moment, so quickly. Yet in the past few months there had been more moments such as that, moments that suddenly turned tense and expectant and made Ellen wonder just what she wanted from Jed, just what she felt for him.

Yet as soon as her mind grasped that idea, it skittered away again. Whatever she felt, it didn't bear much thinking about.

Jed stood up, reaching his hand down to help Ellen to her feet. 'I imagine its dinnertime at the McCaffertys as well as the Lymans.'

'Will you stay?' Ellen blurted, then felt her cheeks turn bright red. Why had she asked that? Jed had already told her his family was having dinner. And why had she wanted him to stay?

'Not tonight,' Jed said, but he walked her back to Jasper Lane, and as Ellen slowly walked up the lane, she felt rather than saw Jed watching her from the copse of beeches at its end.

★   ★   ★

The day of departure came all too quickly. As excited as Ellen was to begin her new life in Kingston, there was something sad about packing her cases and leaving her cozy little room under the eaves.

Rose came in as she was closing her valise. 'Dyle will take you and Peter to the ferry. Lucas is coming too.' She gave a little laugh. 'Actually, we're all coming to say goodbye. I expect half the island will be on the dock to see you three off.'

'Folk go to Kingston every year,' Ellen

protested. 'Surely it's not such an event.'

'And every year we see them off on the boat. You remember last year.'

Ellen nodded. Last autumn Julianna Moore, a slightly snobbish Quebec girl who had moved to the island to live with her grandmother, had gone to Queen's. There had been a crowd of people waving her off as she sat regally in Captain Jonah's little boat.

'The island is a close-knit place,' Ellen acknowledged.

'Yes, and you've become part of its fabric in these last three years.' Rose sat on the edge of the bed, smoothing the worn patchwork quilt. 'Will you go back to Seaton for Christmas?' she asked, and Ellen felt a strange lurch of her heart.

In the last three years she'd been back to Seaton twice, both brief visits. Ellen had been amazed at how removed she'd felt from the town and its inhabitants, almost as if she'd never lived there at all.

Ruth had been coldly impersonal, acting almost as if Ellen's presence was an imposition, and Hamish's jolly bonhomie hadn't been able to cover the tension that crackled in the air.

Visits to Louisa had been surprisingly pleasant, and Ellen suspected this was in part because Louisa had been invited each summer to a camp in the Adirondacks with her cousins, and so had never asked to come back to the island, for which Ellen was grateful.

Also in Seaton, Ellen received letters from Da, as short and uninformative as ever. He still lived in Santa Fe, working on the engines, and once in awhile there was a quarter to be found in the envelope, or even a half dollar.

Sometimes Ellen found she could hardly remember him, beyond a vague sense of his smile or voice. She hadn't seen him in five years.

Still, by the end of her time there, a time spent in stilted conversations and awkward silences, Ellen suspected that her aunt and uncle were as relieved to see her gone as she was to go. Now she considered Rose's question. Would they want to see her?

'I don't think so,' Ellen said after a moment. 'I don't want to impose on Uncle Hamish and Aunt Ruth, and I'd rather be here anyway.'

'Don't you think they might want to see you?' Rose raised her eyebrows in a way that made Ellen squirm a bit.

'They don't seem to want it when I'm there,' she said.

Rose was silent for a moment, her fingers

tracing the vine pattern in the quilt. 'I think you're confusing what seems so with what truly is.'

'How am I to know the difference?'

Rose shrugged. 'It's difficult, especially with someone as prickly as Ruth. But think on things besides how they seem. Didn't Ruth send you a lovely Christmas parcel last winter? There was some beautiful rose wool in it, as I recall, enough for two dresses.'

'Yes — ' Ellen had excused it as a guilt offering, for there had been no invitation to Seaton that year.

'And there have been letters from your aunt and uncle nearly every month.'

Ellen recalled the dry missives from Aunt Ruth, unfeelingly relating the happenings in Seaton without one jot of humour or affection, and always ending with a stern reminder to make herself useful to Rose.

'It feels like duty, Aunt Rose,' Ellen said. 'And I don't want to be a duty, to anyone.'

Rose nodded and patted Ellen's hand. 'I understand that, of course. But sometimes we must think where our own duty lies. Now I think Dyle's hitched the wagon. We should get to the ferry.'

The round of farewells at Stella's dock was a blur to Ellen. She sat in the ferry, crammed between a fidgeting Peter and a sober Lucas, a hatbox balanced on her knees, while everyone she'd ever known called out goodbyes and advice.

'Goodbye, Ellen! Keep an eye on Peter. He's a fine fellow, but he's sure to bring a bit of trouble!'

'Don't step out with those university boys!'

'Don't forget the island!'

'Make sure to write!'

Ellen found herself seeking out Jed in the crowd, and she felt a sharp stab of disappointment when she realized he wasn't there. He'd stayed at home to help with the harvest, which was sensible, and yet saddened her all the same.

Finally Captain Jonah told everyone to stop their noise, and he pushed off from the dock. Still, the cries and farewells followed them until Stella was little more than a speck on the flat, blue-green waters.

A slightly chilly breeze ruffled its surface as they headed into the centre of the lake, and Ellen pulled her shawl around her shoulders. All three of them were strangely quiet, touched by the farewells, Ellen supposed, and contemplating their separate futures.

Captain Jonah eyed them speculatively. 'Don't forget us now, hey?' he said, and Peter smiled nervously while Lucas assured him with a jaunty smile,

'Aye, aye, Captain.'

Ellen didn't register many of the details of the short train ride from Ogdensberg to Kingston, and all too soon they were at the station, and then in a hansom cab, and then Lucas was taking her valise out and bringing it up the steps of Kingston General Hospital's Nurses' Home.

'Well, here you are,' he said brightly. 'Looks a fine place.'

Ellen had to admit it did. The Nurses' Home was a handsome, limestone building with rolling lawns down to the bay. It looked like a stately home rather than the dormitory it was, and Ellen was suitably awed.

She was also homesick, and had to resist grabbing hold of Lucas's sleeve and begging him to stay a few minutes more. It was strange, but since Lucas had gone to high school, they'd grown apart. Ellen feared he was disappointed in her decision to stay on the island, although Lucas insisted he wasn't. Yet neither of them could deny — if they chose to speak of it — that something had changed and cooled between them, even though now Lucas was smiling at her easily.

'First day off,' he promised her, 'I'm taking you out to Kingston's finest tearoom. All right?'

'All right.' The realization that she would

see Lucas soon made her own smile genuine.

'Can I come too?' Peter called out the window of the hansom. He was boarding with a family on Division Street and Ellen knew she would be able to visit him regularly.

'No, scamp,' Lucas replied, 'you get home cooking seven days a week! Ellen can see you another time.'

Peter pretended to scowl, and Ellen quickly kissed Lucas's cheek. He touched his face, surprised, and she blushed, half-regretting her impulsive gesture.

'Thank you, Lucas. I'll write with the date of my first day off. It most likely isn't for ages.'

'I can wait.'

The cab driver cleared his throat impatiently, and with one last wave, Lucas climbed into the cab and Ellen was alone.

She walked slowly up the steps to the Nurses' Home, grabbed hold of her valise, and went inside.

★　★　★

'You will be the twenty-second class to graduate from Kingston General Hospital Nurses' School. This is both an opportunity and a privilege, and I hope you all will take your obligations seriously.'

Ellen instinctively straightened in her seat, as, with eleven other nursing students, she listened to the Nursing Superintendent, Miss Cothill, address them in the Watkins lecture hall at Kingston General Hospital.

'You will have many obligations here. Tomorrow your daily schedules will be given to you. As you probably know, they comprise morning classes and afternoons of service and duty. You will have night shifts on the ward on a weekly basis and you will also do private service in patients' homes, as need requires.' Miss Cothill paused again. She was a tall, spare woman with dark hair scraped back in a bun, but Ellen thought her eyes were kind.

They seemed to soften as she gazed at each nurse sitting in front of her. 'Nursing is a strenuous and rewarding profession, ladies. You will constantly be required to work long, hard hours and give a hundred per cent of yourself, a hundred per cent of the time. There are no guarantees and no promises, except that if you do as I say, giving of yourself selflessly and with total commitment, the rewards will be great. There is no profession, in my opinion, comparable with that of the healer's. Hone your abilities and use them well.'

She cleared her throat, and then began to

recite the many rules required to be kept by nursing staff. Ellen knew that a generation ago, nurses had been seen, at best, as little more than domestic help, and at worse, as slatterns. She felt proud of the reputation nurses had in this modern age, and she hoped only to add to it in the next two years.

'Awaken at six,' Miss Cothill began crisply. 'Classes begin at seven. Uniforms must be pressed and clean. Ankles, wrists, and necks must never be exposed or seen. Caps must be positioned firmly on one's head. Hair must be knotted in a simple bun, no fancy styles allowed. Untidy appearance will result in immediate dismissal. A nurse must walk in a quiet, ladylike way, but always be brisk and efficient. When entering any corridor or hall, a nurse must stop and wait until a superior passes her, if one is walking behind her. When asked a question, a nurse must respond with the utmost courtesy. Impolite behaviour will result in immediate dismissal. A nurse must always consider her patient first. She must never question a doctor's judgement, or do anything in association with a patient without consulting that patient's doctor. Failure to consult a physician in regard to a patient's health or behaviour will result in immediate dismissal. A nurse must be in her dormitory room, in bed with the lights extinguished, by ten o'clock unless she is on duty. Failure to meet this curfew will result in immediate dismissal. A nurse can only have male visitors on her afternoons off, and only for a period of one hour, only in the sitting room. Failure to comply with any of the aforementioned rules will result in immediate dismissal.'

Ellen's face paled with each mention of 'immediate dismissal'. She wouldn't even make it through the first week — the first day!

'A little frightening, isn't it?' the young nurse sitting next to Ellen whispered. Ellen looked over at the girl and smiled tremulously before quickly turning back to Miss Cothill.

'I'm Amity Carwell,' the same young nurse said, introducing herself to Ellen as they filed out of the lecture hall for lunch.

'Ellen Copley,' Ellen replied.

'I do find this overwhelming,' Amity sighed. 'If you want to know the truth, I don't even want to be a nurse.'

'Why?' Ellen exclaimed, finding it hard to believe that anyone would go through such a rigorous programme if she wasn't really committed. Even as this thought occurred to her, another uncomfortable one followed on its heels, that she wasn't sure how committed *she* was.

'Family,' Amity replied. 'No one wants to

marry me, and I don't want to stay at home and turn into a drudge. I had to do something, and I'd rather it was something helpful and trained. I could've been a teacher, I suppose, but I can't see myself droning on to a bunch of children. What about you?'

'What about me?' Ellen asked. They were being carried by the crowd of nurses and medical students who were all making their way to the hospital's dining room.

'Why are you here?'

Something about Amity's frank face, her brown eyes bright and inquisitive, made Ellen reply honestly,

'I didn't know what else to do.'

'Do you like nursing?'

'I think I do,' Ellen said cautiously. 'I nursed my mam when I was younger, and I've been working for the island doctor for the last three years.'

'Island doctor? Where are you from?'

A glowing description of Amherst Island occupied the rest of their journey into the dining room, and Ellen didn't have to think about the seed of doubt so carelessly sown.

Just why was she a nurse? The rigours of life at Kingston General Hospital seemed far removed from her mother's sickroom, or Dr Bandler's country practice.

Ellen tried to imagine her future, serving in

a hospital like this one, or perhaps, as some nurses had dreamily imagined, as a missionary in far-off Asia or Africa. She shivered at the thought, knowing instinctively she was not one for adventure.

Yet what was she for? What did she want to do with her life? What dreams did she still nourish?

Well, Ellen thought with weary pragmatism, she had two years before she had to make a decision.

It was silent that evening as twelve nurses trooped up to their dormitory, exhausted and a little discouraged. They had all been in classes since seven that morning, and the day had seemed twice as long as a normal one. Ellen was relieved to sit on her bed, plaiting her hair as the cool night air blew over her. A shadow fell over the bed, obscuring the lamplight from Ellen's bedside table. Turning, Ellen saw Amity Carwell and smiled.

'You don't look very content,' she said sympathetically, and Amity sat down on the bed, her face bleak and despairing.

'I'm homesick,' she finally confessed after a moment. 'I didn't think I would be. You know, to be honest, I thought I would be glad to leave. And I never expected our dormitory to look so nice — it's grander than home by far! And yet — '

Ellen nodded sympathetically. The Nurses' Home, with its cozy parlour, little library sponsored by former students, and the rows of beds with tables besides and chests at the end was certainly comfortable. She'd heard that the hospital had had such an elegant dormitory built to entice more middle-class women into becoming nurses. It seemed to have worked.

But it wasn't home, not home as she thought of it, with Rose and Dyle and all the children, Jed and Lucas . . . but she wouldn't think of them. She refused to give into despair, not on her first day.

'It's not home,' she finally said to Amity, 'but we'll get used to it, I should think.'

'Our first day off is Sunday,' Amity said with a sigh. 'It seems ages away! What are you going to do, do you think?'

Ellen thought of Lucas. She could send a note to his residence tomorrow, and perhaps he would take her out. Or would he be too busy? She didn't like to impose on him, not when they hadn't been friends, proper friends, for so long.

'I'm not sure,' she said cautiously. 'I have a friend at Queen's College. I might take tea with him.'

'Oh, a beau!' Amity exclaimed, delighted, and Ellen blinked in surprise.

'Not at all,' she said after a moment. 'He's just a friend.' But something in her voice made Amity nod knowingly, and Ellen frowned. Lucas *was* just a friend. She'd never thought of him that way at all, and in truth she hadn't thought of anyone in that way before . . . had she? She'd been solitary and independent for too long to change her ways now.

Yet just the thought of a beau, a proper one, left a strange, yearning ache in her middle, and she found herself inadvertently — instinctively — thinking of Jed. Jed laughing at her, that mocking yet affectionate glint in his eyes, his hands on his hips and his head tilted back as he called her Miss Bossy.

She smiled slightly and the two girls drifted into silence then, each lost in her own thoughts.

A creak of floorboards alerted them to Miss Cothill's presence.

'Lights out,' she called out, and Amity jumped off Ellen's bed.

'Goodnight, Ellen,' she whispered as she hurried to her own bed on the other side of the room.

'Goodnight,' Ellen whispered back. Quickly she blew out her light and snuggled under the covers, too tired to wonder if she was meant to be a nurse — or if she would ever have a beau.

13

The next few days fairly flew by in a flurry of lectures and duty on the wards. The nurses' first responsibility was to change the sheets on patients' beds, the sort of drudgery Ellen was used to and didn't mind, although it was enlivened by another nurse, Harriet McIlvain, knocking a full bedpan straight across the floor.

Superintendent Cothill bore down on her with a frown as both girls froze, caught between hysterical laughter and humiliated tears. 'Clean that up at once, Miss McIlvain. And use the disinfectant.'

Her head seemed crammed full of know-ledge after only one week — lectures in anatomy, physiology, biology, hygenics, and medicine — and Ellen was relieved when Sunday came and she could look forward to the luxury of a whole day to herself.

She'd written Lucas a short note, and he'd replied with alacrity, declaring he'd call for her at one o'clock, after church. Ellen thrilled to think of wearing a proper dress, the rose wool Ruth had sent, and eating fine pastries in an elegant tearoom, in a city no less. It felt like a wonderful, decadent luxury.

'You look lovely, Ellen,' Lucas said when she came into the sitting room where Miss Cothill had had him cool his heels. He wore a frock coat and tie, his dark blond hair slicked back from his blushing face, and Ellen was able to murmur her thanks and reply, 'You look quite the college man, Lucas. I'm proud to be seen on your arm.'

Immediately she wondered if that was too forward, even though Lucas looked only delighted by her remark.

The tearoom he took her to was in the centre of Kingston, and was every bit as elegant as Ellen could have wished for, with fine linen tablecloths and dainty little cups of porcelain.

'Are you surviving?' Lucas asked frankly after the tea had been served.

Ellen wrinkled her nose. 'Just. We're rushed off our feet from dawn till dusk, but I don't really mind. The work keeps me from being homesick. What about you?'

'The lectures are wonderful. I've always wanted this, time to read and learn and just think. It feels such a luxury.' He gave a lopsided smile. 'I feel a bit guilty, leaving everyone at home — '

'They want the best for you,' Ellen objected, and Lucas sighed.

'I know, but sometimes I wonder if it's the best for them.'

Ellen nodded, understanding. 'I know how that feels. Sometimes I wonder if I should have stayed . . . ' Her sigh matched Lucas's. 'Look at Jed, taking care of your mother — '

As soon as she'd said the words, Ellen regretted them. Lucas's face closed up, and she realized with a pang that he must feel guilty for leaving Jed to bear his share of the burden of their mother's care, although his next words belied such a feeling. 'It's what he wants. Jed could have gone to college if he chose.'

'Do you really think so?' Ellen asked. 'How would your father have coped with the two of you gone?'

Lucas's face, usually so open and smiling, hardened briefly. 'He can afford to hire a man, Ellen, or even two. Or a woman to help in the house! He just doesn't want to, because Jed's willing to do it all for free, and work himself to the bone in the process. I won't do that.'

Ellen could only nod, taking a sip of tea, her mind spinning. 'Tell me about college,' she finally said, and seeming as eager as her to lighten the mood, Lucas was soon regaling her with tales of the Freshers Week at Queen's, and the many antics he and his classmates got up to in between their lectures.

'Have you managed to do any drawing?' Lucas asked when the tea things were cleared.

Ellen thought of the sketchbooks and charcoals in the trunk at the foot of her bed, untouched since she'd arrived. There had been plenty of subjects in the hospital, stored in her head, aching to be released onto paper. There had simply been no time.

She shook her head. 'No, I haven't, actually.'

Lucas frowned. 'You need to, Ellen. That's as important as breathing to you.'

'Yes, well, I've managed without breathing for the last week then,' Ellen said with a touch of asperity, and Lucas smiled wryly.

'I never understood why you didn't go to Art School. There's a good one in Toronto — or New York — you could have gone to a hundred different places!'

'If only I had wings,' Ellen said lightly, for she didn't want to dredge up the uncomfortable topics of money or ambition with Lucas. He wouldn't understand the need to be independent, to have security. To not be a burden. She could hardly swan off and do a course that could have no useful purpose, all on someone else's bank account.

Besides, a little voice whispered inside her heart, *what if I'm no good?*

Ellen didn't listen to that voice, instead inquiring brightly after Lucas's lectures, and the people he'd met. He was happy to regale her with several more tales, and the rest of the afternoon passed pleasantly.

The Nurses' Home was half in shadow when Lucas finally walked her home. Ellen knew she'd been gone too long, and hoped she would not suffer the sharp edge of Miss Cothill's tongue, or worse, for it.

'You'll keep writing me, won't you, Ellen?' Lucas asked as he took her to the door. 'I can take you out whenever you've a day off. If you've an evening free, we could even take in a play, or a concert.'

'You don't want to spend all your spare time with me,' Ellen protested.

'Oh, but I do,' Lucas assured her, his eyes gleaming, and Ellen felt a frisson of both excitement and alarm.

'I'll write soon,' she promised and this time, without kissing his cheek, she hurried inside, her thoughts tumbling and whirling inside her head.

★ ★ ★

A month before Ellen was due home for Christmas, she received a letter from Louisa Hopper.

Louisa, Ellen knew, had enrolled at the University of Vermont that year. Ellen had been a bit surprised; she'd never considered Louisa to be an academic.

'I've buckled down since having that fever,' Louisa had confided during Ellen's last visit. 'I like learning now, and I mean to go after it. There's no need in this day and age to get married and have babies as soon as you're out of short skirts!'

'I suppose not,' Ellen agreed, startled, and Louisa gave her one of her coy looks.

'Have you anyone in mind, then, Ellen Copley?'

'No, of course not.' Yet Ellen's contrary brain couldn't help but flash a few images into her head — Jed and Lucas. 'Why, have you?' she asked Louisa, and her friend chuckled.

'Oh, yes, but I don't mean to do anything about it just yet.'

Now Louisa wrote that she was well settled at university, but her father was taking her mother on a Grand Tour of Europe for six months, and so Louisa was at a loss for a place to spend Christmas.

They've entreated me to come to Paris in the spring, she wrote, *and they want me to spend Christmas with relatives in*

Burlington, but they're so stuffy and dull, I couldn't, dear Ellen, not ever! So I wonder if I may be so bold as to suggest I stay with you, at Jasper Lane, for the winter holidays? It would, I dare say, be quite like old times.

'Old times!' Ellen muttered, sinking on to her bed. She wasn't sure why she wasn't pleased by Louisa's invitation. They'd stayed friends over the years, so it could only be natural for her to warmly encourage Louisa to stay. She knew Rose would. And yet Ellen felt a little tremble of trepidation, as if having Louisa to stay on the island now, when they were both so much older, would not be like old times at all, but a different thing altogether.

Yet she could hardly refuse her, especially when Louisa made it so plain that she'd nowhere comfortable to stay, and so Ellen duly wrote Rose, who, as expected, replied in the affirmative, and then replied to Louisa.

Within a fortnight it was all arranged, tickets bought, and Louisa wrote merrily that she would see Ellen on Captain Jonah's 'dear little ferry' on December the twentieth.

'Ice boat, more like,' Ellen muttered, for by that time of year the lake was likely to be mostly frozen.

December twentieth came soon enough. Ellen was looking forward to a fortnight of days spent at her own command, although she would miss the friends, like Amity and Harriet, whom she'd made at the hospital.

'You look like you've been worked to the bone,' Lucas half-scolded when he came to fetch her for the train. He jumped out to haul her valise into the back, and Peter waved madly.

'Hallo, Ellen! Lucas is right, you know. You look far too thin.'

'Thank you very much,' Ellen replied, taking Lucas's hand to help her into the hansom. She'd seen him several times over the last few months, although not perhaps as much as Lucas would have liked.

Their friendship had certainly been rekindled, away from the island, and while Ellen enjoyed the lectures, concerts and teas Lucas escorted her to, she sometimes felt as if he saw something in her that she wasn't sure she saw, or felt, herself.

There had been a few uneasy moments this autumn when Ellen had suddenly feared Lucas might say something momentous, something she knew she would regret, and she'd managed to steer the conversation away from such dangerous topics, although she wondered why she was so afraid.

What did she feel for Lucas? She liked him, certainly; perhaps she even loved him, in a dear, familiar way, but was that enough?

It hardly mattered anyway, Ellen told herself firmly, for she still had a year and a half of nursing, and she could not entertain the idea of a beau until that was finished.

'It will be funny to see Louisa again,' Lucas commented, for Ellen had told him of Louisa's planned visit the last time they'd taken tea together. 'I wonder if she's outgrown her snobbish ways? Jed always said she was too fancy for the island.'

'Did he?' Ellen asked diffidently, unsure what to make of this comment.

'I'm surprised she wants to come back.'

'She hasn't any other place to go,' Ellen said, although if pressed, she would have to admit that Louisa could no doubt have found another agreeable situation. The question of why she had chosen not to vexed Ellen and she put it firmly out of her mind.

'It will be good to see an old friend,' she said, and this time she could even believe it.

Indeed, when Ellen finally did see Louisa waiting at the dock in Ogdensberg, her friend fell joyfully into her arms.

'Oh, Ellen, it's so good to see you!' Louisa cried. 'It's so good to be here!'

Lucas and Peter stood back, bemused,

while Ellen and Louisa exchanged greetings, and linking arms as they had done so many years ago, they clambered into the sledge driven across the ice by Captain Jonah and his two pack ponies.

All of Ellen's doubts about Louisa's visit were quite wiped away in the light of her friend's bubbling good humour and delight in being on the island, and in the McCaffertys' home. Both Ellen and Louisa were pleased at the winter festivities and amusements that had been planned, from an ice sculpture contest in Stella, to a sleigh ride arranged by Jed and Lucas.

Bundled up in their warmest coats and scarves, with thick fur rugs piled over them, Jed led the horse-drawn sleigh down the island's lane transformed by snow and ice into a fantastic fairy land.

If Ellen was nettled that Louisa immediately took the seat next to Jed, and Ellen and Lucas were left to share the back seat, she did not show it, or indeed even admit it to herself.

She smiled at Lucas, conscious of his closeness under the heavy rugs, and he smiled back. She watched as Louisa merrily tucked her arm into Jed's, giving a light, little laugh as she did so. Ellen's stomach clenched as Louisa, giving that irritating little laugh again, brushed a dusting of snow from Jed's dark hair.

'Looks like Jed has an admirer,' Lucas murmured, and Ellen forced herself to smile.

'Louisa loves to be charming,' she agreed, and then turned to gaze at the passing scenery, the evergreens heavily laden with snow, the sky dazzling blue.

The wind nipped their cheeks and ears, and Louisa, Ellen saw, remained cuddled quite close to Jed. Why did she mind? She asked herself fiercely. Why did it *hurt?* It was nothing to her what Louisa did with Jed. Yet no matter how many times she told herself that, she could not acknowledge it as the truth.

She did mind. It did hurt.

Determinedly, Ellen turned to Lucas, giving him her full attention. It was a silly, childish ploy, and one that would only hurt her in the end, she realized too late, as Lucas's eyes brightened and he even dared to rest his arm along the top of the sledge, so although he was not touching Ellen, it was as if he had his arm around her shoulders. Almost.

Once Ellen saw Jed glance back, his eyes flicking along the length of Lucas's arm, but he said nothing — his expression didn't even change — and he turned back to the horses.

It was ridiculous, Ellen thought despondently, to feel this way, to act this way. She was eighteen years old, and yet she felt like a spoiled child, wanting to stamp her feet and cry 'not fair'.

Jed was *her* friend. They'd been together for the last three years, without Lucas or Louisa, and while their friendship hadn't really changed from the teasing mockery and affection of an earlier time, it had deepened and strengthened somehow . . . or at least Ellen had thought it had.

Perhaps it hadn't.

For as the days passed, however, there could be no denying the preference Louisa showed for the older Lyman brother. Ellen watched with slightly narrowed eyes as Louisa always took Jed's arm, lightly and laughingly, yet with a steady purpose all the same. She saw how Jed obliged, even though he seemed to regard Louisa, with her fine clothes and gaiety, with some bemusement.

There was no reason for Ellen to be unsettled by these developments. Why should she care if Louisa and Jed flirted, or even fell in love for that matter?

Yet as Ellen gazed at the oak tree's ice-encased branches outside her window on Christmas Eve, her sketchbook untouched on her lap, she was forced to acknowledge that she did care. She cared a great deal.

Sighing dispiritedly, she leaned her forehead against the cold glass. There could be nothing in Jed and Louisa's moments together, she told herself. Jed hadn't even seen Louisa in three years. He was no doubt humouring her, as she was amusing herself.

And yet . . . and yet . . . what if there was something to it?

What if Jed fell for Louisa, with her glossy hair and dimpled cheeks and fancy clothes?

What would it mean to her?

Ellen knew she had not thought seriously of her feelings for Jed before, and now she knew why. She was afraid. She was afraid that Jed felt nothing for her but a light, brotherly affection that could quite easily be disposed of. It was a fear she did not want to face, and one she certainly did not wish Jed to confirm openly, even as she still stubbornly refused to acknowledge what she felt for him.

'He's rude and oafish and bad-mannered,' she whispered fiercely, and recognized how hollow her words sounded.

Restlessly, Ellen tossed the sketchbook aside and went downstairs. It was nearing supper, and everyone had gathered in the front parlour for games, the light from the fire and the oil lamps casting a cozy glow over the happy, domestic scene.

'Come join us,' Caro entreated, bent over a game of spillikins with Sarah. 'Jed and Lucas have promised to come and roast chestnuts later, too, Ellen!'

'Have they?' Ellen murmured, her heart skipping a beat before beginning to pound.

'Come play,' Sarah called, but Ellen just smiled and slipped from the room. She didn't think she could bear their jolly company.

She heard a sound from the kitchen, and thought it must be Pat, whining to be let out.

It was with something akin to relief that she went into the kitchen, only to then skid to a halt. The room was already occupied, and not by her dog.

Louisa and Jed stood by the coal stove, their arms entwined, kissing quite passionately.

14

The day Ellen was to return to Kingston was clear and still, with a sharp coldness that stole the breath right from her lungs.

She was grateful for the cloak and scarf which kept her warm, and more importantly, hid her features from probing eyes. Although on the surface Ellen had maintained a pleasant, if abstracted air these last few days, inside she felt as frozen as the lake stretching out under a blanket of snow; a hard and brittle layer of ice which covered the churning emotions underneath.

Louisa stood next to her, waiting to get on the sledge. Ellen sensed rather than saw Louisa's tension; it was palpable between them. The friends had not spoken to one another beyond stiff pleasantries for several days. Ellen would not easily forget the conversation they'd had on Christmas morning.

After seeing Jed and Louisa in the kitchen, Ellen had stumbled out, averting her eyes, but not before she saw Jed spring guiltily away, an unusual uncertainty clouding his features.

She hurried upstairs, breathing as fast as if

273

she'd run all the way down Jasper Lane. She didn't want to examine her reaction — its terrible force or the feelings which had caused it — and so she sat numbly staring out the window as twilight fell softly over the barren winter landscape.

She'd hoped to avoid Jed and Louisa for the rest of the holidays — the Lymans would be having Christmas celebrations at their own house — but of course it proved impossible.

There was church on Christmas morning, and as everyone exchanged greetings in the frosty air after the service, Louisa walked determinedly up to Ellen.

'Ellen, you must talk to me.'

'I think I've said Happy Christmas, Louisa,' Ellen replied with a small smile.

'Don't speak such nonsense. Ever since you saw Jed and me in the kitchen, you've been strung tighter than a bow. I can only wonder at the reason why.' There was a hard glint in Louisa's eye that Ellen did not like at all. She lifted her chin.

'You surprised me, that's all. Admittedly, it was a bit uncomfortable, but I dare say I shall recover in time.' As a joke, it fell flat.

'If you had set your cap at Jed,' Louisa said in a hard voice, 'you should have made your feelings known. I told you how I felt about him all those years ago.'

'You told me you could make him fall in love with you!'

'And I did, didn't I?'

Ellen made a disgusted sound. She did not want to ask if Louisa was in love with Jed.

'Are you jealous?' Louisa asked without spite. 'Do you want him for yourself, or do you just want no one to have him?'

'Want him for myself!' Ellen sputtered indignantly. Her cheeks were flushed with cold and humiliation that she should be having such a discussion with Louisa, especially when it was obvious where Jed's affections must lie. 'I should think not! He's had nothing but mockery or scorn for me from the day I met him. I'd never fall in love with Jed Lyman, never.'

Louisa's eyes were bright with a strange satisfaction. 'You almost talk as if you don't like him.'

'I don't!'

'Yet you've been friends these last three years — '

'You can have him, Louisa,' Ellen said firmly, although there was a ragged edge to her voice and she could not help but add, hurt and humiliation spiking her words, '*if* you think your parents will be best pleased! Do they want you courted by an ignorant farm boy who hasn't even been to high school?'

Louisa's mouth opened soundlessly, but it wasn't her friend's reaction that drained the colour from Ellen's face. It was Jed's.

He'd approached them without either woman seeing, and he stood in the snow, his hands shoved into the pockets of his overcoat, his face quite expressionless.

Ellen struggled to form a coherent thought or word, but her mind was numb. Her scornful words seemed still to reverberate in the air, a terrible echo.

Louisa shut her mouth and swept towards Jed, linking arms with him, her eyes blazing.

'If you plan to snitch to my parents, Ellen Copley, you can tell them I am very happy, and proud, with my choice!' She shook her head slowly, her voice shaking. 'I never took you for a *snob*.'

With that, Jed and Louisa walked out of the churchyard, and Ellen was left standing there, blinking back tears of rage and misery.

The injustice of it burned rawly in Ellen's soul — she, the lass from Springburn, a snob! And yet the words she'd so harshly spoken were the words of a snob, and patently untrue. She'd spoken them from malice, and hurt, and fear. And she'd never, ever wanted Jed to hear them.

Yet he had, and there could be no taking them back. There could be no going back,

Ellen quickly realized, for both Jed and Louisa avoided her, and for the first time she looked forward to leaving the island with a quiet, miserable desperation.

For the sake of the family and the anticipated celebration, Ellen pulled herself together to participate in the opening of presents, the grand goose dinner, and the parlour games and sledge rides that no Christmas would be without.

Yet her distracted air, the pall of misery that hung around her like a grey cloak, did not escape Rose.

'Are you quite well, Ellen?' she asked quietly one evening when the two of them were seated by the fire.

Ellen looked up from the novel she'd been trying to read; she'd barely turned a page. 'Oh, yes, Aunt Rose. It's been a lovely holiday.'

'Has it?' Rose pursed her lips in a knowing way, but left it at that. Ellen was suddenly aware of Louisa's absence in the cosy parlour; Jed had taken her for a sledge ride. Lucas had invited Ellen, but she'd pleaded a headache.

'It's never too late to mend things,' Rose said quietly, and Ellen looked up in uncomfortable surprise. The last thing she wanted was for her falling out with Jed to be noticed, or did Rose just mean Louisa? Ellen didn't know, and she was not about to ask.

'I'm just tired, Aunt Rose,' she said firmly. 'Nursing school has quite fatigued me. I'm sorry if I don't seem myself.'

'No, child,' Rose replied with a weary smile, 'don't be sorry.'

Now all the farewells had been said, and Ellen and Louisa, Lucas and Peter were climbing in the sledge to take them back to the train and Kingston.

Ellen pulled the travelling rug over her; the air was freezing and still. Louisa sat next to her, and Ellen handed her a bit of the rug.

'All ready?' Captain Jonah called cheerfully, and then he cracked his whip and the ponies began their methodical trotting, the sleigh skimming across the hardened crust of snow.

'You haven't asked,' Louisa said into the silence, her voice low enough to reach only Ellen's ears, 'so I'll tell you. I love Jed and I hope to marry him.'

Ellen stared out at the flat stretch of snowy lake. 'Has he asked you, then?'

'Not yet, but I think he will.' Louisa grabbed Ellen's sleeve with one mittened hand. 'Ellen, look at me! You've been as pale and lifeless as a ghost these past few days. What is wrong with you? Is it because of Jed? I promise you, I didn't know — '

'Louisa, please!' Ellen glanced quickly at Lucas, who was engaged in a conversation about ice fishing with Peter and Captain Jonah. 'You must stop these theatrics! I'm not in love with Jed, and never have been. I was surprised, that is all. You must admit you are an unlikely pair.'

'Then why have you been so pale, so withdrawn?'

Ellen met Louisa's gaze, and saw the genuine anxiety in her friend's eyes. She dredged up a smile from the depths of her soul and used the excuse she'd given Rose.

'The work at the hospital tires me. I've been tired and — ' she took a breath ' — that's all. Really, Louisa.'

Louisa did not look convinced, but Ellen thought she might be persuaded simply because it was easier to believe than the truth.

The truth. Even Ellen did not want to face the truth. She drew her cloak tighter around her shoulders and closed her eyes against the stark beauty of the day, and the memory of two lovers which had seared itself into her brain.

★　★　★

The Nurses' Home was alive with chatter and laughter as Ellen settled back into her dormitory. Everyone had presents to show, stories to tell.

Everyone, it seemed, but Ellen. She couldn't face the crowded parlour with its laughter and music, and so she retired early upstairs, thinking once again that she would sketch.

Except she couldn't. For once, the riot of colour and action she loved to put on the page wouldn't come. She felt nothing; there was nothing in her head or heart, no idea waiting to be given life. She sat with the sketchbook unopened on her lap, a pencil clasped loosely between her fingers, staring into space.

'Ellen?' Amity stood in the doorway, slightly flushed from the warm parlour, an uncertain look on her face. 'You've hardly said a word since supper. Are you ill?'

'No. A bit tired, perhaps.' The lie was becoming thinner, even though it held a fragment of truth. She certainly wanted nothing more than to climb into bed and pull the covers over her head.

Amity came into the room. 'Well, here's the gossip from downstairs. Cynthia Parlin is engaged — he asked on Christmas Day. Gladys Traipine isn't coming back — she's a second year, do you know her? Apparently her father said she hasn't learned a thing here and he won't let her return.' She sat on the bed. 'And there's a new doctor, a surgeon, Dr Trowbridge. No one seems to have seen him yet, but apparently he's very handsome.' She paused, frowning. 'You do look peaky. And going back home was meant to be a rest, you silly thing!'

Ellen gazed down at her sketchbook. 'Yes,' she said quietly, 'I am a rather silly thing.' She was horrified to realize she was quite suddenly near tears, and she blinked them back, her throat raw and aching with the effort.

'Ellen?' Amity lay a hand on her arm. 'Ellen, whatever has happened?'

A tear plopped on to the cover of her sketchbook, and Ellen wiped it away with her thumb. 'Nothing, really,' she said raggedly, 'except that I've been a terrible, blind, *stupid* fool.'

Amity gave an uncertain little laugh. 'That doesn't sound very good.'

'No, it isn't.' Ellen took a deep breath, the effort of holding the howling misery within her making her sides ache. 'Amity, have you ever been in love?'

'No, not a bit. It's why I decided to become a nurse. I'd rather fancied having a husband, children, the lot, but it hasn't happened and I don't think it will.' She smiled slightly. 'I know I'm only twenty, but I feel as if it's passed me by already.'

'Yes,' Ellen agreed, 'I know what you mean.'

'So, you must be in love with someone, then.' Amity kept her voice light, although there was real concern in her dark eyes.

'Yes, and I've only just realized it. I should have seen it ages ago, years perhaps, but I never did. I didn't want to. I . . . I suppose because I was afraid.'

'Afraid? Why?'

Ellen looked up, her eyes bright with both tears and understanding. 'Because everyone I've loved has left. That's putting it a bit too strong, I suppose. Just Mam and Da, but still.'

Amity frowned. 'You were afraid this man would leave you?'

'No, not exactly. I just didn't even *consider* loving him. Loving anyone. I've never really thought about getting married, even. And yet somehow it has all crept up on me, and been the most awful surprise.' She managed to laugh, just a little, and the sound trembled on the air.

'I think it could be quite a pleasant surprise, depending on the circumstances.'

'Ah yes, the circumstances. Those are just this: he's in love with my friend Louisa, and I found them together in an embrace.' Ellen flushed at the memory. 'I was so shocked and horrified — and then I realized. I would never have felt that way if — '

'If you didn't care for him.'

Ellen nodded miserably. 'I expect they'll get married. I could live with that, I suppose, since I never planned on getting married myself, but I'm afraid I've lost Jed's friendship as well. I said some horrible things — about him. I didn't know he was listening.' She looked up, her eyes bleak. 'But he was, of course. And I don't see how anything can ever be the same between us again.'

Amity was silent for a moment. 'It probably won't,' she said quietly, 'but you can move on. These things can heal over. There's still a scar — you've seen it in surgery! — but you can be almost new again. Can't you?' She looked anxiously at her friend, and Ellen nodded slowly.

There was no point going back, living in regret for lost dreams she'd never even known she'd had. She was made of sterner stuff than that — the years in Springburn, in Seaton, attested to that.

Ellen smiled wanly. 'Yes,' she said, and this time her eyes were dry. 'Yes, I can.'

The next few weeks kept Ellen too busy to dwell on her feelings for Jed, or the events over Christmas which had made her aware of them. There were lectures to attend, ward duties to perform, and the general hectic affairs of life at the hospital and in the Nurses' Home.

Halfway through January, Ellen was called upon by the new surgeon, Dr Trowbridge, to assist in surgery.

She quailed under his imperious summons, for she'd never been in the operating theatre, with its rows of wooden seats for the medical students, the operating table below as if on a stage.

'It's a simple amputation, Nurse,' Dr Trowbridge informed her briskly. His normally spotless grey suit was now covered with a white coat and apron, and the surgical instruments, sprayed with carbolic acid, lay gleaming in their tray.

In the last decade Pasteur's Germ Theory had gained wider acceptance, and Kingston General Hospital had been practising sterilization techniques for several years. It made Ellen feel strange to think of all those little germs flying through the air, like some kind of invisible yet deadly poison, yet she'd seen herself the positive effect of washing hands.

'Nurse Copley, you will hold the appendage.'

Ellen, standing quietly to the side, looked

up, startled. 'The — ?' she began, and then realized what he meant. She was supposed to hold the leg that Dr Trowbridge planned to amputate.

Swallowing the bile which had risen in her throat, Ellen grasped the patient's leg as another doctor dripped ether into the cone above the man's face.

'The right leg is gangrenous,' Dr Trowbridge intoned to the medical students leaning forward in their seats, their faces bright with curiosity, 'and will be amputated above the knee. I expect the amputation to take no more than two minutes.'

There was a murmur of admiration, and the assisting surgeon announced that the patient was unconscious.

Dr. Trowbridge brandished his metal, serrated saw, and Ellen closed her eyes.

She didn't dare look as she heard the doctor's methodical sawing, first a soft, easy sound and then with a loud, harsh grinding noise as he cut through the bone.

Her hands grasping the leg were slippery, and she felt light headed. In her six months in nurses' training, she'd had to do a fair number of unpleasant and menial tasks, but nothing quite as bad as this.

Standing there, trying not to sway as spots danced before her eyes, Ellen wondered what she was doing there . . . in the theatre, in the hospital, in Kingston. Had she chosen this path simply because it was safe? Familiar?

Nothing about this moment felt either of those things. She swallowed the bile in her throat, determined not to make a fool of herself, or worse, endanger the operation.

Then it was finished. Ellen stumbled backwards, the appendage still clutched in her hands.

The students were clapping, Dr Trowbridge was smiling easily, and Ellen was left holding someone's leg. She felt faintly ridiculous as well as sick.

The assisting surgeon mopped up the blood as Dr Trowbridge began to sew the wound, and another nurse nudged Ellen towards the bucket in the corner.

It looked like a slop bucket, and she dropped the leg in dubiously, wincing as it landed with a dull thud.

'I think I'm going to be sick.'

She hadn't realized she'd spoken aloud until the nurse, one of the second years, grasped her by the elbow and steered her towards the door.

Ellen stumbled out of the theatre, gasping in lungfuls of air that did not smell of blood and carbolic.

'I don't think I was meant to be a nurse,'

she told Amity rather flatly as they sat in the parlour that evening. 'I nearly fainted when Dr Trowbridge amputated that poor man's leg.'

'I'd faint if I were near Dr Trowbridge,' Harriet McIlvain giggled, and Amity rolled her eyes.

'It happens to all of us. It's a shock, the first time. You'll get used to it.'

Ellen shuddered. 'I'm not sure I want to get used to it.' She thought of the students, craning to see Dr Trowbridge's handiwork, the smell of antiseptic covering the sweet rot of gangrene. Just the memory was enough to make her stomach turn over unpleasantly.

'You will, though,' Amity said with the confidence of someone who had already endured this particular trial and succeeded.

Ellen leaned back against the settee and closed her eyes. She wasn't sure she wanted to admit to Amity how much the experience in the operating theatre had shaken her, not simply because of the nature of the operation, but rather because it made her question her vocation.

What vocation? an inner voice mocked, and Ellen was forced to listen to it . . . to acknowledge that she might not, after all, want to become a nurse.

'I'm going to get some fresh air.' She stood

up, to the surprise of the other nurses cosily ensconced in the parlour.

'Go outside?' Harriet squeaked. 'It's got to be well below freezing, and pitch dark! You wouldn't!'

'I would,' Ellen replied firmly, and Amity, watching her with a rather knowing expression, simply said, 'Don't forget your cloak, then.'

Outside, it was every bit as cold as Harriet had said, and Ellen strode through the hard, frozen snow until she came to the shore of the bay. It was strange to think this icy little bay was part of the same lake that surrounded Amherst Island so many miles away, that Rose and Dyle, yes, even Jed, might at this moment be staring at its flat, frozen surface, the moonlight casting the untouched snow in silver.

A wave of homesickness and longing swept over Ellen so she had to blink back tears. It wasn't longing for the island, which had been made strange by her new feelings for Jed, or Seaton, which had never been a home. It wasn't a longing for the stuffy little flat in Springburn, or any home she'd known.

Rather, it was a longing for a home she'd never had, a warm, comfortable place with a mother and father who were healthy and whole and happy to be there. A proper home.

'It's too late to want that now,' Ellen said aloud, trying to be sensible even though she felt far from it inside.

Inside she felt as lost as the little girl coming off the train, with a Scottish burr and tangled hair.

Perhaps she hadn't changed so much after all.

And then she realized afresh what she really wanted — Jed. Jed's love, the security of his arms around her, his face smiling down into hers. That would be a proper home, and it would never, never be hers.

Yet the force of wanting it did not subside, and for a moment it seemed as if her whole body would shake with unfulfilled longing before Ellen straightened her shoulders, as she had so many times before when presented with an insurmountable obstacle. She couldn't travel any farther down that road, so she would choose another.

And yet what path would — could — she follow? The thought of being a spinster nurse, living in the Nurses' Home and spending her days changing sheets and slop buckets, assisting in surgeries as she grew older and lonelier, made Ellen shudder. She couldn't. She wouldn't.

A few months ago such a path, vague as it seemed, appeared possible, probable, even desirable, yet now, knowing how she loved and wanted to be loved, it seemed like the worst sort of prison. A life sentence.

So what *would* she do? By this time the moon had gone behind a cloud, and the bay was in shadow. Ellen's feet were numb and her gloveless fingers were stiff with cold. There was nothing for her out here, no one, no answers. Slowly she turned back to the dormitory, her future as uncertain and undecided as ever.

★   ★   ★

'There's a visitor for you in the parlour.' Harriet's face was flushed with inquisitive excitement. 'He's quite handsome, and he seems so eager to see you! Have you a beau, Ellen?'

'Not the last time I looked,' Ellen replied with a little smile. She had no idea who might be waiting for her in the parlour, and she could only summon a brief spark of curiosity. The last few months she'd been so consumed with her duties, as well as her growing determination to find another course for herself . . . although what that was to be, she still had no idea.

Shrugging aside the familiar fog of those worries, Ellen checked her appearance in the small mirror above the nurses' communal wash basin. Her reflection revealed that her hair hadn't quite fallen from its pins, and quickly straightening her cap and skirt, Ellen hurried downstairs.

'Lucas!' She moved forward warmly, truly glad to see him. Their busy lives and schedules had kept them apart for several months, although secretly Ellen wondered if Lucas had guessed her feelings for Jed, and stayed away for that reason.

The thought made her flush, and she pushed it aside resolutely.

'I'm sorry I haven't come sooner, Ellen. I always meant to — '

'It's a busy time,' Ellen dismissed quickly. 'Are you well?'

'Yes. Very well. Can you take a stroll with me?' Lucas looked nervous, and his fingers crept towards his collar to give it a self-conscious tug.

Ellen hesitated for only a moment. 'Of course. Let me get my shawl.'

Outside, the sky was a delicate blue, wispy clouds scudding across its surface. The lake was choppy and bright, and the grassy lawn leading down to it was studded with buttercups.

'Kingston is beautiful this time of year,' Lucas said as they strolled down to the bay.

'I've never seen so many cherry blossoms before in my life.'

'I wish I had more time to see it,' Ellen replied ruefully. 'The hospital has kept all of its nurses busier than ever. I fear the only sights I see are rows of beds and slop buckets needing to be emptied!'

'You do like it, though?' Lucas asked a bit anxiously, and Ellen smiled. She was not about to admit any of her doubts to Lucas, or anyone. Not until she'd decided for herself what her own future was to be.

'You don't think I'd do it otherwise?' she said with mock horror, and his smile was touched with relief.

'Have you been drawing?'

Ellen forced down a bubble of irritation. She knew Lucas was concerned for her, but sometimes it felt like nagging.

'When I have the time. A few sketches.'

'I'd like to see them — '

'Oh, they're not much. Another time, perhaps.' Actually, they were nothing at all. Ellen had not opened her sketchbook once since she'd returned to the hospital after Christmas. She hadn't even tried; the thought filled her with something close to nausea.

'Ellen — ' Lucas looked down, nervously scuffing his shoe through the soft, spring grass. 'There's a smoker at Grant Hall

Saturday after next — '

'Smoker?' Ellen interrupted, startled, and Lucas looked up from his contemplation of the lawn, abashed.

'Sorry. It's a college term. A dance, I mean. A social. A party.'

'I think I understand,' Ellen said, smiling. She had a feeling where this conversation must be headed.

'I'd like it if you came with me,' Lucas said in a rush. 'That is . . . if I could escort you — '

'I don't know if I shall have off that Saturday,' Ellen replied. She was trying to untangle the rush of emotions tumbling through her: the pleasure at being invited and the thought of a dance, the nervousness at what going might mean for both her and Lucas, and the disappointment not that Lucas was asking her, but that she couldn't be more enthused.

'Perhaps you could make a special arrangement?' Lucas suggested hesitantly, and Ellen nodded.

'Yes, I could ask, at least. Superintendent Cothill can be quite understanding when she chooses.' Impulsively, Ellen touched Lucas's hand. 'Thank you for asking me.'

He blushed with pleasure, and something in Ellen's heart eased. She'd decided months ago she would not pine for Jed, and she didn't think she had been. She would find a way to go to this dance with Lucas, she decided right then, and moreover, she would enjoy it. Immensely.

In the end, Superintendent Cothill gave permission easily, and Ellen was soon surrounded by envious and excited nurses clamouring to know what she would wear, if she was in love with Lucas, and what he looked like (Harriet gave everyone a rather embellished picture of Lucas's fair looks).

'You can't wear that,' Marjorie Henley declared, aghast, when Ellen took out her rose wool to inspect. 'It hasn't any lace or trim, and besides, it's wool. You can't wear wool to a spring dance.'

'A smoker,' Harriet corrected excitedly.

'Smoker or dance, I haven't anything else,' Ellen replied sensibly, to which a cry rose from her comrades.

'Between us all, we can come up with something,' Amity said, and so they did.

The dress, in the end, was a castoff of Marjorie's, who had plenty to spare, with lace and trim deftly added by Harriet, who possessed an unknown skill with needle and thread. Amity donated gloves, a gift of an elderly aunt, and Sally Fenwick lent her best kid slippers, as long as Ellen promised not to scuff them too badly.

When the evening finally came, Ellen felt she was dressed as elegantly as a princess, even if it was all borrowed finery.

She twirled in front of the other nurses and glanced down at herself in admiration for the resourcefulness of her friends.

'It really does look quite splendid,' Amity said in amazement, and Ellen laughed.

The dress was pale green silk, with a vee of lace crossing in the front, and then descending in ruffles to the hem, which was a good half-inch above Ellen's ankle, displaying Sally's kid slippers to great advantage. The sleeves were also trimmed in lace, capped quite short, so Amity's long, elbow-length gloves could be put to good use.

She was missing a hat and a reticule, not to mention a shawl, but Ellen didn't mind. Marjorie had dressed her hair in a loose, upswept style, and had given her a pearl necklace as well.

'Don't lose it,' she warned, and Ellen nodded.

'I promise. I'll take care of everything. You've all been so good to me.'

She glanced round at the happy, excited faces of her friends, and felt emotion rise like a tide within her. Her friends. She'd made a life for herself here, she realized; it had been

made for her. She'd been accepted, welcomed, and loved, and the enormity and
value of it hit her now so she had to blink
back tears.

'Ellen, you look as if you might cry!'
Harriet exclaimed, and Ellen gave a trembling
little laugh.

'Now that wouldn't do! Then my nose
would turn red and my eyes would puff up
— I'd send Lucas running before we made it
out of the parlour. No,' she finished, blinking
back more tears, 'I'm just so grateful to you
all.'

'Show us some gratitude by having a
wonderful time,' Amity said, 'and telling us all
about it when you return!'

'Promise.' Her heart fizzing with anticipation, the rest of the nurses crowding the stairs
and trying to peer into the parlour, Ellen
fairly floated down to meet Lucas.

'Ellen!' Lucas stood, straight and tall in his
evening wear, his fair hair slicked back from a
high, broad forehead. His eyes glowed with
admiration and perhaps a little more. 'You
look lovely, lovelier than I ever could have
imagined.'

Ellen felt like a blossom opening to the sun
under his praise, and she smiled as he took
her hand and led her out into the warm,
fragrant night.

The walk to Queen's was a short one from the hospital, although Ellen stepped slowly and rather carefully in her borrowed slippers.

Even in the few months since she'd been at KGH, Queen's and even Kingston had changed, new buildings constructed out of the famous grey limestone, motorcars trawling the streets.

'Everything moves so fast,' Ellen said as they walked to Grant Hall. 'I feel as if the world is growing right up around me.'

A car honked its horn, and Ellen jumped in surprise. Lucas chuckled.

'It is growing, and faster every day. It's a new century, a new decade.'

Ellen nodded thoughtfully, although the rapid change made her a bit uneasy. Hemlines were higher, motor cars more commonplace, and there was even talk of installing a telephone in the Nurses' Home. Yet where, Ellen wondered, did this leave her? Or Da? Or even Uncle Hamish and Aunt Ruth? Would Seaton General Store have a telephone, Uncle Hamish an automobile? One day, perhaps, and yet it seemed hard to imagine. Hard to bear, somehow.

'Florence Nightingale died this year,' Ellen said quietly. 'Nursing has moved on a great deal from her day, of course. It is, as you said, a new century.'

'There are only good things to come, Ellen,' Lucas promised, his voice ringing with sincerity, and, putting his arm around her, he ushered her into the hall.

Ellen's first experience of a Queen's College 'smoker' was overwhelming. The room was crowded and hot, the music loud, the dancing surprisingly raucous. Everyone was there for a good time, and she shrank back slightly at the sheer noise and activity.

She supposed she'd expected stately waltzes as the music gently swelled, but the reality was a lively ragtime piano playing as couples performed such new, and rather strange, dances as the turkey trot and Texas Tommy.

'I'm afraid I won't be any good,' Ellen confessed with a little laugh, for although Rose had taught her to waltz in the parlour to Dyle's humming, that was the extent of her experience with dance. The country dances enjoyed at island weddings and parties seemed another thing entirely.

'Don't worry,' Lucas said, grinning, 'I'll show you.'

And show her he did. Ellen would never have expected Lucas to be such an accomplished — or energetic — dancer, but he was wonderfully light on his feet, and confident enough to direct Ellen's own faltering steps.

Laughing, she found herself getting quite

in the mood of the thing, and Lucas shed his jacket as the ragtime carried on.

'Oh, I need a breath,' Ellen gasped after Lucas had taken her through the turkey trot.

'A breath of fresh air?' he said with a smile and led her outside.

The night was balmy for May, moths fluttering under the gas lamps and the distant sound of a woman's laughter floating on the evening breeze. Couples mingled in the shadows, murmuring or involved in something more.

Ellen wrapped her arms around herself, taking a few steps away.

'Cold?' Lucas came up to her and rested one hand on her shoulder. 'I could lend you my coat, if you like.'

'No, thank you. I'm fine. It's a lovely evening.' Ellen was suddenly conscious of Lucas's closeness, the way his hazel eyes had flecks of gold, the little smile that quirked his lips — and then she was conscious of nothing but his kiss.

He pressed his lips to hers gently, almost reverently, and Ellen's hands came up to rest on his shoulders as a matter of instinct. Then he stepped away.

'I don't know if I should apologize,' he said, his voice a bit shaky. He ran a hand through his hair as Ellen blinked at him.

'I've never been kissed before.' She flushed

at this admission, but Lucas only smiled.

'Me neither.' His smile became a wry grin. 'It wasn't so bad, was it?'

'No.' Ellen touched her fingers to her lips. 'No, it wasn't.'

There was a moment of silence, broken by a high-pitched yelp followed by a feminine squeal of laughter. Lucas shoved his hands in his trouser pockets.

'Ellen, I love you.'

Ellen stared. She had suspected Lucas might harbour some feelings for her, but a declaration of love took her completely by surprise and robbed her of speech.

'I know you don't love me,' he continued matter-of-factly.

'Lucas — '

He held up one hand. 'Not the way I love you, at any rate. I still hope that you may come to love me, in time. Nothing would make me happier than being your husband.' His face turned red. 'I know I shouldn't say that now, and I'm no good with flowery words. I keep those for the books. But . . . would you consider . . . my suit? In time? Knowing that I care for you very deeply?'

Ellen felt a lump in her throat. She wished she loved Lucas, loved him with the passion and intensity that he seemed to love her. He was so perfectly suitable for her, he encouraged her and understood her far better than anyone — certainly Jed — did.

And she did love him . . . but not in the way that he wanted. Not, Ellen realized sadly, in the way she wanted. Although his kiss had been very nice, it had been nothing more, and she knew it would be unfair to both of them if she were to pretend it had, or think it ever could be.

'Lucas, you do me too much honour,' she began unsteadily, and his twisted smile made her realize he knew he was being let down.

'Never mind,' he said. 'Don't answer me now. I shouldn't have spoken. I knew it was too early. Just . . . just know that I love you, and if you ever change your mind — or your heart — I'll be there. Waiting.'

'That's not fair to you,' Ellen protested, and Lucas shrugged.

'It's not as if I'd be doing anything else, Ellen. I don't mind.' He held out his hand, and Ellen put hers into it. 'Now, shall we go back into the dance?'

She nodded, but as they entered Grant Hall the raucous ragtime music and lively dancing seemed a world apart, a light, carefree place where you weren't given someone's heart to safeguard . . . a precious thing, Ellen thought, looking sadly at Lucas, that her own heart didn't seem to want.

15

By mid-June most of the Queen's students were stretched out on the meadows by the lake, halfheartedly looking at books but mostly enjoying the sudden, summery weather.

The nursing students watched them enviously from the wards, for they had far less leisure time than those who studied at Queen's.

Still, there were summer holidays to look forward to, and Ellen was surprised and relieved to realize she was looking forward to returning to Amherst Island, despite the awkwardness of Lucas's declaration and Jed and Louisa's romance.

Louisa had written her a few weeks earlier to inform her that the Lymans had invited her to their farm for the month of August, 'and I hope a proposal will be forthcoming at the end of it!'

Ellen found that this information neither surprised nor pained her; she was blessedly numb, and there was a small part of her that even looked forward to seeing her friend.

As for Lucas, he'd been every bit the solicitous friend he ever had been, and there was no mention of the evening of the Queen's smoker, and his words of love.

Sometimes, in an idle moment, Ellen imagined herself married to Lucas, living on the island perhaps, and it was not an unpleasant scenario. Sometimes she wondered if she could grow to love him in time, as he clearly hoped.

She knew better than to speak of it to him — for false hope was worse than none — but she still treasured his friendship and vowed that was not a bridge to burn, not like she had with Jed.

Ellen was packing her valise for the journey home, the windows of her dormitory thrown open to the summer air, when Harriet McIlvain hurried into the room.

'Ellen, Superintendent Cothill wants to see you in her office.' Harriet looked anxious, and Ellen felt her own sharp pang of nervousness. To be summoned to the nursing superintendent's office was never a good thing.

She walked slowly down the stairs to the little room adjacent to the parlour. Miss Cothill stood in the doorway, a piece of paper in her hand, her expression grave.

'You wanted to see me?'

'I'm sorry to be the bearer of grim tidings, Nurse Copley,' Miss Cothill said quietly, 'but a telegram has just been delivered to my care.

It regards your aunt.'

'Aunt Rose?' Ellen's mouth was dry and her eyes widened.

'No,' Miss Cothill corrected, 'your Aunt Ruth. She's very ill and you're summoned home to Seaton immediately.'

'Aunt Ruth?' Ellen repeated, and found she could not quite believe it. She hadn't known Ruth ever to be ill; somehow she could not imagine her stern countenance made pale and tired in illness. Yet, she realized, she had not seen her aunt and uncle in over a year. The thought grieved her.

'I'm sorry, Nurse Copley,' Miss Cothill said, her voice gentle, and Ellen could only nod.

With a numb heart she finished packing, and made arrangements for a train to Seaton.

She watched the trees and towns speed by, changed at Rouse's Point, and finally, a bit grimy, her hair beginning to fall from its pins, she alighted at Seaton Station.

'Ellen Copley, it's good to have you back.'

Ellen took the station master's hand with some surprise as she stepped from the train on to the platform.

'Thank you, Mr Fairley.'

'I'm glad you've come,' Orvis Fairley continued soberly, 'considering your Aunt Ruth.'

Ellen felt a prickle of alarm though she kept her expression and voice calm. 'Is she very ill, then?'

He took a step backwards, his face suffused with embarrassed colour. 'It's not for me to say, Miss Copley. It's not for me to say — '

Ellen nodded in acceptance. The last two days of travel from Kingston had left her in a quagmire of doubt and fear. The telegram had been so brief; she had no idea just how ill Aunt Ruth really was. Part of her mind told her that Hamish would not have sent for her unless Ruth was truly unwell; another part insisted that Aunt Ruth was invincible.

She would simply have to find out for herself.

'Do you mind if I leave my valise at the station? Uncle Hamish can fetch it for me later.'

'Oh, there's no need for that, miss,' Orvis said quickly. 'I'll bring it up to the store. There's not another train coming for twenty-three minutes.'

That was the first time such an offer had been made, and it took Ellen by surprise. She wasn't used to people being so nice to her in this town, and it made her uneasy. Aunt Ruth must be truly ill, she thought.

'Thank you, Mr Fairley.'

They walked quietly up the street. A heavy,

humid pallor hung over the town, making the weather hot and oppressive. Ellen murmured greetings to several people she recognized, the regretful looks on their faces making her more and more nervous.

When she arrived at the general store, it seemed forlorn somehow, even though it was not noticeably different. The same barrels and bins lined the wide front porch as they had six years ago, when Ellen had first arrived with Da.

There were a few new additions, Ellen saw after a brief moment of inspection: gloves and goggles for automobile riding on one shelf by the door, with a hand printed sign, 'Don't Get Left in the Dust!'. Displayed in the window were a telephone and a typewriter, both gleaming and black.

Inside, the store had its familiar smell, both musty and sweet, and Ellen blinked as her eyes adjusted to the light. A few people browsed through the aisles; Ellen heard their murmured helloes with only part of her mind.

Uncle Hamish was not at the counter.

Ellen couldn't remember a time when he hadn't been there, his apron white and spotless, his cheeks rosy, his smile bright. Now, a thin young man with sharp eyes and greased hair lounged against the worn marble, and he straightened his bow tie as Ellen approached him.

'Do you know where Hamish Copley is?' she asked politely, although what she really wanted to know was who this fussy young man actually was. She recognized him vaguely, but that was all.

'He's back at the house, tending to your Aunt Ruth.'

'You know who I am?'

'Of course.' The young man smiled smugly. 'You're Ellen Copley. I was in school with you, when you went to the upper class. I'm Artie Dole.'

Ellen remembered a cheeky boy who yanked her plaits, and she smiled coolly. 'Yes, now I remember. Has Uncle Hamish hired you to work the counter?'

'Yes. I've been here since September.'

Ellen blinked in surprise at this news. Why had no one informed her? When, she suddenly wondered with a dawning panic, had she last received a letter from her aunt and uncle? She couldn't remember, and she felt even more disconnected from her life in Seaton, from Uncle Hamish and Aunt Ruth.

Someone grasped her arm. Ellen turned and saw it was Elmira Cardle, her face heavily powdered and her eyes bright. 'We're so sorry, Ellen. You did the right thing, coming home.'

'Thank you,' Ellen murmured, disconcerted. 'I think I'll just go see Uncle Hamish, now.' She excused herself and crossed the yard to the house.

It was quiet and dim when she let herself inside. 'Uncle Hamish?' she called softly, and moved into the kitchen.

He sat slumped at the table, his head in his hands.

'Uncle Hamish?'

Hamish looked up blearily, managing a weary smile when he saw Ellen. 'We knew you'd come.'

'I had no idea — ' Ellen trailed off, unable to finish her thought, not wanting to explain the shock her uncle's appearance gave her. Hamish was unshaven and untidily dressed, a shadow of the man she knew and respected.

'You'll be wanting to see your aunt,' Hamish said as he struggled up from the table. 'The doctor's been this morning. Said she was no better, but no worse. It's been like that for days.'

'What . . . what is it?' Ellen asked hesitantly. 'Does she have the influenza?'

Hamish shook his head. 'If only. Although that kills off people too, I suppose. No, she's had stomach pains — for months, she says now, though she never did tell no one. The doctor said it's a cancer, eating away at her insides. He doesn't think she'll last very long, another week or two at most. That's why I sent for you . . . I knew you'd want to pay your respects. And I didn't know what else to do.'

Ellen could only nod, one hand reaching for the table to steady her. Even in her worst imaginings, she hadn't dreamed of anything quite so dire. Ruth on her death bed! As ill as that! It seemed impossible, and Ellen realized, with a bit of surprise, that the emotion filling her, trickling through her, was sorrow. Grief, deep and real.

'I'll go see her.'

Ellen climbed the stairs, noting the layer of dust on the banister Ruth normally kept polished and shining.

She went to the front bedroom, a room she'd only entered once or twice, and knocked on the door.

There was no answer.

Hesitantly, Ellen pushed it open. She saw Ruth inside, lying on the bed, pale and still.

'Aunt Ruth?' After a moment, her aunt's eyes fluttered open. It took her a moment to focus on Ellen, and when she did she smiled faintly. 'It's Ellen. May I come in?'

Aunt Ruth nodded. 'Yes, of course.' Her

voice was low and raspy.

Ellen went to the side of the bed. She'd had experience of many sickrooms in her year at KGH. She'd seen people die, had closed their eyes and dressed them for burial. On more than occasion she'd wheeled a corpse on a gurney down to the morgue in the basement.

Yet none of that prepared her for this moment. Looking into Ruth's faded eyes, seeing the sharp lines and angles of her face both softened and clarified in illness, being the subject of her wispy smile, brought Ellen right back to the coal dust and smoke of the kitchen in Springburn, her mother's frail hand grasping her own. She remembered the confusing rush of despair and love and she swallowed with difficulty, her throat thick with tears.

'I'm glad you've come.'

'Of course I would,' Ellen said, her voice coming out choked. 'I'm sorry I didn't come sooner.'

'Never mind that.' Ruth's eyes fluttered closed then struggled open again. 'I wasn't going to send for you,' she said after a moment, each word laboured and slow. 'Hamish said to, but I told him it wasn't right.'

'I'm glad he sent for me, Aunt Ruth,' Ellen

said. 'I want to be here.'

Ruth shook her head, barely a movement against her pillow. 'Why should you waste your summer in a sickroom? You've spent enough time there.'

Ellen touched her hand, a fleeting gesture. 'I don't mind.'

Another shake of her head, and Ruth's eyes fluttered. Just these few moments of conversation clearly exhausted her. She looked at Ellen with pain-clouded eyes that still saw all too much. 'It isn't right. What am I to you?'

The words echoed in the still room, in Ellen's still heart. Yet she couldn't respond; even if she'd known what to say, Ruth had already fallen back asleep.

The question kept up a haunting refrain in Ellen's mind as she went back downstairs. She busied herself with chores, tidying the kitchen and parlour, making supper. Within a few hours, the shell of a house seemed like a home again, if only in the trivialities of a lighted fire and a meal on the table.

What am I to you?

Ellen closed her eyes briefly as she saw Ruth's knowing look. It shamed her unbearably to think that Ruth wouldn't expect her to come, perhaps wouldn't even want her to come. Admittedly, Ellen had fled Seaton before for the comforts of Amherst Island

and life with the McCaffertys ... her own palpable relief at leaving Seaton time and time again both humbled and shamed her now. Ruth had obviously known how she felt, but then hadn't Ruth been relieved too? What was *she* to Ruth?

Still, Ellen knew, Ruth was her aunt. The Copleys had sheltered her when her own father had chosen a different path, a life apart. They'd fed her, clothed her, offered her opportunity, even if it had been without affection. Without love.

Had it?

What am I to you?

They were questions, Ellen realized painfully, she could not truly answer.

That evening, Ellen pulled the overflowing mending basket towards her while Hamish sat in his favourite chair in the parlour, staring into the empty grate.

'How long has she been like this?' Ellen asked quietly, and he shrugged.

'A few weeks.'

'You could've sent for me sooner.' She was obviously needed, Ellen thought, if just to keep Hamish looking presentable and food on the table. The residents of Seaton had brought hams and casseroles by the barrowful, but Hamish hadn't seen fit to do anything with it all.

312

He shrugged again. 'Ruth said not to.'

'Don't you think I would've wanted to know? To be here?' Ellen could not keep the reproach, the hurt, from entering her voice, even though she blamed herself. Her actions in the past few years had shown otherwise. She'd only been to Seaton twice in all that time, and the visits had been brief and awkward.

Perhaps they truly believed she wouldn't have come, wouldn't have wanted to.

'Ah, Ellen.' Hamish's voice was thick. 'What am I going to do without her? I know she was sharp, and some thought she was cold, but she was dear to me. She was the soul of this store, even if I was the heart. She was my soul.' He wiped his sleeve across his eyes, unashamed. 'I don't know why I loved her so much, I honestly don't! When I told Douglas — your father — that I aimed to marry her, he laughed right out loud. Told me she was too prickly for his taste, and he was right. She is prickly. But you know, after all these years, I wouldn't have it any other way.' He turned to Ellen, smiling sadly. 'I wouldn't have her any other way.'

Ellen's eyes filled with tears and she knelt in front of her uncle, putting her arms around him. 'Of course you wouldn't, Uncle Hamish. And I wouldn't either.'

As soon as she spoke the words, Ellen knew them to be true. Aunt Ruth was prickly, and difficult, and proud. She was hard and stern and strict, and yet she was more. It was only now that Ellen saw it, and knew it to be true. A tear slipped down her cheek as Hamish returned her embrace, and she laid her cheek on his shoulder.

★ ★ ★

The next week saw Ellen occupied with familiar tasks, caring for Ruth who drifted in and out of consciousness, sometimes not noticing Ellen and the small duties she performed, at other times all too aware of Ellen moving quietly in her room, changing sheets or filling the water pitcher, bathing her forehead, bringing clear broth for her to drink.

She watched Ellen with bright, knowing eyes, but rarely spoke, and neither did Ellen.

One afternoon when the heavy weather had broken so the sky was clear and the air fresh, Hamish told Ellen to take a walk.

'You've penned yourself inside, and there's no need. Ruth is sleeping, and I can be on hand. I know for a fact Louisa Hopper would like to visit with you. She's home for the summer, although I've heard she's going to

314

that island of yours later in the season.' From somewhere Hamish found a smile. 'What's that about, then?'

Ellen managed to find a smile as well. 'Louisa's found a beau, Uncle Hamish. I reckon we'll be hearing wedding bells soon.' She surprised herself by how little it hurt to say it.

'How about that, then!' Hamish slapped his knee. 'Another bloke likes them prickly as well! Go see her, Ellen. I'm sure it will do you good to hear her news.'

Ellen did not really want to hear Louisa's news, but she knew her uncle meant well. In truth, she'd barely given her friend a thought since her return, so occupied had she been with her duties towards Ruth and Hamish. Now she felt a different foreboding fill her, for she wasn't quite sure she wanted to speak with Louisa, not with the memory of their words at the New Year still fresh in her mind.

'Go out, enjoy yourself,' Hamish urged, and Ellen smiled thinly. She would have to see Louisa at some point; perhaps it was best to get it over with it.

She changed her dress, instinctively smartening herself just a bit, and walked towards Water Street.

Mrs Hopper answered the door, but this time she greeted Ellen warmly, taking her arm and drawing her forward into the house.

'Ellen, we've been so sorrowful to hear about Ruth. The doctor says she isn't long for this world. Do you think it's true? I know you're only a nurse, and in training at that, but — ' Mrs Hopper trailed off, vaguely aware she'd said something insulting.

'I couldn't tell you how long it will be,' Ellen answered with quiet dignity, 'as only the Lord knows. But we'll be by her side until she passes.'

'Of course you will,' Mrs Hopper murmured. 'So dedicated, despite you rushing off to Canada like that. I'm sure Louisa will be thrilled to see you. Did you know she is spending all of August in Stella? The Lymans invited her. We'll be coming ourselves at the end of the month, to meet them, and Jed, of course. Louisa tells me they have one of the most prosperous farms on the island.'

That was exaggerating a bit, Ellen decided, but she was glad Mrs Hopper was pleased for her daughter, and so she smiled politely. 'How very exciting. Louisa did mention it to me, I believe.'

A moment later Louisa came down the stairs, stiffly, a look of caution on her handsome face. She looked older, Ellen saw, more dignified. All traces of childish bad humour were gone, and she was a young

316

woman indeed, beautiful and proud. No wonder Jed loved her.

Louisa held both her hands out to Ellen, who clasped them in her own with awkward grace. 'I'm so glad you came, Ellen.'

'Shall we all take tea in the parlour?' Mrs Hopper suggested cosily, and Louisa gave a little laugh.

'As delightful as that sounds, Mother, Ellen and I haven't seen each other in a long while.' She turned to Ellen, her eyes bright. 'I know what we'll do. We'll go to the soda fountain on Main Street. Have you been, Ellen? It's new, and all the rage.'

'Soda fountain?' Ellen said dubiously, and Louisa giggled.

'It's 1910, you know! You must keep up with the times!'

They didn't have a chance to speak until they were in Welton's Druggists, a smart new building with stone steps and ornate scroll-work flanking its glass doors. Ellen vaguely remembered that the building there before had been an old brick one, a blacksmith's whose services were obviously no longer needed.

Louisa pushed confidently through the glass doors, striding towards the back where a row of high, cushioned stools stood in front of a long, marble counter, similar to the one in the general store, save that behind it was a young man in a white apron and cap, and there were rows and rows of taps and bottles.

'I'll have a strawberry fizz,' Louisa said with a flirtatious, little smile, and she turned to Ellen.

'Have you ever had a soda?'

Ellen thought of the bottles of sarsaparilla Hamish sold in buckets of ice in the summertime, and had a feeling this was another notion entirely. 'Not really.'

'You must try a black cow! They're simple delicious.'

'Black cow?' Ellen repeated dubiously, but the soda jerk was already making her drink in a tall, frosted glass. He put it in front of her with a flourish, and Ellen gazed down at the dark, foaming drink with some trepidation.

'Chocolate syrup and root beer,' Louisa informed her. She took a sip of her own bubbling, pink soda. 'Like I said, it's really delicious.'

Ellen took a sip, and the bubbles went right up her nose. 'Oh!' She clapped her hand to her face, startled, and Louisa laughed.

'You are old-fashioned, aren't you, Ellen? Don't they have soda fountains in Kingston?'

'I'm sure they do, but I've been kept too busy to sample their delights,' Ellen said a bit shortly. She pushed her drink away from her and glanced around the store, its high glass cabinets lined with bottles and boxes.

She read a few of the brand names — Lydia Pinkham's Vegetable Compound, Wampole's Tonic — and realized with a jolt that these were items Hamish normally stocked, now with a store to themselves. 'I'd no idea Seaton was becoming such a metropolis,' she said after a moment. 'Having a druggist! It's moving up in the world, I suppose.'

'Moving with the times,' Louisa corrected. 'Most towns have drugstores now, and department stores. Things change, you know. I go to the soda fountain all the time in Burlington. I've been to three different ones.'

'Do you like college?' Ellen asked, and Louisa shrugged.

'It's good fun. I didn't really know I had a brain! I can't imagine ever using it in that way, though.' She gave a little laugh. 'Some of the girls there are dreadful bluestockings. I don't suppose they'll ever get married.'

There was a pause too full of meaning, and Ellen prodded her drink with the straw, watching the brown bubbles churn and foam. 'And shall you get married?' she asked eventually.

Louisa took a breath. 'You know I'm going to spend the summer with the Lymans? Jed

319

asked me. It seems sensible, considering how we've been so far apart since Christmas. I'm hoping,' now she gave a giddy, little smile, 'that there's a proposal by September!'

It was no more than Ellen expected, and she nodded. 'Do you think,' she asked, 'you will like being a farmer's wife? There are no soda fountains in Stella, you know, and I doubt there ever will be.'

'You're mistaken if you think I hold soda fountains that dear!' Impulsively, Louisa leaned forward, putting her hand on Ellen's arm. 'Oh, Ellen, I love him! That's what makes all the difference. I know you think you love him — or loved him — I saw it in your face when you saw us in the kitchen. But you don't! When you love someone, it's so consuming, so wonderful — '

Ellen thought of the last six months, her determination to forget Jed and the many lonely, miserable hours she'd spent towards that end, and had to agree with Louisa that it was consuming. Wonderful she'd yet to experience.

She smiled stiffly and even took a sip of her drink, the bubbles buzzing on her tongue. 'Louisa, I told you before that I didn't love Jed,' she said firmly, setting her glass down. 'You might fancy I do because I was a bit cold after Christmas, but I can tell you it wasn't that. The truth is, I thought the island and all of its residents were, well, mine. I didn't want to share them with anyone. You know well enough I was reluctant to have you come that first summer. Childish jealousy, I know, but there it is.' Ellen shrugged, and Louisa looked both uncertain and relieved.

'You will come to our wedding, then?' she asked with a little smile. 'Although Jed must ask first, as you know!'

'Of course I will.' Ellen occupied herself by taking another sip of her drink, and then instantly regretting it. The bubbles were too much, and went right up her nose.

'And what will you do?' Louisa asked. 'Go back to nursing school, I suppose? Will you stay at the hospital there after you graduate?'

The picture Louisa painted, which Ellen had already imagined far too many times, was as bleak as ever.

'I don't know what I shall do,' she said. 'I shall have to wait and see.' She thought of Ruth, waiting to die, and Hamish's store, perhaps becoming a thing of the past, and she wondered if anyone's future was certain, even Louisa's, waiting as she was for a marriage proposal that had yet to come.

16

As July moved into August, the fields turned dry and brown under a blazing sun and Ruth's health continued to worsen. Ellen and Hamish took turns sitting by her bed, bathing her wasted, feverish skin, trying to get her to take a little broth, although it barely wetted her lips before she turned her face away.

One evening as twilight began to settle over the fields, Ellen sat by Ruth's bed while the older woman slept. In sleep, Ruth's face was relaxed instead of taut with pain.

Ellen breathed in the smell of cut grass from the open window. She heard a child run with a hoop down the street, the tinkling laughter floating up to the room like the sound of bells. As dusk deepened, the sound of crickets began in earnest, a chorus that could become deafening in the middle of the night.

Ellen smiled in memory of when she and Da had first arrived in Seaton. She'd never heard such a ruckus before, and had slept with a pillow over her head those first few weeks, as had Da.

Until he left. Ellen's smile faltered slightly

as she thought of her father. The letters from New Mexico had been less and less frequent, and sometimes Ellen forgot she even *had* a father. It was hard to remember his face sometimes, his Scottish burr. It was hard to remember Mam as well, Ellen realized.

She felt as if she were drifting farther and farther away from her memories, her past life, and she did not yet know what, or whom, the future held.

'Ellen.'

Ellen started in surprise. Ruth had wakened, and was looking up at her with a faint smile.

'I'm glad to see you're awake.' She smiled back. 'Will you take some broth?'

'No, I'm not hungry.'

'You need to keep your strength up — '

'No, I don't.' Ruth smiled again. 'At some point, Ellen, there's no need for that anymore.'

Ellen paused, swallowed. 'Is there anything I can get you?'

'Yes, there is.' Ruth's hand reached for Ellen's own. 'Your sketchbook.'

Ellen stared, speechless.

'You didn't think I knew, did you? Hamish told me. He showed me the drawing you'd done of me. It was like looking in a mirror, only better. You saw me as I didn't even see myself. Didn't even know I could.' This speech caused Ruth to close her eyes briefly, a sheen of sweat on her forehead.

'Sometimes I don't know what I'm going to draw,' Ellen confessed quietly, 'or why.'

'I'd like to see your other sketches,' Ruth said, 'if you'll show me.'

Ellen nodded. This was the last thing she expected, yet it was a request she could not deny. She'd brought her sketchbooks to Seaton, though she had not opened them. She went quickly to her room to fetch a sketchbook. There was a pile of them now, in her trunk, and after a second's hesitation Ellen took the ones from her first years in Seaton.

'I haven't drawn much of anything in this last year,' she confessed. 'I've been too busy.'

'That's just as well. I have enough to catch up on.'

Ellen helped Ruth sit up a bit in bed, propped by pillows. She was amazed at how fragile Ruth had become; it was as if her bones were hollow.

With trembling hands Ruth began to turn the pages. She studied each sketch carefully, the ones of the robin on the tree outside Ellen's window, the rows of sweet jars in the store, the brook encased in winter ice.

When the sketches became more personal, Hamish laughing at a joke, Elmira Cardle pursing her lips fussily, she only smiled.

'You've got a good eye,' she said once, at the sketch of Elmira, and then turned the page.

At the back of the first book, one Ellen had filled a long time ago, there was a folded sketch. Ellen had almost forgotten about it.

Ruth unfolded it, and they both stared at the picture of Da. He was laughing, happy — the picture she'd meant to give him as a goodbye present, but he'd never allowed her the chance.

'I . . . I'd forgotten that was there,' Ellen said after a moment. 'I haven't looked at it in years.'

'It's a good likeness,' Ruth said in a raspy voice. 'I can tell how much you love him.' She closed the book and leaned back against the pillows. 'Thank you for showing me.'

'I'm glad you wanted to see them,' Ellen admitted, and Ruth gave her a ghost of a smile.

'Did you think I wouldn't want to?'

Ellen was at a loss for an answer, and Ruth shook her head. 'Of course you wouldn't. I know I've been hard with you, Ellen, and it wasn't always fair. But I knew I had to be, for my sake as well as yours. I've never been a mother, the Good Lord didn't see fit to make me one, and I accepted that over the years, as did Hamish.' She took a deep breath which rattled through her chest like air through an empty cage. 'But I still had something of a mother's love in me, I suppose, because I knew I could feel that with you. And I knew I was the last kind of mother you needed, and this life here with us in the store, in Seaton, I saw what it was doing to you. Taking your pride, your joy, what little you had back then. I always knew you'd do better in Stella . . . with Rose.'

Ellen shook her head, amazed and saddened by this confession. 'I could've been happy with you,' she whispered.

'Perhaps,' Ruth allowed after a moment. Her voice was harsh and ragged with the effort of speaking. 'Perhaps I've just been selfish. I was afraid of showing I loved you, because I knew you could never love me back, not the way a mother loves her daughter. You had that for your own mother, and Lord knows I'm not very lovable. Oh, Hamish loves me, I know he does. Thank heaven for that. He'll need you, Ellen, when I'm gone. Just for a little while. Don't tie yourself to him, not for my sake, or his — ' she shook her head, her voice trailing off, and Ellen clasped her hand.

'Oh, Aunt Ruth,' she choked, 'I do love you.'

Ruth's eyes brightened. 'Well, that's something to take with me.' She was silent, struggling for the strength to go on. Ellen held her hand as tightly as she dared, willing her fingers to somehow show Ruth what her actions and words never had.

She did love her, and, she realized, Ruth had always loved her. It was both strange and wonderful to think of it, to know it, to feel its truth in her bones, in her heart.

'What about your Da?' Ruth weakly motioned to the folded sketch with one hand. 'You need to see him. He's your family, Ellen. Always will be.'

'I've written him. But I don't know him any more, Aunt Ruth. I haven't for a long time.'

'You always know your family,' Ruth said. She closed her eyes, her voice little more than a whisper. 'I did.' Her fingers faintly squeezed Ellen's before she fell asleep once more.

★　★　★

Ruth died three days later. At least half of Seaton stopped by with condolences and casseroles, until a week after the funeral Ellen stood in the kitchen, surveying the stocked larder and wondering just what was supposed to happen now.

Hamish had held up admirably. It was, Ellen thought, as if he'd grieved already, and now knew he must soldier on. They all had to go on, although Ellen wondered just where.

The screen door slapped open and closed, and Ellen heard Hamish's familiar, shuffling tread.

'There's a letter for you. From New Mexico.' He stood in the kitchen doorway, a bit paler and thinner, but Ellen was glad to see that his eyes still twinkled, if only a little bit.

'I wrote Da a few weeks ago,' she murmured, taking the letter. 'I didn't think word would come so soon.'

She opened it while Hamish waited, scanning the few lines with a wrinkled brow.

'Well? What does my brother say?'

'Dear Ellen,' she read in a halting voice, 'I'm sorry to hear about Ruth. I know Hamish loves her, and it's a terrible thing, being parted from a wife. It makes me realize even more how frail we all are, and I want to see you before you've grown up completely. I'd like to invite you to visit me in Santa Fe. Perhaps you'll stay awhile, even. I have a small house and a good job, which is more than most can say. Please write when you can visit and I'll send the fare. As ever, Your Da.'

Hamish was silent, and Ellen folded the

letter back into the envelope.

'You'll go, then?' he asked, and she looked up at him.

'I don't know.'

'He's your father, Ellen.'

'Yes, but you wouldn't know it.' She thought of what Ruth said about family. Yet right now, Rose and Dyle, Hamish and Ruth were her family. Da had left that responsibility with them.

Hamish nodded slowly, his expression thoughtful. 'Are you angry with him?'

'No,' Ellen said after a moment, realizing it was the truth. 'But he's a stranger. And I don't want to leave you alone so soon.'

Hamish shook his head. 'I'll do fine. The people of Seaton will see me right, and I've always got the store.'

'Still — '

Hamish held up a hand. 'Don't make this house into another sickroom, Ellen, taking care of me. Ruth told me you'd try to do that, and I'm warning you, I won't have it.' He looked so determined that Ellen had to smile.

'You're hardly ill, Uncle Hamish.'

'You're darn right I'm not! I'm fit as a fiddle, and I don't need a nurse. You go to Santa Fe. See your Da. What he's done or not done doesn't matter. He's still your Da, and he wants you now.'

'Now,' Ellen repeated with a trace of bitterness, and Hamish awkwardly put his arm around her.

'Ah, Ellen. We can't choose the way people love us. They just do.' He paused, frowning. 'A trip to Santa Fe will take a month at least. What about nursing school?'

'Well.' Ellen took a breath. 'I'm not going back. I've realized this last year that I don't want to be a nurse. I may have spent a good part of my life in a sickroom, but that doesn't mean it's the only place I'm meant to be.'

'No, indeed.' Hamish looked pleased. 'I always thought myself you should do something about those sketches.'

Ellen smiled slightly, thinking of Lucas's similar encouragement. And why shouldn't she do something? She'd spent so much of her life hiding from truth, from opportunity, and all because of fear. She would not do that any more, not if she could help it. 'Perhaps I will.'

Hamish smiled, pleased, and Ellen smiled back. Suddenly the road in front of her seemed, if not bright with possibility, then at least not so shadowed in uncertainty.

Later that evening, as Hamish closed up the store and the sun began its lazy descent, Ellen dug out her most recent sketchbook and flipped through its pages. She took a pencil, her fingers closing around it awkwardly. It had been so long. She hadn't even had the faintest spark of ambition or desire in her heart to draw; it had been as if she'd shut away that part of herself. Yet now, shyly, gently, she opened it once more. She did it not just for herself, but for those who had encouraged her: Lucas, Jed, Hamish, Ruth. She thought of Ruth's wispy smile, the bright look in her eyes, and began to draw.

★ ★ ★

A week later Ellen returned to Amherst Island. Hamish had insisted she visit Rose, especially as he knew his sister would want to hear Ellen's news.

Indeed, Rose came running down Jasper Lane even before Dyle's wagon had drawn up to the front door.

'Ellen! I'm so pleased to see you!' Rose wrapped her in a warm embrace. 'We were all saddened to hear about Ruth. We wish we could have been there.'

'Hamish knows of your regard,' Ellen murmured. 'The distance was too far.'

'Still — ' Rose bit her lip. 'You look completely worn out! We must get you well fed before you return to nursing school.'

'Yes, about that.' Ellen smiled. 'I'm not

331

staying long, for there's a train leaving Kingston for Chicago in a week's time and I plan to be on it. And I'm not returning to nursing school, either.' And as Dyle and Rose both gaped at her, she prepared to explain.

It was lovely being back on the island, and if Ellen was avoiding visiting the Lymans and seeing Louisa, she didn't acknowledge that to herself. Or when she did, she told herself they needed space and privacy.

She was content to spend time with the children, playing games and picking berries, enjoying the moments of stillness and peace which seemed to have come so rarely to her this last year.

And she drew. After a year of blank paper, Ellen felt her spirit was again unleashed. She drew everything, yet she found herself drawing several sketches of Ruth from memory; images of Ruth she didn't know she possessed. Ruth smiling, laughing, looking thoughtful or sad. Humour lurking in eyes that Ellen had once believed only to be flinty and hard. Whether it was the Ruth she remembered or the one she wished she'd known, Ellen couldn't say. But she drew the images as they came, unbidden and plentiful.

Late one afternoon she found herself walking down Jasper Lane to look for a stray chicken, when she saw a familiar figure ambling slowly towards her.

Her heart leapt within her and her mouth turned dry as her heart and soul both seemed to frame one word: *Jed*.

As the figure came closer, she saw it wasn't Jed at all. It was Lucas.

'I've been wanting to see you,' he said with a smile as he approached, and Ellen smiled back.

'I'm sorry I haven't stopped by, Lucas.'

'I know you've been busy. I was sorry to hear about your aunt.'

'Thank you.' Ellen swallowed. 'It was hard.'

Lucas's expression softened. 'Poor Ellen. You've lost so many people.'

'As have many others. You needn't feel sorry for me.' Ellen lifted her chin. 'I'm strong.'

'I know you are. I heard from your aunt Rose that you won't be going back to Kingston.'

'No, I've decided not to be a nurse.'

'Do you know what you'll do instead?'

Ellen shrugged. 'I'm considering a few options,' she said, and then to her surprise, Lucas took her hands in his.

'Well, perhaps you will consider one more.'

'Lucas — ?'

'I told you I'd give you a bit of space and I have now, haven't I?'

Ellen's hands felt cold in his. 'I suppose you have.'

Lucas looked both intent and nervous, and Ellen felt a stirring of trepidation. Then he spoke.

'I don't know how else to say it, so I'll come straight out with it, Ellen. Will you marry me?'

Ellen's hands, still encased in Lucas's, were numb. She stared at him, his eyes sparkling with hope, his expression rapt and so very serious.

'Marry you?' she repeated, trying desperately to frame a response that would be both accurate and gentle. 'Lucas, this comes as a surprise.'

'I thought I made my feelings clear the night of the smoker,' Lucas said with a slight frown. 'Ellen, I love you. And I must admit that I have hoped, given time, you might love me.'

'But you still have two years at Queen's left,' Ellen said, stupidly, for it gave Lucas hope she knew she couldn't offer him.

He smiled. 'We can have a long engagement. And then — ! Think of it, Ellen. The world will be open to us. I want to travel, I want to *dream*, with you at my side.'

He looked so excited, so serious, and so vulnerable with his hair flopping boyishly over his forehead, so sweet and so familiar. So dear. Gently he released his hands from hers. 'Ellen, *do* you love me?'

Ellen bit her lip. She realized she'd been afraid of this moment coming for some time; she was afraid to give an answer because she knew the truth in her heart, and feared it wouldn't be enough for Lucas. Yet she also knew she didn't want to lose him.

'I think,' she said slowly, 'I could come to love you, in time.'

Lucas was silent. In the distance Ellen heard the baleful lowing of the cows, waiting to be brought in, and the sudden, frenzied barking of her dog, Pat. The sounds of home, familiar and comforting, and yet she felt as if she and Lucas were in a world apart.

'I don't suppose,' he finally said with a wry little laugh, 'that is exactly what I wanted to hear.'

Ellen sighed heavily. 'No, I don't suppose it is.'

He pushed his hair off his forehead, raking it back with long, slim fingers. 'I thought it might be enough,' he said after a moment. 'When I spoke to you in May, I thought all you needed was time. I was prepared to give you that.'

Ellen could only nod, and Lucas managed a rueful smile.

'But now that the moment is here, and I've declared myself, I realize I want a little more than a wife who may or may not come to love me in time. Is that too awful of me?'

'No,' Ellen choked, her throat now thick with tears, 'it isn't. Lucas, you deserve someone to fall in love with you, head over heels.'

'I don't know about deserve. But I couldn't bear living side by side with you, Ellen, and knowing I wasn't making you happy.'

Ellen brushed at her eyes with an impatient hand. At that moment she wished she was in love with Lucas — passionately, deeply in love — more than anything else. She wished she could change the leanings of her treacherous heart.

Yet she knew she couldn't.

'I'm sorry,' she whispered.

'So am I.' Lucas shoved his hands in his pockets. 'Tell me, is it because of Jed?'

Ellen jerked back. 'Jed?'

'I'm not blind. And I know you better than perhaps anyone else. I don't mean to sound arrogant in saying that, but I think I'm right. Do you love him?'

'I thought I did, at Christmas,' Ellen confessed unsteadily. 'When I saw him with Louisa, I suddenly realized. It took me completely by surprise. I wasn't expecting to ever — '

'Fall in love?'

'No, I wasn't.' She gave a small smile. 'And now I'm not certain if that's what it was, or if it was just hurt pride, or . . . I don't know. I couldn't even say. But it doesn't matter, Lucas, because that has nothing to do with you. What I feel for you.'

'Or what you don't feel for me.'

She nodded sadly. 'Yes.'

'Well, then. I suppose I'm sorry I asked.' His voice was gentle, but Ellen's heart still ached.

'How long are you on the island for?' Lucas asked after an awkward pause.

'Only a week. I'm going to New Mexico, to visit my father.'

He nodded slowly. 'Then I suppose I won't see you much until the autumn, when we're both back in Kingston.' He shook his head, conscious of his slip. 'Except you're not coming back. What are you going to do, Ellen?'

'I really don't know,' Ellen admitted, trying to smile.

Lucas raised his eyebrows in tender mockery. 'Well, you know what I've always told you to do.'

Ellen gave a little laugh. 'Who knows? Perhaps I will go to art school, one day.'

'You should. Don't sell yourself short,

Ellen, or what you're capable of.'

Ellen smiled, her heart aching — breaking — wanting to love Lucas. Wishing they would return to the farmhouse with happy news, with excitement and joy instead of this endless, aching sadness.

'I'll walk you back to the farmhouse,' Lucas said.

He offered her his arm, and as Ellen slipped her hand into the crook of his elbow, she wished she could have accepted Lucas's proposal. She even wondered if she should have.

★　★　★

Several days later Ellen was packing in her bedroom. She lay her few dresses carefully in her valise, smoothing the fabric. Most of them had been cut down from Rose's, although she still had the rose wool that had been a Christmas present from Ruth.

The memory of Ruth's quiet kindnesses brought a sting of tears to Ellen's eyes. She hadn't truly appreciated her aunt's affection towards her, she saw now. She'd only seen the stern look, the harsh word, without pausing to consider what these might have hidden . . . or protected.

Ellen sighed. She wanted to put the past

behind her, as much as she could without forgetting those who loved her. This was a new start, even if she wasn't certain where precisely she was going.

'Hello, Ellen.'

Ellen turned in surprise. Jed stood in the doorway, his hair rumpled, his expression both anxious and uncertain.

'Jed!' His name came out as a little yelp, so astonished was she to see him in her little bedroom, filling up the small space with his presence and energy. He looked the same, she saw, wonderfully the same. His eyes glinted grey and his hair was as scruffy as always, as scruffy as it had been that day he'd come for her in the wagon, and her whole life had changed, had begun.

'I didn't mean to startle you. Rose said to come on up, as you're leaving on the morrow. I feel I haven't seen you all summer.'

'No, you haven't,' Ellen murmured. She straightened a dress in her valise that had already been perfectly folded. Her cheeks were warm and she found she couldn't look at Jed again.

'I was sorry to hear about your Aunt Ruth.'

Ellen nodded, still not looking at him. 'Thank you.'

There was an awkward pause. Ellen risked looking up and saw Jed was staring at the floor as he twisted his cap between work-roughened fingers.

'Lucas told me you're not going back to Kingston,' he finally said. 'Will you stay here?'

'I shouldn't think so.' Ellen finally felt able to meet his gaze directly. 'I'm not sure what I'll do, but I want to go somewhere. Be something. After all, there's nothing for me here . . . is there?'

The silence, the heavy meaning, was palpable between them. Ellen hadn't meant to issue such a direct challenge; it had come without warning. She gazed down at her valise, her words spilling out in a rush.

'Besides the McCaffertys, of course, and Jasper Lane . . . this will always be home to me.'

'Yes.' Jed was silent, gnawing his lip. He looked up. 'Yes.' Another pause as he took a step forward. 'Ellen, I wanted — '

A brisk knock sounded at the door, and Ellen and Jed both started. Rose poked her head round the door, smiling with determined cheer. 'I've a pile of handkerchiefs for you, Ellen. You always seem to lose yours, so I thought I'd hem a few more for you.'

Rose's bustling, motherly concern made Ellen smile gratefully. 'Thank you, Aunt Rose.'

Jed shifted uncomfortably. 'I should be going.'

'Why don't you stay for supper?' Rose suggested. 'We've seen you little enough, although I suppose you have Louisa to attend to. You're both welcome to stay, of course.'

Jed's face flushed a dull red. 'Yes, perhaps. Another day.'

Rose glanced between the two of them and then quietly shut the door once more.

'Will you take a walk with me?' Jed asked suddenly, and Ellen's heart leapt with both hope and fear.

'I don't — '

'For old times' sake,' Jed said, his smile crooked, and Ellen nodded silently.

Outside the sun was sinking low in the sky, sending long, golden rays across the fields, and touching the tops of the oaks arching over Jasper Lane with bronze.

They walked slowly, silently, needing no words. Perhaps, Ellen thought, not knowing what words to say.

The farmhouse was nearly lost to view, hidden by the oak trees, before Jed spoke. 'What do you reckon New Mexico will be like?'

Startled from silence, Ellen gave a little shrug. 'I really couldn't say. The photographs I've seen make it look near to desert.'

'Will you stay out there awhile?'

'I shouldn't think so.'

Jed shoved his hands in his pockets. 'So then what will you do?' He sounded a bit surly, and Ellen almost smiled.

'I've no idea, Jed, but it hardly matters to you?'

He turned to her suddenly, the movement sharp and quick. 'Is that what you think?'

Ellen shrugged, holding her hands up in a defensive gesture. 'I only meant you're busy with your own things, with Louisa — '

'And aren't we friends?' Jed demanded. 'Has that changed?'

Ellen slowed, and then stopped completely. 'I should think it has, a bit,' she said quietly. She studied Jed, the surprising storm of emotion in his eyes, the way one hand raked through his hair, making it stand rather ridiculously on end.

'I never meant for that to happen,' he said, his head bent, his voice so low Ellen struggled to hear him.

'Nor did I,' Ellen agreed, just as quietly.

Jed looked up at her, his expression bleak. 'Yet it did, all the same.'

Ellen tried to smile. 'I look around at the motor cars and soda fountains and realize everything changes, Jed. You can't stop it.'

'I'm not talking about soda fountains.'

Ellen swallowed. 'Then what are you talking about?' She shouldn't ask, shouldn't want to know. Shouldn't want to hope, even now, and yet she did.

'Just — ' Jed shrugged helplessly, and Ellen knew he was caught. Perhaps he felt something for her, perhaps even more than she'd ever hoped or feared. Yet it wasn't enough, not nearly, not when Louisa had been invited for the summer, when their engagement was already the news of the season, and it hadn't even been announced. She knew it, and she could see from the desperation in his eyes that Jed knew it too.

'Don't.' Ellen lifted one hand, and Jed caught her fingers in his own. The simple touch shook her to her core, and her mouth opened soundlessly as he gently brought her fingers to his lips.

He released her hand before they'd done more than brush his mouth, but the tiny action sent tremors straight through, and she could only stare.

'Then I won't,' he said, sadly, and raised one hand in farewell. 'Goodbye, Ellen.'

Ellen still had not found her voice as Jed turned and walked down the lane, the sun bathing his head in shoulders in light, his back forever to her.

17

It seemed as if half of Stella came out to bid Ellen goodbye. As she stepped into the ferry, Captain Jonah, grizzled as ever, standing with one arm on the helm, she wondered if everyone realized what a momentous journey this was. It was the beginning, she thought, of the rest of her life.

'You will write,' Rose reminded her with a catch in her voice.

'Yes, although I might be back before my letters arrive,' Ellen replied with a little smile. 'I don't think I shall stay too long. It would be an imposition on Da.'

'Yes, of course — ' Rose trailed off, and Ellen knew what she meant. She was asking Ellen to keep in touch, and more than that, to consider the island her home, no matter how far she went or what distant dream she pursued.

Ellen reached out to clasp Rose's hand before settling in the little boat. 'I'll write, and more,' she promised, and Rose smiled in acceptance.

Ellen saw Lucas in the crowd at the wharf, smiling his farewell with wry sorrow. Jed and

Louisa were there as well, in the back, both of their faces blank and closed although they smiled.

So many dear faces, Ellen thought, so many memories. She wondered when she would be back, and what would have happened by then.

Ellen waved one last time, and amidst a chorus of farewells, Captain Jonah headed into the ruffled, blue waters.

'You travel more than any islander I know,' he said as the boat bobbed gently on the waves. 'I don't know why you don't stay put, Ellen Copley.'

'You think me an islander?' Ellen asked in surprised gratitude, and Captain Jonah gave her a considering look from under his bushy brows.

'Aye, I suppose I do, at that,' he admitted gruffly.

Ellen smiled. 'There's no higher compliment than that, Captain Jonah.'

He grinned toothlessly at her. 'You're right there.'

It took two days for the train from Ogdensberg to reach Chicago. At first Ellen gazed out the window at the changing scenes, the trees that fringed the track touched with scarlet and gold.

Then the trees gave way to flat prairie,

endless grass, with farms bare specks in the dry distance, and Ellen slept, leaning her head against the glass pane of the window. She hadn't realized how weary she was, how her bones and muscles and even her heart ached with fatigue from doing and feeling too much.

The click-clack of the train's wheels soothed her, and she slept through hour after hour of endless grassland, until the train slowed and she awoke to a changing sight. The prairie gave way rather suddenly to buildings, first shanties and warehouses, and then Chicago's elegant Union Station, the wide flowing river at one side. Ellen blinked in surprise at the glorious façade. The building looked more like a castle than a depot.

A few minutes after the train had chugged to a stop, Ellen stood on the platform, clutching her valise and looking around with obvious uncertainty.

Although she'd arranged by telegram to stay at a boarding house nearby, she realized she had not considered transport to that establishment, or just how big the city of Chicago actually was. It had been no more than a small, black dot on a wide stretch of empty map, yet now it sprang around her, a city fully grown, more of a city than anything she'd seen since that first frightening day in New York.

People bustled by her in a continuous, indifferent stream; a few jostled her shoulder with muttered oaths. She took a step backwards, willing herself away from the noise, the crowd. She hadn't felt like this since she and Da had stepped off the boat into the seething reaches of Manhattan over six years ago, excited, overwhelmed, and just a bit afraid.

A porter carrying two heavy valises jostled her elbow, and someone else pushed by on her other side. Before Ellen could stop herself she found herself falling hard on to her knees, her hands flat out in front of her.

'Oh!' The breath had been knocked from her, and as people continued to stream by with indifferent ease she knelt there, her knees aching, her hands scraped.

'Can I help?' She heard a kind voice, vaguely familiar somehow, at her side, and then someone was helping her from her inelegant position on the pavement. 'Are you quite all right?'

Ellen turned and saw a young gentleman, perhaps in his thirties, dressed in a fine style, his hat, an elegant topper, in one hand as he surveyed her in kindly concern. His hair was jet black but his eyes were bright, blue, and rather merry. 'That was quite a fall. Please, let me take your bag and bring you somewhere more comfortable.'

'I don't — ' Ellen began uncertainly. He smiled with the confident ease of a person born to wealth and privilege. 'There is a ladies' lounge in the main hall. May I escort you there?'

Ellen decided that seemed safe enough, and she liked the look of the man. There was no guile in those blue eyes, no calculation in his smile. 'Yes, thank you,' she accepted. 'That would be very kind.'

He hoisted her valise along with his own, and soon she was following him through the crowds to a discreet, wood-paneled door on the side of the hall. 'You can rest here,' the man said. 'Are you waiting for a train?'

'Actually, I just got off one,' Ellen admitted. 'I need to find my hotel . . . I didn't realize what a big city Chicago is.'

'Over a million people living here now,' the gentleman confirmed. 'May I direct you to your hotel if you are not in need of the ladies' lounge?'

Ellen hesitated again. She knew it wasn't proper to chat with a strange gentleman in the middle of Union Station, but she felt she had little recourse. She was lost, she was overwhelmed, and she didn't know how to get to her boarding house. She smiled bravely.

'Yes, you can.'

'Splendid.' He held out one hand. 'Henry McCallister, at your service.'

Ellen introduced herself and then quickly told him her predicament, and he insisted on hiring her a hansom himself.

'Am I correct, Miss Copley,' he asked as they walked towards the entrance of the station where a dozen hansom cabs waited in a gleaming black line, 'in believing I hear a bit of the Scots' burr in your voice?'

Ellen glanced at him in surprise before realizing why his voice had sounded familiar — he was Scottish! She hadn't heard such an accent in all her years in America, not even from Rose, Ruth or Hamish, all Scots born.

'Yes, I am. I came from Springburn, originally.' To her surprise, she found she said this proudly.

'But how wonderful!' Henry McCallister exclaimed. 'I'm a Glasgow man, myself. I'm only visiting here briefly, for a bit of business.'

They'd reached the queue for the cabs. Ellen gazed around with wonder. Buildings a dozen stories tall towered over them. She could hear the tooting horns of at least twenty cars on Van Buren Street, more automobiles than she'd ever seen before in one place.

'I must look a right greenhorn, gawping at all this,' she said with a little laugh. 'I haven't been in such a big city for awhile.'

'You know the address of your hotel?' Henry asked, and she nodded.

'Yes. Thank you for your help. I think I shall be all right now.'

She was at the head of the queue, and the driver of the hansom jumped down to take her valise.

'In that case, Miss Copley, will you have dinner with me tonight?'

The invitation was so genuine and heartfelt, it tore at Ellen to refuse. Yet she surely could not dine unescorted and alone with a strange man, in a strange city.

'I fear, Mr McCallister,' she said, 'that would not be appropriate.'

A faint blush tinted his pale cheeks as he smiled in apology. 'Of course, I quite see what you mean. I don't mean to be forward . . . only as one Scot to another, perhaps we could enjoy a meal? I'm staying at the Congress Hotel on Michigan Avenue. They have a pleasant restaurant, plenty of diners to serve as chaperones.' His smile was winsome and just a tiny bit rakish, mockingly so, that Ellen found herself laughing.

She was in a strange city, no one knew her, so she could do as she pleased. She knew she would conduct herself with propriety, and she believed Henry McCallister would as well.

'All right, Mr McCallister, in light of your fine arguments, I accept.'

'Where to, miss?' The driver asked, and Ellen told him her address. Henry McCallister spoke briefly to the driver, and then helped Ellen into the hansom. 'I've arranged for the driver to bring you to the Congress Hotel at seven o'clock, and return you to your boarding house at nine. Is that suitable?'

'Perfectly.' Ellen suppressed both a laugh and a thrill of pleasurable anticipation. Henry McCallister was clearly a man who got things done.

That evening Ellen entered the foyer of the elegant Congress Hotel with more than a little trepidation. After some consideration, she'd dressed in her rose wool. Although it was too warm for the season, she had nothing else suitable. The gown she'd worn to Lucas's smoker was packed in a trunk at the McCafferty farmhouse. She thought of the ruffled silk with longing, and then shrugged. Henry McCallister was obviously a gentleman of fine tastes and some wealth. Ellen could hardly hope to impress him, no matter what she wore.

Not, Ellen told herself sternly, that she was trying to impress him.

The Congress Hotel was an imposing building, boasting, the cabby told her, a thousand guest rooms. It seemed an impossible number to Ellen, and she entered the lobby with some trepidation.

The lobby of the hotel was large and luxurious, with sumptuous carpeting and sparkling chandeliers. Ellen saw that there was even a grand piano in one corner. She'd never seen such elegance and she looked around uncertainly for Mr McCallister, already feeling quite out of her depth.

'Miss Copley! I'm so glad you came.' She turned around at the sound of his voice; he stood before her, his dark hair slicked back, dressed in an excellently cut evening suit.

Ellen smiled, pleasure and anticipation unfurling within her. 'Did you think I wouldn't?'

'I wondered,' Henry admitted candidly. 'After taking my leave of you, I realized the boldness of my invitation. The last thing I want is for you to be uncomfortable.'

'I'm not,' Ellen lied, for her sumptuous surroundings were already making her feel a bit gauche and stupid. She smiled again. 'This certainly is better than the modest fare offered at my boarding house.'

'The food here is excellent,' Henry confided as, with one hand on her elbow, he led her into the dining room.

After they were seated at a table for two, crisp linen napkins laid on their laps by the white jacketed waiters, Henry turned his brilliant blue gaze on Ellen.

'Where are you travelling to, Miss Copley?'

'New Mexico. I'm visiting my father.'

'He lives there?'

'He works on the railway.' As soon as she said it, Ellen realized how poor that sounded to someone as wealthy and well-connected as Henry McCallister seemed to be. She pursed her lips in a frown. Why was he dining with her this evening? Slumming with a working class girl? A blush stained her cheeks at the thought.

'You must be looking forward to seeing him,' Henry said smoothly, ignoring the awkward pause that Ellen's admission had created. 'Has it been some time?'

'Six years. I've been living with my aunt and uncle.' Ellen did not want to talk about Amherst Island, or Ruth and Hamish. A lump of homesickness had lodged in her chest like a stone and she was afraid if she started describing the places she'd been — those she loved — she would shame herself by weeping or worse.

Instead, she glanced around the dining room, the light glinting off the crystal chandeliers and wine glasses, and wondered how she would paint such a scene.

At the table next to them a woman in ivory silk and diamonds looked exquisitely bored. Ellen drew her in her mind in a few quick strokes — the way she propped her chin in her hand and gazed irritably at her surroundings, impressed by nothing.

'You look,' Henry said quietly, 'as if you're memorizing the room.'

Ellen started in surprise. 'I am,' she found herself admitting. 'I'm sorry, I didn't mean to be rude.' Then, impulsively, she found herself admitting, 'As soon as I get back to my room, I shall draw it all.' She so rarely spoke about her art, Ellen wondered why she'd mentioned it so suddenly to this man. Yet it hardly mattered, she decided; she was unlikely to ever see him again. Perhaps that was why she'd mentioned it in the first place. There was something safe about anonymity.

'Draw?' Henry repeated, interest sharpening his voice. 'Are you an artist, Miss Copley?'

'Hardly. I sketch, that's all.' Ellen shrugged, uncomfortable. 'Artist' was surely too fancy a term for what she did; it suggested ambition, experience. She had neither. Still, Henry was not deterred. He leaned forward, clearly unwilling to dismiss the subject as she would like.

'What do you draw?'

'Anything that takes my fancy. People, animals, an empty room.' She smiled faintly, surprising herself by elaborating. 'I like to catch the unexpected moments, the little thing that you wouldn't think of unless it was right there in front of you, on the page.' Ellen's cheeks warmed and she balled the napkin in her lap, embarrassed. Why was she talking like this to this man? The only other person she'd shared her art with really was Lucas.

Lucas . . . for a moment she remembered him as she'd last seen him, smiling sadly, his own dreams turned to dust, and it was her fault. She felt a wave of longing — for the island, for family, for home — that crashed over her and left her feeling lost and alone, wondering why she was sitting in a strange hotel in a strange city, with a strange man.

'That's all very interesting,' Henry murmured, and Ellen's gaze slid away from his own speculative one.

They gazed down at the menus, and Ellen stared at the unfamiliar dishes with a faint sent of unease. She had no idea what to order, and she'd a feeling Henry knew it.

Consommé Olga, paté de foie gras, roast squab . . . it all sounded elegant rather than appetising. Ellen swallowed, scanning down the menu with mounting panic. She didn't want to make a fool of herself, and yet . . .

Henry knew she was out of her depth. She'd just told him her father had laid rails!

She glanced up and met his bright gaze with a candid smile. 'I've no idea what any of these things are. Can you order something simple for me?'

Henry, charmed, smiled easily. 'Of course.'

It was only after their first course was served, paté for Henry and cream of celery soup for Ellen, that he asked her again about her drawing.

'Have you ever been to art school?'

'Heavens, no.' Ellen shook her head, smiling with firm dismissal. She wasn't about to tread this old road as she'd done with Lucas. 'I wouldn't even know where to begin.'

He nodded, a knowing glint in his eyes. 'It's just a hobby, then? Something to pass the time, that you could discard easily?'

There was no contempt or judgement in his voice, yet strangely Ellen felt it. She'd 'discarded' her art for several months that year, and it had felt like part of her soul had gone missing. It was only once she began again, the images and memories and ideas returning unbidden, that she realized how much she'd missed it, how numb she'd been, and she knew she didn't want to be without it again.

'Well?' Smiling, Henry raised his eyebrows, waiting.

Ellen laid down her spoon. She was strangely chilled by his words, and the possibility they conjured. 'No,' she said slowly, 'it's not like that.'

'Then tell me how it is like.'

Ellen glanced at him a bit sharply. 'Why are you so interested?'

'I'll tell you in a moment.' Henry waved a hand in dismissal. He seemed almost impatient, eager, and Ellen couldn't help but wonder why. 'Tell me what it is like, please, Miss Copley.'

She shrugged, discomfited. 'It's like breathing. You don't go to school to learn how to breathe.'

Henry was silent for a moment. 'Indeed not,' he finally said, 'yet perhaps you can learn to — breathe — better?' He laid down his own fork, so they were gazing quite openly at one another, Henry in interest and Ellen in confusion. 'Let me be frank, Miss Copley. I'm a trustee of The Glasgow School of Art. I'm here on business with the Art Institute of Chicago; we are attempting to establish ties with American schools and emerging artists. And we are always looking for new talent.'

Ellen gave a little laugh of disbelief. 'Do you mean me?'

'Possibly.'

'You haven't seen my work.'

He nodded, smiling. 'No, you're right. It might be terrible.'

A bubble of choked laughter escaped her. 'It might be,' she agreed, swallowing.

'Has anyone seen your work, Miss Copley?'

She toyed with her spoon, uneasy again. 'A few people, family and friends. But I can't really trust what they say, can I? They wouldn't tell me if it was awful.' She smiled and Henry smiled back at her, humour lighting his eyes.

'No,' he agreed, 'they wouldn't. Perhaps you would show me one of your drawings?'

Ellen thought of her sketchbook, tucked in her valise. Showing a stranger her sketches was like giving him glimpse into the workings of her heart . . . her soul, stripping herself bare for his scrutiny, and perhaps his contempt. 'I . . . I . . . don't — ' she stammered, and Henry smiled in understanding.

'I am bold once more, and perhaps making you uncomfortable. Forgive me.'

Ellen nodded dumbly, for what he said was true and she did not know how to respond.

The waiter came to clear their plates, and

Henry smoothly moved the conversation on to safer topics. Before long, Ellen was at ease and enjoying herself once more.

Nine o'clock came all too quickly, and after enjoying the crème brûlée and coffee Ellen found herself reluctantly rising from the table.

'I thoroughly enjoyed your company,' Henry murmured as he escorted her to the entrance of the hotel. 'And I hope we meet again.'

Ellen thought that unlikely, but merely murmured her own thanks in return as Henry pressed a crisp white business card into her hand.

'In case,' he said, 'you change your mind.'

As she climbed into the hansom he touched his lips to her fingers, and Ellen couldn't help feel she was in a fairy tale, for one evening at least.

'Cinderella, about to be turned back into a pumpkin,' she murmured as the hansom drove off with Henry still watching from the kerb.

Ellen glanced down at the business card. It simply read, 'Henry McCallister, Trustee, Glasgow School of Art.' She stared at the elegant script for a moment before slipping it into her reticule. She doubted she would ever return to Glasgow now, and certainly not for art school. There was no money, for one thing, and her future, whatever it held, was surely in this country.

Still, Ellen thought, leaning her head back against the seat cushions, there was no harm in keeping the card.

★ ★ ★

It took two more days for the train from Chicago to reach Santa Fe. Ellen felt as if she'd been travelling forever, residing in dusty third-class cars and spartan boarding house rooms.

By the time the train rolled into the Santa Fe depot, the track had been winding its way through rocky gorges, crossing perilous chasms on narrow iron bridges, with Ellen's nose fairly pressed to the glass. She'd never seen such sights — an endless blue sky stretching above the canyons and arroyos of a sculpted, foreign landscape.

The depot was impressive in its own way, yet completely different from Chicago's palatial Union Station. Made of adobe with brick archways and Spanish roof tiles, it made Ellen feel as if she'd left the United States entirely.

As she stepped off the train, the crisp, dry mountain air hit her in full force, seeming to suck the breath from her very lungs.

There were few people getting off the train, and even fewer on the platform, yet she still didn't recognize Da. She looked around nervously, aware of how strange a place this was, how far from home she had travelled.

She'd sent a telegram informing Da of her arrival, yet who knew if he'd received it?

'Ellen?' The uncertainty in the Scottish accent had Ellen turning. A man stood before her, a man she'd passed over in her search for Da, a man, she saw now with a lurch of her heart, who was her father.

'Hello, Da.'

He looked at her in wonder, and took a shuffling step forward as if he wanted to embrace her but was afraid to reach out and touch her.

Ellen moved as well, putting her arms around him. He was thinner, stooped, his hair grey under his greasy cap, his jaw stubbled.

'You've changed,' he said in a voice choked with emotion as they stepped back from each other. 'I've never seen you so fine.'

Ellen inclined her head, unable to put into words that her father had changed as well. Of course, she should've expected him to be older, greyer. She had not anticipated how worn and work-weary he would seem, as if the joy of life had been stolen from him.

There was no sparkle in his eyes, no spring to his step. He had become an old man.

Ellen remembered their hopes from the ship, the house they would build, the life they would lead together, the dog and the garden, and swallowed past the lump of regret in her throat.

'I'll take you home,' Da said with a little smile. 'We're together now, Ellen. It'll be good for us.'

She nodded mutely, wondering how this place could ever be home.

Da shouldered her valise as they stepped out on to Front Street. All of the buildings in Santa Fe were similar to the depot, built mission-style with mud bricks and terracotta roof tiles.

'You'll like it here,' Da said with a bit of his old confidence as they walked along the wooden platform that served as a pavement. 'There's nowhere with cleaner air, healthier living, I warrant you.'

Ellen nodded again. Her father did not look as if he'd had enough healthy living, to her eyes.

'I wanted to get a cab for you,' he admitted sheepishly, 'or at least a mule. But these are hard times for everyone. It was enough scraping the cash to get you out here.'

'I'll pay you back for that,' Ellen said

swiftly, although she had very little money herself.

'There's no need.' A shadow flickered in Da's eyes. 'I know I paid little enough for your keep over the years. I never thought things could be so dear.' He looked away, embarrassed, and Ellen's heart ached.

After a few more minutes of walking, the breath searing Ellen's lungs from the mountain air, they reached a row of mud-brick shanties huddled against the rail line, the bleak shape of mesas jutting against a crystalline sky in the distance.

'Here we are,' Da announced cheerfully, and ducked into one of the buildings.

Ellen blinked as she adjusted to the dim light of the hut. The dwelling comprised two rooms, crude windows cut into the mudbrick walls, the floors made of packed earth and covered with bright but threadbare woven rugs.

There was a pot-bellied stove in one corner, a table with two stools, and in the back Ellen saw a cot with some woven blankets thrown over it.

It was, she thought sadly, poorer than anything they'd had in Springburn.

'It's not much, I know,' Da said, 'but it's home. I'll make us some tea.' He picked up a tin kettle and went out to the pump for water.

Ellen sank on to a stool and pressed her fists to her eyes. She wasn't sure what she'd expected, but not this, the pitiful remnants of the life Da had carved out for himself from this harsh and unforgiving land.

He'd wanted so much from this country, for himself, for her. Why had he settled for this? Why hadn't he come back?

'You must be tired,' he said, injecting some determined cheer into his voice as he lit the stove. 'This will set you right.'

'Thank you.'

Her father put the kettle on, busying himself with the small, mundane task for longer than necessary. The silence stretched between them, and Ellen was conscious of how little she had to say. There had been so many words, so many dreams and regrets, hopes and griefs, she'd wanted to share with him over the years, yet now she had no words for this stranger.

Finally Da turned from the stove, smiling awkwardly, and joined Ellen at the little table. 'I wish there were some biscuits — ' he trailed off, hunching his shoulder, and Ellen shook her head, smiling.

'It's all right. I ate on the train. I'm not very hungry.'

'We can go to the caff for a slap-up meal later,' he told her. 'I've enough for that.'

'Good. Lovely.' Ellen nodded, still smiling, but the silence was there again, heavy and palpable. 'Are you happy here, Da?' she finally asked. 'I could tell so little from your letters.'

He glanced down at his hands folded on the table, knotted and work worn. 'Happy enough,' he said at last. 'Happy as any man can be.'

'You like working on the engines?'

He shrugged. 'It's work.'

The kettle boiled with a shrill whistle, and Da set about making cups of tea.

Ellen cradled her tin mug in her hands and blew on the hot liquid.

Da settled himself in the stool across from her once again and they drank in silence.

'Sometimes I wonder what would've happened, if I'd stayed,' he said after a moment.

'In Seaton?'

He shook his head. 'No, in Scotland.'

Ellen gazed at him in surprise. 'You've always wanted to get away from there.'

'I've wanted to get away from everywhere I've been,' Da admitted ruefully, although a deeper regret laced his words and shadowed his eyes. 'It's just the way I'm made, I suppose. The only reason I haven't set off from this place is there's nowhere else for me to go. And I wanted to see you again, I wanted to be together again.' He was silent for a moment, his expression brooding. 'I know I haven't done right by you, Ellen, and I expect you've grander plans than keeping house for me in this mud hut. I'm not to keep you here. Ruth's written me with all the things you've done, the schooling you've had.' He reached out one gnarled hand to rest it on top of hers. 'I'm proud of you, Ellen. Real proud. You know that, don't you?'

Ellen nodded, her throat tight. 'Yes,' she whispered, 'I know.'

'Of course, if you were to stay with me — ' Da smiled sadly. 'But this is no place for you, is it? It never was. That's why I didn't bring you in the first place.' He stared down at his mug of tea, shaking his head. 'I always felt badly you had to nurse your mam and miss your own schooling. I didn't feel I did right by you in Scotland, and I was afraid the same would happen in America. You'd be keeping house for me again, if I brought you out here . . . or anywhere.'

'And if you'd stayed in Seaton?' Ellen asked quietly.

Da looked up, smiling wearily. 'Ah, Ellen, I could never do that. There wasn't a place for me there. Ruth wouldn't have me behind the counter, not with my accent and rough ways.

She polished Hamish up, I know, but I'm a different kettle of fish altogether.'

Remembering her father's snapping black eyes and ready grin, she had to agree. 'There could have been something else for you,' she said, even as she knew it wasn't true. It never could be.

'Maybe,' Da said, 'but I wasn't happy there, Ellen, and I didn't want to bring you down with me.' He paused, and there was blatant need in his voice, on his face as he asked, 'and you've been happy, haven't you? Aunt Ruth and Uncle Hamish, Rose and Dyle, they've all been good to you, haven't they?'

Ellen stared at him, remembering the misery of her first months in Seaton, alone, abandoned. But there had been so much happiness to follow. There had been joy. She thought of Ruth the last time she'd seen her — you know your family — and she smiled. 'Yes, I've been happy.' There was no point blaming Da for what he'd done or who he was, not now, when it was far too late. Whatever relationship they might have had was a thing of the past, a figment of her imagination. Ellen saw the naked relief on her father's face, and she reached for her valise, thinking of the long-ago sketch she'd once meant to give him.

'Da,' she said, 'I have something for you.'

★ ★ ★

The leaves were drifting from the trees in lazy, scarlet circles when Ellen walked up Jasper Lane in early October. She'd left her valise at the ferry, as she hadn't sent word of her arrival. The walk was a long one, but she didn't mind. The sky was hazy and blue, the breeze warm, and she wanted to be alone. She wanted to think through everything that had happened, and finally decide the first steps towards her future.

It had been good to see Da, Ellen realized, because in a strange way it had set her free. She loved him, and she knew he loved her. That would have to be enough, because she knew now they would have no life together. They'd changed too much, grown too far apart as they pursued separate destinies, and it would continue to be so.

After leaving Santa Fe, she'd stopped at Seaton and stayed for a few weeks, to see Uncle Hamish. He was coping well, the townspeople surrounding and supporting him.

'What will you do?' Ellen had asked one evening, and Hamish smiled.

'Stay here. I don't know what else I'm good for, really. I know the world is changing, and the days of the general store might be nearing

368

an end. What with the catalogue store right on Main Street. Sears Roebuck, it's called, and it sells more than I ever could.' He sighed. 'But I'm still making a living, at any rate.' He paused, his eyes bright. 'And speaking of that, Ellen, there's something I want to tell you. Your aunt left you something, a legacy I'd call it although that might be too grand a word. It's not much, enough to see you through a few years perhaps, with whatever you want to do. The details are with the bank. I didn't know about it myself till she passed on, but she wanted it for you.' He paused, his voice choking with emotion. 'She did love you, Ellen.'

'I know,' Ellen said quietly. 'And I loved her.'

They'd just both had strange ways of showing it.

Now as Ellen saw the McCafferty farmhouse in the distance, heard Pat's barking and a faint trill of laughter, she smiled. No matter where she went, this was home.

Ellen squinted and saw a figure in the distance down the lane. For one hopeful moment she thought it was Lucas, but then she remembered he would be in Kingston by now, at Queen's.

The figure came closer, and Ellen saw it was Jed. He was leading a pig by a rope.

'Ellen!' He smiled with some of the old ease and affection they had lost. 'World traveller that you are! You've been to New Mexico and back! How is your father?'

'He's well.' Ellen pointed to the pig. 'You're not leading that poor old sow to the slaughterhouse, I hope?'

'Not yet. She needs some fattening up. No, she's wandered into our garden and I'm bringing her back to yours. Ma'd be right cross about it if our pig wasn't doing the same.'

'How is your Ma?' Ellen asked, and Jed shrugged.

'As ever. She holds on, but we never know how long for. I suppose you just need to be grateful for what you're given.'

'Yes,' Ellen agreed, 'I suppose.' She fell into step with Jed, the pig trailing reluctantly behind them, with Jed giving the beast a tug forward every now and then. 'How have things been here? Any news?'

'The old Togg farmhouse burned down; most said it was a blessing. And the McClellands are bringing a motor car to the island; they're going to drive it over on the ice when the lake freezes over.'

'I expect everyone on the island will have a motor car, sooner or later,' Ellen said and Jed shook his head in disbelief.

'It doesn't bear thinking about. I'll stick to horses, thanks very much.'

'And what about Lucas and Peter?' Ellen asked. 'They're off to Kingston?'

'Yes, they went last week. Half the island saw them off, as usual.'

Ellen smiled, picturing it. 'Good.'

Jed cleared his throat. 'Louisa took the same ferry. She travelled back to Vermont.'

Ellen nodded, her eyes on the ground and her measured steps. 'You had a good visit?'

'Yes.' Jed was silent, and Ellen waited, knowing there was something more to be said.

'There's a bit more news,' he finally said, a certain awkwardness to his words. 'The thing is . . . Louisa and I are engaged.'

Ellen nodded, silent for a moment. She'd expected no less. Yet she found the news didn't hurt as much as she'd thought it would. It still hurt, there was no denying that, but not with the crippling pain she'd felt a few months ago. She looked up, meeting his gaze, and smiled. 'I wish you happy then, Jed.'

Jed jerked his head in the semblance of a nod. 'She's going to leave school,' he continued almost painfully, 'and live here. We'll be married in December. She says she doesn't mind being a farmer's wife.'

'And so she shouldn't.'

Jed looked down at the ground, one worn boot scuffing the dirt. 'I can't help but think there's things that haven't been said between us, Ellen,' he said in a low voice.

Ellen's heart skipped a treacherous, hopeful beat but she managed to reply lightly, 'Then they should remain unsaid, don't you think?'

He nodded slowly, lifting his eyes to exchange a bittersweet smile. 'I reckon so.'

And that was that, Ellen thought with a pang. That chapter of her life — her hopes — was closed and finished. Jed glanced up the lane. They were near the house, yet still far away enough to remain unseen. 'You coming up?'

Ellen nodded. 'In a minute.'

She watched him go up the lane, such a fond, familiar figure. She didn't know why she felt like she was losing him now, when surely if she'd ever had him; she'd lost him long ago.

Yet with that pang of loss came another emotion, one Ellen let fill up her heart like her sail. Hope.

A chapter of her life might have finished, but a new one was just beginning, a crisp, blank page upon which to write her fledgling dreams and ambitions.

A wind blew off the lake, a crisp wind of

autumn, ruffling her hair and promising frost. The wind of change, Rose would call it. Ellen thought of the catalogue store in Seaton, the motor car coming to Amherst Island, the sketches she'd sent Henry McCallister, and his reply, encouraging her to apply to Glasgow Art School for admission. With the legacy from Aunt Ruth, art school was now a distinct — and wonderful — possibility. Yes, the winds of change were blowing.

The sun was setting fire to the horizon as she lifted her face to the breeze.

'Blow, Winds of Change,' Ellen whispered with a tremulous smile, 'and take me with you.'

TRAVEL WRITING

Peter Ferry

Pete Ferry is driving home when a car, swerving dangerously on the road, over-takes him. The driver is a beautiful woman, half-naked — something's clearly not right. Cautiously, he follows her. What should he do? Then, at the traffic light, he's next to her car. He must act now — but he hesitates, the lights change and her car lurches forward straight into a tree, killing her instantly . . . In Chicago, Pete tells this story to the students in his class where he teaches. But, is this just an elaborate tale which illustrates the power of storytelling? Or did this actually happen?

ON THE HOLLOWAY ROAD

Andrew Blackman

Unmotivated and dormant, Jack is drawn into the rampant whirlwind of Neil Blake, who he meets one windy night on the Holloway Road. Inspired by Jack Kerouac's famous road novel, the two young men jump into Jack's Figaro and embark on a similar search for freedom and meaning in modern-day Britain. Pulled along in Neil's careering path, taking them from the pubs of London's Holloway Road to the fringes of the Outer Hebrides, Jack begins to ask questions of himself, his friend and what there is in life to grasp. Taking on speed cameras and CCTV, motorway riots and island detours, will their path lead to new meaning or ultimate destruction?

HALF-TRUTHS & WHITE LIES

Jane Davis

When Tom Fellows proclaims that a Venn diagram is a far better way of illustrating modern family ties than a traditional tree, his young daughter Andrea has no idea that he is referring to their own situation. It is only when she loses both parents in a shocking car accident that she takes an interest in her own genealogy and begins to realize that her perfect upbringing was not all that it seemed . . .

THE BLUE NOTEBOOK

James A. Levine

Batuk is a fifteen-year-old girl from rural India. When she was recovering from TB in hospital she learned to read. Her only possessions are a pencil and a blue notebook in which she writes her journal . . . She records that her father sold her into sexual slavery when she was nine. And how, as she navigates the grim realities of the Common Street — a street of prostitution in Mumbai where children are kept in cages as they wait for customers — she manages to put pen to paper. Her private thoughts and stories are all put down. Through the words that Batuk writes in her journal, she finds hope and beauty in the bleakest of situations.

V   EP